RALPH COMPTON

—————————◆—————————

THE SALTWATER TRAIL

A RALPH COMPTON WESTERN BY

JACKSON LOWRY

BERKLEY
New York

BERKLEY
An imprint of Penguin Random House LLC
penguinrandomhouse.com

ISBN: 9780593334096

First Edition: January 2022

Printed in the United States of America
1   3   5   7   9   10   8   6   4   2

Book design by George Towne

THE IMMORTAL COWBOY

This is respectfully dedicated to the "American Cowboy."
His was the saga sparked by the turmoil that followed the
Civil War, and the passing of more than a century has by
no means diminished the flame.

———◆———

True, the old days and the old ways are but treasured
memories, and the old trails have grown dim with the rav-
ages of time, but the spirit of the cowboy lives on.

———◆———

In my travels—to Texas, Oklahoma, Kansas, Nebraska,
Colorado, Wyoming, New Mexico, and Arizona—I always
find something that reminds me of the Old West. While I am
walking these plains and mountains for the first time, there
is this feeling that a part of me is eternal, that I have known
these old trails before. I believe it is the undying spirit of
the frontier calling me, through the mind's eye, to step
back into time. What is the appeal of the Old West of the
American frontier?

———◆———

It has been epitomized by some as the dark and bloody
period in American history. Its heroes—Crockett, Bowie,
Hickok, Earp—have been reviled and criticized. Yet the
Old West lives on, larger than life.

———◆———

It has become a symbol of freedom, when there was always another mountain to climb and another river to
cross; when a dispute between two men was settled not
with expensive lawyers, but with fists, knives, or guns.
Barbaric? Maybe. But some things never change. When
the cowboy rode into the pages of American history, he
left behind a legacy that lives within the hearts of us all.

—*Ralph Compton*

CHAPTER ONE

H E's COUGHING UP blood again. You think he'll last 'til we get to Bozeman?" Clayton Forsythe looked out of the corner of his eye at their suffering boss, Henry Oakes. The old man bent double and leaned away from his wranglers to hide how close he came to hawking up a lung in his latest bout with consumption.

"Ain't nuthin' we kin do 'bout it, other 'n bury him," the trail boss said in a low voice. "That's a damned shame, too. I've worked for him nigh on eight years. Last year was bad out on the trail right after we left Colorado, but this year?" Vic Reedy shook his head. "He's been bad the whole way."

"It's looking a lot like the end of the trail for him," Clay said slowly.

He hadn't expected working for the Rocking O to be his life's work. This late in the year, the best he'd expected was to leave the trail hands in Bozeman, get a list of Montana ranchers and farmers willing to put up a cowboy for a few weeks during the winter before he'd have to move along to the next homestead. A few chores, maybe a dollar or two, and most homesteaders were eager to see a man willing to sleep in the barn and not disturb the family too much. Life during the fierce Montana winters was never easy, and an extra hand often meant the difference between freezing to death and seeing the spring sunshine.

If he had any luck, Clay hoped to find a farmer unable to get around the way he used to. A man with a gimpy leg or a sore shoulder wasn't as likely to chase off a cowboy looking to help out. He smiled a bit grimly. Now and then there was even a pretty young daughter of just the right age and inclination to burrow down with in the hay during long, frigid nights.

"You'd better count on it. This is the last Rocking O herd. Mr. Oakes will get good money for it, but it all has to go back into the ranch."

"For his son?"

Reedy snorted contemptuously and shook his head.

"He'll drink it all up. You saw how he was, and you'd just blowed in a couple weeks before we started the drive."

"I hoped," Clay said, "that he was on a bender to celebrate."

He pushed his broad-brimmed tan Stetson back and wiped the sweat on his forehead. For this time of the year, it was mighty warm. It was way too early for the Chinooks to be blowing, though there was no disputing the hot air gusting around them at the moment. Such a fickle wind made the cattle real nervous.

"Most all of us hoped Soused Sully'd amount to more than a hill of beans. Ain't happenin'. No, sir, not happenin'. He'll drink away the Rocking O inside a year. Before spring maybe since I heard tell he'd taken up with the youngest Snider girl. She's a peck of trouble, and she's hardly seventeen."

Clay ignored the trail boss as he rambled on about the woman's lack of morals and her interest in picking Henry Oakes' bones clean. Clay had drifted in from over in Nebraska, found nothing in Denver and crossed the Front Range into Middle Park, hunting for work. Henry Oakes had rounded up close to five hundred head of cattle, mostly his but also including a fair number of strays wandering the range, just begging to have a brand pressed into their bovine flanks.

He hitched up his gun belt and looked hard at the rancher. Blood trickled down his chin from his mouth and nose. Oakes' ashen face told the story. This was a dead man riding along at the head of the herd, too stubborn to die in the saddle. Force of will carried a man only so far. It was now a matter of when the rancher passed on, not if.

Clay took off his Stetson and ran his fingers through long, lank black hair, then shook his head around enough to let the hot wind dry him off.

"Should I see if there's anything I can do for him?" Clay asked the trail boss, anxious when Oakes hawked up a bloody gob and sprayed it like a shotgun blast.

"You're no medicine man, and I don't remember seein' you walk on water."

"Nope," Clay said, smiling at the memory. They'd crossed a river—he never even heard its name—and he had been swept away. If Reedy hadn't spotted him and used his lariat, Clay figured he'd still be washing down the river. Or his corpse would. The trail hands had joshed him about how Reedy had snared himself a fish and Clay was lucky he didn't get tossed back for being too small.

Clay had learned a long time back not to let such joking about his diminutive height chew at him. He stood five foot five in his Mexican leather boots and was as sturdy as they come. There wasn't a man on the drive he hadn't bested arm wrestling. He'd even taken on Lanky Lou Larson, about the tallest, biggest man he'd ever seen, in a bout of Indian leg wrestling. Lanky Lou had had the advantage of leverage, using his long leg, but when they'd linked arms lying on the ground, raised their legs and locked at the knee, Clay knew he had the other man beat. He was stronger, had better back muscles and, with a powerful surge, had extended his short leg to send his opponent somersaulting backward.

He'd won close to five dollars on penny-ante bets that night. After that, the kidding about his size had stopped, except for a few things like being washed down the river and getting fished out by the trail boss. For once, Clay felt he fit in.

That made it a doubly damned shame about Henry Oakes. Clay could have seen fit to ride with the Rocking O crew another season or two. They were good trail hands and performed their jobs well without too much grousing. Most complaints he heard were mild and more often than not said in jest.

"Leave him be," Reedy warned, reaching out to grip Clay's brawny forearm. "It'll only make him ornery. When he gets upset, the coughin' gets worse. Don't rush him."

Clay understood. He tugged on his gelding's reins and trotted off to see if the herd needed tending. Lanky Lou's quarter horse cut back and forth in front of a steer that thought to wander off on its own. The expert cowboy slowly moved the cantankerous animal back until it once more bounced about, crowded by a dozen others.

"How much longer?" he called out to the open range, not expecting an answer.

Clay had to laugh when a half dozen cowboys all shouted back, "When we get there!"

He had never ridden this trail before, but from the look of smoke on the horizon, they weren't more than ten miles out of Bozeman. The town produced the dark cloud from simply being there. Woodsmoke, even sooty billows from burning coal, marked their destination as surely as any X on a map.

Clay worked his side of the herd. It was as if the beeves sensed the end of the trail, the long days walking and the sparse grass coming to an end, and yearned to be penned up and fed grain. He wondered if he was any better at planning his future. The cattle wanted feed and water and not to be tromping along, no matter that their next stop was a cattle car taking them back East to a slaughterhouse. For the immediate future, they were content.

He should be, too. The only one on the drive with a definite future was Henry Oakes, and he might be dead before the cattle reached their destination.

Clay fell into a daydream, riding along, half paying attention to the cattle, as he considered where to head next. Wintering in Montana to get ready for the next season was hard. Maybe he'd turn back south and head for Mexico right away, before the winter clamped down like a vise on the mountainous terrain. There were towns just over the southern border that appealed to him. Or they had in the past. With the recent revolution, he might not be as popular there, though if he had a pocket full of silver dollars, that bought a passel of goodwill.

"There it is, men," Oakes called out. He wiped the last bloody spittle off his lips with a swift pull of his sleeve. "You'll be paid by nightfall!"

That brought a resounding cheer. To his surprise, Clay found himself whooping and hollering, too. The drive hadn't been difficult, but boring routine had worn on him, as it had on all the rest. Their cook had died a week along the trail, and they'd taken turns preparing the food. For his part, Clay was tired of little more than beans for dinner, with a slab of beef alongside, and then oatmeal for breakfast. Only Lanky Lou had skill enough to make decent flapjacks, but that was all he knew how to cook. The others weren't any better. Because the men were pulling double duty, there wasn't time for whoever was stuck with being chef of the day to find vegetables or fruit along the trail.

It took the better part of an hour once they reached the town to herd their beeves into pens. By the time Clay had finished with his part, Henry Oakes came out of the shipping agent's office with a large leather sack jingling with coins.

"Line up, men, and collect your due. You've earned it." Oakes held back a cough. His hands shook a mite as he parceled out their wages. Clay took his, counted them and started to speak.

"You earned it, son."

"There's a gold double eagle along with my pay."

"A bonus." Oakes sighed, then shuddered. He turned rheumy eyes onto Clay and said in a voice so low, Clay wasn't sure he heard him properly, "If only you coulda been my son, things wouldn't look so bleak for the ranch." Louder, Oakes said, "Move along. I wish you luck wherever you go."

As Clay walked off so Oakes could pay off the rest of the cowboys, Vic Reedy came over and put his arm around his shoulder.

"Let's you and me wash away some of the trail dust. The Pouncing Panther Saloon's the best."

"Pouncing Panther, eh," Clay said. "I like the sound of it. Are you buying?"

"The first round. Then you gotta buy me one. That's the way it works. Of course, if you want to keep buyin', I ain't gonna tell you no!"

They walked down the middle of the street, passing by the boisterous laughter and loud music echoing from a half dozen saloons. Clay wondered if Reedy had a reason for choosing the particular drinking establishment he did since all the others afforded the same allure.

The Pouncing Panther was the last in a long row, almost at the edge of town, and looked as prosperous as the others. They entered and looked around. All the tables were crowded with poker games. It took Clay only a glance at them to know his chances at any of them were slim. Each was presided over by a well-dressed man with keen eyes, quick fingers and the look of a professional card sharp. Along the wall to his right, a bored-looking woman in a stained red dress with a low-scooped neckline bent over a faro table. The gamblers across from her had the look of sex-starved miners. They stared more at the woman's cleavage than they did at their bets or how she raked in some of their winning wagers, keeping them for the house. The few soiled doves at the rear of the saloon provided better value, or so Clay thought. The faro gamblers lost dollars or tens of dollars on every bet. They could have hired one of the other ladies for a fraction of that.

"There's a spot at the bar. Come along, old son. Let's sample James' newest brew."

"You know the barkeep?" Clay saw the stolid man behind the bar working his way from one end to the next, refilling glasses and taking money with the precision of a well-oiled machine. Clay frowned. The man looked familiar.

"He's my younger brother. But don't expect that tightwad to stand us for a free drink. I do declare, he can squeeze a nickel so hard, the buffalo squeals in agony." Reedy pushed Clay forward.

Clay moved so his right hip turned toward the room,

letting him lean on the bar with his left elbow. After such a long time on the trail, the crowd made him uneasy. He wasn't a gunman with lightning reflexes, but he knew his accuracy once he dragged that hogleg out of its holster was as good as any man's.

"Two shots of the real stuff, James. The bottle you keep under the bar for that no-account mayor you voted into office will do us just fine."

"Don't go ragging on Mayor Kenny, you old reprobate."

The barkeep poured two shot glasses so they brimmed with amber fluid. Just looking at the liquor made Clay's mouth water. The only liquor on the trail was carried in the cook's wagon for medicinal purposes. The Rocking O cowboys had honored that scrupulously, another mark of an experienced crew. Dealing with balky cattle required a sharp eye and a clear brain. Otherwise, somebody'd surely die.

"How is my little brother?" Reedy picked up the glass and eyed it, as if expecting to find salvation in it. Then he knocked back the shot and let out an earsplitting cry. "That's fine hoochinoo!"

Clay sipped tentatively, then drank his down. The liquid burned all the way to his gullet and puddled in his belly, the warmth spreading throughout his midriff. The aches and pains of so much time in the saddle slipped away. A few more shots and they would be a long-forgotten memory.

"Good," he said, his voice raspy. "What'd you call it?"

"Vic's harkening back to our days up in Alaska. The Tlingit Indians make firewater they call hoochinoo. This ain't it."

"No, sir, not at all. This is better, James. Much better now that you stole that old reprobate Finnigan's secret recipe." Reedy smacked his lips in appreciation.

"You say Kenny's not been strung up for robbin' the town treasury yet?"

Clay took another shot and let the crowd of others working to the bar move him away from Vic Reedy and the homecoming with his brother. From the sound of it, the Reedy family had the town in a bear hug. The saloon keeper, the town mayor, maybe others all hailed from the same parents. If the Rocking O disbanded here, Vic would be among his kin.

Clay had been a drifter so long, he hardly remembered where to call home. For someone young in years, he had put a lot of miles behind him. The far horizon always beckoned, promising just a little more adventure or money or . . . what? Someone to settle down with?

He licked his lips and tasted a lingering drop of whiskey. Another shot or two would cure him of that pipe dream. He was a wrangler. A drifter. Someone always on the trail to somewhere else.

The crowd carried him away like a leaf caught in a slow-running stream. He was content enough to let Vic Reedy get on with his family reunion. Clay saw a couple men from the drive at the back of the saloon, negotiating with the ladies of the evening. He considered partaking of those lovely ladies' charms, too. It got mighty lonely out on the drive, riding night herd, singing to the cattle to keep them soothed. The daytime chores weren't any less lonesome, and this trail drive had been doubly so since they had been shorthanded. He had done the work of two men, and the beeves never noticed or cared.

Lanky Lou caught sight of him and came over. Sharing a drink or two with the tall cowboy would go a ways toward chasing away the loneliness. Lou was someone, other than Reedy, that Clay had gotten along well with out on the trail.

"Come on and join us, Forsythe," the tall cowboy invited. "We got about the purtiest little fillies in Bozeman waitin' fer us."

Clay considered.

"If you weren't so bowlegged, you'd be twice as tall," Clay said. "Are those legs hollow? Let me buy you a drink and then—"

"I don't think Lulu Belle's inclined to wait. This whole place is full of gents linin' up to find exactly what she can offer."

Clay started to answer when a whipcord-tough, weathered, thin man came over and eyed them like he was getting ready to guess their weight the way traveling carnival barkers did.

"Just off the trail, you two?"

"Herdin' the Rocking O brand," Lou said. "Just got into town and lookin' to have some fun."

"Before you get too soused, hear me out. I'm hiring for another outfit. Good pay and you'd both be in line for a signing bonus."

"Now, what might that be?" Lou paid scant attention as he made eyes at Lulu Belle.

"Her. I'll hire you on and see that you and her spend the night gettin' to know each other real good." The man's dark eyes fixed on Lou like a snake watching a mouse. Clay felt uneasy at it. "Top wages and a night with her? How can you go wrong with that?"

Clay studied the man closer. He was too insistent. He wore fancy duds for a cowboy, but Clay told himself some men dressed up to come to town. What bothered him the most was the way the dark man wore the Peacemaker at his right side. The holster was tied down and the six-gun looked well used. Cowboy? Or gunfighter?

"I ain't got anythin' else to do now that we're at

the end of the trail," said Lou. "Nothin' but corralin' Lulu."

"If you sign on with my outfit, you can collect the bonus right now. It looks as if she's hankerin' as much for you as you are for her." The dark man turned.

Clay tensed for a split second. He thought the man was going to throw down on him. His hand rested on the ebony butt of his six-shooter and he bent forward slightly, balancing on the balls of his feet.

"You in, too? She's got a friend just itching to spend time with you."

"Got other plans," Clay lied. "I wasn't looking to sign on with another outfit just yet. Which one are you recruiting for? A local rancher?"

"Not local," the man said.

"Not interested, then," Clay replied.

However the man answered, Clay was inclined to dodge the opposite way. He put enough edge into his words that the man couldn't miss the rejection. Again Clay thought the man was going to draw. Instead he laughed. There was enough mockery that Clay took half a step back.

"Come along, my good man," the recruiter said, putting his arm around Lou's bony shoulders. "I just might join you. It'd be a shame to let her friend pine away all alone."

"Clay, you sure?" Lou looked back at his old trail companion as his new boss guided him to the rear of the saloon where the girls waited. "It'd be good to ride with you again."

Clay lifted his glass in salute. Then Lanky Lou found himself engaged with Lulu Belle and ignoring everything else in the world. They slipped out the rear, going toward a row of cribs behind the saloon. Clay felt as if he should stop Lou, and he didn't know why. The

Rocking O had paid them off. There weren't horses to drive back south into Colorado. The job was over.

That job was over, but Clay found that the drinking had just begun when Vic Reedy and his brother waved for him to rejoin them. Dawn cracked the sky by the time he'd had enough of the tarantula juice that James Reedy had concocted.

CHAPTER TWO

CLAY MOANED AS he turned over. He squinted as warm sunlight bathed his face. He rubbed his eyes and tried to sit up, but the way his head throbbed forced him to lie flat on his back in an attempt to quell the pain. He struggled to remember what had happened. He felt as if a locomotive had plowed into him and knocked him smack into the next county. Only supreme effort forced his eyes open. The light hurt.

"Forsythe, get your drunk carcass up."

"Vic?" He recognized the trail boss' voice and worried that he was caught in a terrible dream, that they hadn't reached Bozeman at all and were still on the trail. How much more did they need to ride before he could rest? "Did I get thrown? That wild mustang, was he the one that did me in?"

"Rise and shine, Forsythe. You're hungover, but it prob'ly feels like a mule kicked the tar out of you after you guzzled a full bottle of that joy juice last night. Come with me." Reedy poked him with the toe of his

boot until Clay finally relented and got to his feet. He
wobbled a little, then steadied himself against the wall.

He had finished the night curled up in a corner of
the Pouncing Panther. He remembered seeing the first
faint fingers of pink-lit wispy clouds warning him that
he had drunk the night away. But it was hardly an hour
past that promise of a new and more sober day.

"Let me find somewhere to go back to sleep."

"You'll feel better walkin' off the popskull still in
your belly. The exercise might even drain those bloodshot eyes of yours."

Reedy shoved him toward the swinging double
doors and out into the light of day. The sunlight, faint
as it was, threatened to blow his head apart like a keg
of black powder had been planted and set off behind
his eyes.

"Tlingit. I remember you saying it was some witch's
brew the Alaska Indians conjured."

"That's what my brother tells everyone. Or not. It
depends on what it takes to get them to sample his
whiskey. He conjures it all up in his back room, every
drop, no matter what the bottle label says. Now
come on."

"Where are we going?"

Clay cringed with every step. The impact of foot
against sunbaked dirt street sent an earthquake through
his body and set off a volcano in his brain. Reedy was
right about one thing. He felt better by the time they
reached a doctor's office. The neatly painted shingle
swung to and fro in the morning breeze.

"Doc Quinton's the best in town," Reedy said. He
opened the door and held it for Clay. "Don't go makin'
too much noise. It'll disturb him."

"The doctor? You're taking me to him for some
hangover cure? There's no call pouring some potion
down my gullet. I'm feeling better."

"Ain't the doctor I'm worried 'bout you disturbin'. It's Mr. Oakes."

Clay tried to figure out what the trail boss meant, but he stepped as quietly as he could into the surgery. He winced as floorboards squeaked. In his condition it sounded like the crack of doom with every footfall.

A youngish man with thinning sandy hair and a worried expression pushed though curtains and came into the office. Pale blue eyes peered out of bloodshot orbs.

"You look as bad as I feel," Clay said.

"I've been up all night with Mr. Oakes." The doctor sighed and sank into a chair behind the desk. He held his face in both hands for a moment, then looked up. "I did all I could for him. His lungs filled with blood. That was the end for him. I'm sorry."

"He died?" Clay looked at Reedy.

The trail boss ground his teeth together the way he did when things went wrong.

"Tuberculosis," the doctor said. "He should never have made the drive. It took too much out of him. There are plenty of sanatoriums in Colorado where he could have recuperated." Dr. Quinton shook his head. "His lungs were in such bad shape, maybe they couldn't have cured him, even at the Glenwood Sanatorium, but at least his final days would have been easier." He coughed, hinting that his own condition wasn't much better than Oakes'. "He might have lived another year."

"Did he say anything 'fore he up and died?" Vic Reedy sounded desperate.

"Not a thing. You want to arrange for a funeral or should I get the undertaker to handle the burial?"

"The undertaker ought to handle the details," Reedy said quickly. "We worked for Mr. Oakes 'til we got to town. Then he paid us off."

"So you don't work for the ranch any longer?" The doctor nodded, understanding the situation. The only people willing to take responsibility were back in Colorado, Oakes having let all his employees go.

Clay tried to find something to say, but words galloped away. He let Reedy herd him from the office. They stood just outside. The warm morning sun felt uncomfortable now.

"Why'd you bring me over here? Did you think I could do something for Mr. Oakes if he was still alive?" Clay had no idea what that might have been.

"I hoped he'd tell the doctor he was leavin' the spread to me. I've worked for Henry Oakes long enough. We'd been through thick and thin."

"You expected him to give you the Rocking O instead of his son?"

"Something like that. We don't call him Soused Sully for no reason. That boy's never sober. Sullivan Oakes never showed any interest in the finest ranch anywhere in Colorado. His pa was everything Sully's not."

"I wasn't around much, but his son never showed much ambition."

"That's a polite way of sayin' he's a wastrel. I had thought to ride back. No reason to leave Bozeman now that Mr. Oakes has passed on."

Clay thought on it, then said, "You wanted me to witness Oakes willing the ranch to you?"

"I did," Reedy said. "That doesn't make me a bad man." He sighed. "If he had, I'd have offered you the chance to be the foreman. You're good, Forsythe, about the best trail hand I ever rode with. You have the skill to break broncos that nobody else kin ride. Ropin' 'n' brandin'? You showed me a thing or two, and I've been on the range for nigh on twenty years."

"Those are mighty kind words," Clay said, unsure

what more to say at such praise. Reedy hadn't mentioned his admiration out on the drive. If anything Clay thought the trail boss had badgered him worse than any of the other hands, including a couple who had spent more time looking to get out of work than actually riding herd.

"Truth. You've got years left in you that I don't. Maybe my brother Kenny can set me up with a decent job. He's mayor of this here town. He owes me. There's no way I'll ask James. Running a saloon takes a special kind of crazy. He's got it. I don't." Vic Reedy smiled crookedly. "If I didn't drink away all the profits, I'd lose my temper when the first drunk called me out. Puttin' a few bullet holes in the payin' customers is *real* bad for business."

Clay wasn't sure why he mentioned it but he did. He said, "There was a fellow recruiting for another trail drive last night in the saloon. You might hire on with him."

"Are you fixin' to join up?"

"Lanky Lou did, I reckon. He had some powerful incentive to with the sign-up bonus being offered." Clay paused, thinking how good Lulu Belle had looked. Her friend hadn't been anywhere near as ugly as a mud fence, either. "I didn't like the look of the recruiter."

"Was he a local? I know most of the ranchers in these parts."

"He said he wasn't."

Reedy shook his head. "It's a poser, then. Why should somebody come to Bozeman to hire a crew? He'd be better off going down into Jackson's Hole."

"Why there?" Clay perked up a mite. He had no intention of staying in Bozeman, not like Reedy. He had no family here and wasn't inclined to while away the time until the snows came and made any travel impossible. Better to find another job until it was time to drift south. A lot farther south where the snow wasn't a problem.

"I heard tell of a rodeo there. There's supposed to be big prizes for the winners. Maybe you should see if bein' best in bulldoggin' or calf ropin' isn't in your future. You're good enough."

"But am I the best?" Clay considered the matter.

There was only one way to find out.

CLAY ENTERED JACKSON'S Hole from the east, through Togwotee Pass. He sucked in clean, pure air and coughed. The high mountains took his breath, just a little. Riding rodeo at such altitude would be a chore, but he was used to high country on the western slopes of the Front Range. Would others entering the contest find themselves gasping for breath? To Clay it didn't matter. Competing for prizes meant being at his peak, no matter the weather, the altitude or the competition.

He rode on into Jackson's Hole and turned south. The countryside appealed to him, but then he was more a rancher than a farmer. The soil was worthless for raising crops, even if the vicious winters allowed for a decent growing season—which they didn't. There might not be farms all around but wildlife abounded. For the first time in weeks, he found hunting easy along the trail from Bozeman and knew why the mountain men favored this region.

The rivers were dammed by armies of beavers, deer poked their noses out from behind every juniper and ponderosa pine and smaller game fed packs of wolves that gave Clay a wide berth. Why tangle with a human with a rifle when rabbits were plentiful and easy or a half dozen wolves could bring down an elk and dine for a week?

By the time he rode into the town of Hoback, he felt ready to whip his weight in wildcats. Clay rode slowly down the main street already festooned with banners and signs proclaiming the upcoming gala rodeo. From the business being conducted in the half dozen saloons at midday, nearly every cowboy in the Rockies was raring to go.

Thirst from being on the trail so long made him veer toward a likely-looking watering hole. Ironically named Paradise, the saloon was hardly more than a tent. Canvas had been nailed to wood uprights. The entry was nothing more than strips of an old horse blanket sewed to the canvas roof, but the tinny sound of a piano blared from inside and barely drowned out the roar of men drinking and carousing.

Clay fastened his horse to an iron ring not already filled with other reins. He settled his six-gun and then pushed aside the tattered blanket strips and looked around the smoke-filled room. More than twenty customers darted around like fish in a stream. They guzzled beer in huge mugs and some carried almost empty bottles of whiskey. The bar was a long rough-hewn plank balanced on two sawhorses. Where most bars had brass cuspidors for their patrons' use, this one had dug foot-deep pits in the spongy ground. The hollows were almost overflowing.

Walking carefully around those spit pits, Clay went to the bar and dropped a silver cartwheel. It spun and finally came to rest after creating a satisfying ring against the wood. The barkeep drew a beer and snatched up the coin. It disappeared into a bulging pocket on his canvas apron. He made no move to give back one red cent.

"Hey, where's my change?"

"A dollar for the beer."

Clay moved around to get a better grab on his pistol. He knew when he was being cheated.

"Don't work yourself up into a lather. Prices on everything in Hoback have gone sky-high." The barkeep gestured to show the crowd inside the Paradise. "This time of day, we'd be empty, save for maybe old Gus. I swear that man's britches are glued to a chair. He never budges."

"That's the truth, mister," said the cowboy next to him at the bar. The man grinned, showing a gap in his yellowed front teeth. "Old Gus never stirs." He laughed at his answer and tried to elbow Clay in a show of hilarity. He missed and went to his knees. He thought this was even funnier.

The prices might have been exorbitant but that hadn't stopped this patron from drinking too much.

Clay sipped his beer and joined the endless current of bodies around the room. He listened hard. Most of the others were cowboys come to town for the rodeo. Sizing them up made him more confident. There were cowhands who did their job, ate their chuck and caroused. They had no ambition to do better at any of those things. A few of the men showed more gumption, and those Clay studied closely.

They had a hard look in their eyes. They concentrated on their jobs and were likely good at roping and riding. Competition. Serious competition.

He finished appraising them and their possible strengths, drained his beer and stepped back into the sunny Wyoming afternoon. From information on the signs along the street, he had to sign up for the events. Glad to be out of the saddle for even a few blocks, he ambled along, taking in the sights. The rodeo was likely the biggest thing to ever blow through Hoback.

Every vacant lot was filled with tents and cowboys. Without his inquiring, that told him the town's lone hotel was packed to overflowing. He had no call to share a single room with a half dozen others and pay ten or twenty dollars for the privilege.

As he neared the tent set up to take entrants' money, he saw a sight that made him grin. Two cowboys decked out in flashy duds held forth under the board-walk overhang for a gunsmithy. They strutted about like peacocks and with good reason. Their wildly col-orful clothing, shining silver conchas and boots made out of some gray skin the like of which Clay had never seen before put any plumed bird to shame. And like a peacock's feathers, their outrageous attire drew the ladies.

Clay considered going over to listen to what they had to say since the ladies all laughed or hid grins be-hind genteel hands or open fans. The pair of Beau Brummells knew how to attract and fascinate the town's more desirable womenfolk.

"You fixin' on enterin' the rodeo? Step on up and fork over yer entry fees," a grizzled old man called from inside the tent. Clay went in and almost backed out. Behind the clerk stood two guards with shotguns resting in the crooks of their arms.

"Are they entering, too?" Clay eyed them closely. From the cut of their clothing, they weren't cowboys and didn't spend much time astride a horse. More likely, they were lawmen, although neither showed a badge.

"They're makin' sure nobody gets the bright idea of robbin' me. What's yer pleasure? Bulldoggin'? Calf ropin'? Ridin' the goldangest, orneriest broncos what ever went sunfishin'?"

"All of them, I reckon," Clay said.

"Thirty dollars. Coin, no greenbacks. Not even

scrip issued on the local bank. It's not that I don't trust banker Boxleitner, but, well, metal don't fade like the ink on his printed bills, if you know what I mean."

"Thirty?" This princely sum would take almost all of his pay left from riding herd for the Rocking O.

"You got to bet big to win big. A hunnerd dollars first prize in each event. That means you're riskin' one dollar in hopes of rakin' in ten."

"I know what it means," Clay said.

"Good, an eddy-cated wrangler. And from your look, one what kin walk away a sight richer than he is now. Thirty dollars wins you three hunnerd." The crafty gleam in the old man's eye warned Clay.

"How many have entered already? And how many more do you expect?"

"Oh, a few, a few. You look to be the best of the lot. Did you get a gander at those two across the street?"

"The Mexicans?"

"Them's the ones you got to beat. All hat, no cow, that's what my ole pa used to say 'bout folks that get gussied up like them."

"They've certainly got the hats," Clay admitted. "But how many others will enter?"

"Close to a hunnerd so far. Won't be many more since the competition starts tomorrow afternoon. There's not room enough in Hoback to hold stragglers."

Clay considered the odds. A hundred or more vying for the prizes, but the old man was right. How many were real cowboys and how many of that number were more than adequate? If those Mexican peacocks were any guide, he'd sweep the three events.

"Here you are," Clay said. He fished out the twenty-dollar gold piece and reluctantly stacked ten cartwheels beside it. The die was cast. He was committed to competing, but they were skills he had honed over the past few years. Hadn't Vic Reedy said he was about the best he had seen in twenty years of riding herd? Hadn't Henry Oakes considered making him trail boss?

Even if he didn't win all three events, walking away with the top money in just one tripled his money. That was better than he could do playing faro.

Clay stepped out of the tent and cast a covetous eye at the two Mexicans in their gaudy finery. They each had a pair of young ladies, one on each arm, to admire their plumage. After Clay won the rodeo's top prizes, the ladies would flock to him instead.

He sauntered off to fetch his horse and find a vacant patch of ground to sleep on that night. Tomorrow was going to be his day to shine.

CHAPTER THREE

PACING BACK AND forth, Clay tried not to watch the other cowboys as they exploded from the chute. He tried not to watch because so many were so good, but the whistle of a lariat sailing through the air, the thud as a calf was yanked off its feet, followed by pitiful lowing as a couple quick turns of rawhide were whipped around three of its hooves drew his eyes like a compass always points north. The crowd cheered and a timekeeper shouted out the seconds required for the hog-tying.

The precious few seconds.

"They are pretty good."

Clay jumped a foot. He had been concentrating so much on the event in the arena that he missed the cowboy coming up beside him. A quick glance told him this wasn't a cowboy. This was a vaquero dressed in typical Mexican range gear.

The vaquero laughed and slapped him on the back.

"You do not recognize me without all the fine *chicas* hanging on my arm, eh?"

"I didn't recognize you without the bright clothing."

"Ah, you noticed. *Bueno*. It is meant to draw attention."

The man leaned on the corral fence and peered through at the next contestant, who had erupted from the chutes. His lariat had tangled and the calf scooted away unroped. The calf stopped at the far side of the arena and let out a sound of bovine derision. At least it sounded that way to Clay.

"You succeeded," Clay said.

"He leaned too far when the gate flew open. Even if his rope had not caught on his own boot, he would have taken too long. The secret is bringing the calf down quickly. The rest?" The man shrugged. "Tying is the easy part."

"That's all there is to it?" Clay laughed harshly.

He had roped and thrown hundreds of calves. It was a complex dance, every part demanding complete concentration. Taking your eye off the calf might mean missing a twitch that warned of a sudden spurt of speed in an unexpected direction. A toss of the head? That caused a miss. Hitting the ground running after the calf was upended was important, too. Step on a rock, turn an ankle in a hole, slip in the dirt—the calf might as well be on the moon for all the chance of tying its hooves. Then the rawhide strip carried in clenched teeth had to be expertly wound. Two turns usually secured the thrashing calf. Only the most skilled knew when to take time for a third. If the calf kicked free, the entire rundown, roping and tying was wasted.

Do it all just right; do it all faster than everyone else. There wasn't any part that came easily.

"That is all. See my partner? He is in the chute. Watch how he works."

Clay climbed onto the lower rail to get a better look. The vaquero's friend had also forgone the flashy clothing in favor of more traditional work clothing. Still, something looked amiss and Clay couldn't put it into words. They were Mexican vaqueros, but their clothes looked different somehow. The fabric carried a sheen he had never seen before on cowboys' duds from south of the border, and the cut was different. He wasn't enough of a clotheshorse to detail the differences, but the two men weren't—quite—the same as others he'd ridden with. Before he could consider the matter further, the calf burst from its chute. A precise time later, the rider's gate snapped open.

The roping was over in a flash. For a moment Clay wondered if he had closed his eyes. Then the announcement came. The vaquero had posted the fastest time so far.

"See? It is all in the roping. And José is slow."

Clay stared skeptically at the man beside him and then said, "Slow? He's leading everyone else."

"That is because I have not roped yet." The vaquero laughed. "I am Leo Suárez and my slowpoke *amigo* is José Vasques."

"Vaqueros?" Clay asked, not sure what else to say. Vasques' quickness and skill left him unable to think clearly.

"Not us. We are *paniolo*."

"What's that?" Clay spoke to thin air. Suárez rushed off to climb the rails and settle astride his horse in the chute. He patted his horse's neck, then came the explosion of frightened calf, horseflesh and rider.

Clay stared in disbelief. Suárez had beaten his partner's time by a fraction of a second. The two vaqueros—*paniolo*, whatever that was—were in first and second place.

He started to push through the crowd to find the men and congratulate them when he heard his name called.

"Clayton Forsythe! You're up next!"

He waved to the official with the list, snared his horse's reins and went to the chute. A cowboy ahead of him successfully roped and tied the calf. And his time was twice that posted by Leo Suárez. Clay edged his horse into the chute, then mounted. Worrying about the two Mexicans and their lightning times was a sure path to defeat. He had done this more times than he could remember. He bit down on the rawhide strap, edged forward in the saddle just enough to grip with his knees and ran out a loop in his rope.

A quick nod and the world turned to molasses around him. His horse thundered after the calf. The loop trailed out with painful slowness to land around the calf's neck. It jerked high into the air, all four legs leaving the ground at the same instant. Still moving in the curious slowness of heightened sensation, his gelding dug in its front hooves. At the same instant he secured the lariat around the saddle horn. He hit the ground, spat out the rawhide as he spun about. He threw his hands high in the air.

For an instant Clay thought he had gone deaf. No sound. The crowd had frozen. Then he heard the cheers and saw how the crowd responded. He freed the calf and let it run as he coiled his rope and secured it to his saddle. A quick pat on the well-trained horse's neck ended when he heard his time.

He had never reacted faster.

And he'd still been a fraction of a second behind Vasques. Third. With leaden feet, he exited the arena leading his horse. The two *paniolo* waited for him.

"You took my advice. You were speedy," Leo Suárez said.

"But not fast enough to beat you. Either of you." Clay thrust out his hand and shook both of theirs.

"You are a good loser, eh?" Suárez pointed. "There

is no one remaining to ride who can beat any of the three of us."

"You won the hundred dollars," Clay said.

"True, and José rakes in fifty. You will win twenty-five. Not bad for ten seconds' work, eh?"

"How's that?" Clay tried to understand what they said. "Third place wins money?"

"Ah, a man who sees only first prize and the rest is for losers," Vasques said. "He is like you, Leo."

"He thinks like me but he ropes like you," Suárez said. "Too slow!"

The men laughed. Clay hesitated, then had to join in.

"I know when I'm beat—at least, in the calf roping. There're a couple more events."

"Do not spend your prize money too soon, eh?" Suárez spoke rapidly to his partner, causing Clay to perk up.

"I know a little Spanish. What are you speaking?"

"We are not Mexicans," Vasques said. "My papa was, and so was Leo's grandmother. We are Hawaiian now."

Clay stared at them in disbelief. "I've heard of that place. An island out in the Pacific somewhere. You're from there?"

"Both of us were born on Oahu. We ride for the biggest ranch in all Hawaii," Suárez said proudly.

"The Barker Ranch," added Vasques. "We run more than five thousand head of cattle."

"What are you doing in Wyoming? This is a long way from Hawaii, isn't it?"

"Very far, but we have come here for the rodeo. Others from the Barker now buy breeding stock nearby. We will herd them to the smaller ranch in northern California, then sail them to Hawaii to improve the stock." Vasques sounded proud of his outfit.

Clay had heard of most of the big spreads, especially down in Texas, but never one like this.

"It's big? How many acres?"

Suárez and Vasques exchanged rapid words in Hawaiian; then Suárez said, "More than a hundred thirty thousand acres."

"That's a mighty good size. So you call yourselves *paniolo*? That's Hawaiian for vaquero?"

"For *español*. There is no ess sound in Hawaiian, so our ancestors became *paniolo*." Suárez started to say more but Vasques nudged him.

"We must go win more money. You will bulldog and then ride the broncos?"

"I paid good money to do that," Clay allowed.

"Then you will lose good money to us!" Together Suárez and Vasques hurried off, leaving Clay to trail behind.

The bulldogging went better for Clay than it did for the Hawaiians. Again he finished third, but they failed to come close to a winning time. Suárez lost his grip and was trampled by his steer. Vasques wrapped his arms around his steer's horns but could not twist around hard enough to throw it. The two cowboys who bested Clay were luckier than they were good, but he had to admit they deserved their prizes. He pocketed another twenty-five dollars.

The final event claimed one rider after another. Clay had never seen broncos buck so hard and send so many riders flying through the air.

"They have chosen the most vicious stallions for us," Vasques said. "This will be a serious test."

Clay took a deep breath. He was next up and the bronco selected for him looked like a real killer. The huge coal-black stallion's nostrils flared and whites showed around his eyes. He snorted and pawed and looked ready to take off like a Fourth of July skyrocket while still in the chute.

"There ain't no horse what never can't be rode," he said.

Unfortunately both of his companions knew the rest of the saying. Together they said, "And there ain't no rider what never can't be throwed."

Suárez slapped him on the back and said, "We will pick up your pieces."

"If you ever come down from spinning so high," added Vasques.

"Your encouragement makes me want to go right on out there and show you how it's done." Clay climbed the fence and straddled the horse as it bucked and kicked at the stall. He wrapped the rope halter around his hand, then dropped down. The instant he hit the horse's back, the gate flew open.

And Clay was in for the ride of his life.

The stallion twisted in midair, landed so hard, it jolted his teeth, then kicked upward and tried to take flight. It bent close to double in midair, sunfishing and turning. When the horse crashed into the ground from that bucking, Clay was a goner. He sailed away, barely avoiding the back hooves kicking out to smash him in the head. He hit the ground and rolled, but the impact dazed him.

Stunned, he was unable to move. Then he went airborne again. Strong hands gripped his arms and lifted him out of the arena. When his vision cleared a little, he saw that Suárez and Vasques had rescued him.

"Did I stay on?" Clay started to repeat it, then realized the bronco had gotten the better of him.

"It was close, my friend, but that villain proved better than you this day."

"I could ride him. I could break him, given another chance."

"See what landing so hard does to a man's head, Leo? It knocks out all common sense."

Suárez and Vasques argued about Clay's recovery until breath came normally again and the ache in his body faded just a little. He needed another bottle of James Reedy's whiskey to get knee-walking drunk to chase off the last of the aches and pains. He wasn't in line for any prize money here, but he had earned a total of fifty dollars after forking over thirty as entry fees. He felt good enough about coming out that much ahead.

"It is our turn to show you how this is done. Watch and learn," said Suárez.

José Vasques' ride went the needed two seconds longer than Clay's, but like Clay, Leo Suárez also failed. Suárez went flying at the first buck. The three of them huddled together, waiting for the final decision. Of all the entrants, only two had successfully ridden that afternoon. Vasques was named the top bronco rider, showing more skill than a cowboy from a nearby ranch.

Clay was the first to congratulate Vasques when he was declared the grand-prize winner and claimed a fancy belt buckle worth more in bragging rights than in money.

"We have done well," Suárez said. "Of nine possible cash prizes, Leo, between us we have won four."

"Add in my two third prizes and together we claimed six of the top nine. You should buy me a drink."

Clay surprised himself and didn't feel at all bad after being bested by the two Hawaiian cowboys. They had won fair and square. He had done his best, and today, they were better.

"Do they have tequila in Hoback?" Suárez looked around as if hunting for someone to ask. "I have never had a shot of tequila."

"What do you drink in Hawaii? Something rare and exotic?" Clay reclaimed his horse and walked with them to find their cow ponies.

"Rum. We drink rum. Sailors bring it in large kegs. That is better than the native fermented coconut milk!"

"I get tired of guava juice and rum," Vasques said. "Always it is rum and some fruit. Passion fruit, orange, guava. We should be real Wyoming cowboys and drink whiskey!"

"This looks like as good a spot as any," Clay said.

The crowds were building after the rodeo. He wondered if the two Hawaiians would be mobbed by admirers for their outstanding skills and two first-place wins.

"Go in and find us a place of honor. We will change our clothing and join you in a few minutes." Vasques held the belt buckle at his waist to see how it would look. His broad smile told how he enjoyed showing up the local cowboys by winning it.

"Change your clothes," Clay said slowly. "You're going to put on your fancy duds? The ones that make a man squint because the colors are so loud?"

"It makes a man squint and a woman squeal in pleasure. Did you see our boots? They are made from sharkskin. That is us. Two sharks swimming about, looking for prey. Our female prey!" The pair laughed uproariously at this and took the reins to Clay's horse.

"See you inside," he said.

He tried to find the name of the saloon, but it had been put up so hastily, the proprietor hadn't bothered with a sign. For all Clay knew, there might not even be a name. It hardly mattered if the whiskey was potent and didn't entirely drain his winnings. The dollar beer the day before had made him wary of being cheated.

He pushed his way through to the bar and considered himself lucky that the barkeep charged him only ten dollars for a full bottle. A quick sample convinced him the price was right. The liquor ran down his gullet as smooth as silk and warmed his gut. By the time he got to a table with three chairs, the booze was well on its way to erasing his new aches. One hard landing in particular had jolted his spine. Riding broncos wasn't for the faint of heart. The whiskey even eased those twinges.

He knocked back his second shot, then hesitated before taking a third when he recognized the man standing outlined in the doorway. He doubted the recruiter had trailed him from Bozeman. If he wanted to hire on cowboys for his spread, coming to the Hoback rodeo was a clever way to do it.

But Clay wished the man had picked another saloon. His presence cast a dark cloud over the festivities. The man made his way along the bar, talking to one cowboy after another. Most ignored him, a couple at least listened to his spiel but none signed up for the man's crew. Everyone in the saloon wanted nothing more right now than to celebrate the rodeo and swap stories about how they could have won if only . . .

The man spotted Clay. His grin was enough to chill a priest's soul. He started over, then halted halfway to the table when Suárez and Vasques made their entrance. Clay waved for them to join him.

They settled into chairs and cupped their glasses in both hands as if warming them.

"This is rye whiskey? This is what *norteamericano* cowboys drink?" Suárez asked.

"I can't tell if it's rye. I doubt that it's bourbon. It's powerful rotgut, though."

"That is enough for me," Vasques said. He wet his lips, made a face, then knocked back the shot. For a moment he sat as if paralyzed, then let out a raucous cry of delight. "That is a real drink! No more rum for me!"

Suárez was more subdued, but barely, when he declared, "It is stronger than rum. Even the dark rum. I like it. It is good that you bought an entire bottle, my friend."

Clay looked past the two gaudily dressed *paniolo* to where the recruiter stood as if nailed to the floor. The anger on the man's face caused Clay to worry that he was going to grab for the big Peacemaker slung low at his hip.

"Do you know that man? The one dressed in black?" Clay lifted his chin to point, Navajo style.

Both Hawaiians turned. They tensed and both moved for their six-shooters. Before anyone cleared leather and opened fire, the recruiter spat, pivoted and stormed from the saloon. Suárez and Vasques turned back to the table and carefully poured themselves another drink. Neither said a word.

"Do you know him?"

They glared at Clay. Their dark eyes burned with a fervor that gave him his answer.

"To being the best cowboys in Wyoming!" Suárez called out.

The two made sure the ladies in the saloon noticed them, saw their colorful clothing and came flocking over. Clay didn't mind at all that, as he had in the rodeo, he finished in third place to them.

But he wondered how the two Hawaiians and the gunslinger knew one another.

CHAPTER FOUR

I NEED TO find the outhouse," Clayton Forsythe said.
He knew his words slurred and the hubbub in the
saloon erased most of his heartfelt statement. Neither
Leo Suárez nor José Vasques acknowledged it when he
got up and made his way toward the rear of the room.
The door out back had fallen off its hinges.

Clay knew how it felt. He had drunk too much whiskey, but he felt good for having done it. The torment
racking his muscles and bones had vanished after the
fourth or fifth shot of the tarantula juice. He managed
to get through the doorway without further damaging
it. He stepped out into the cool, cloudless night. His
shadow stretched like a compass needle in front of
him, pointing to his destination. The wooden structure
with the half-moon carved in the door beckoned.

He hadn't taken two steps when he realized he
wasn't alone. He reached for his six-gun, but a strong
hand clamped on his wrist and twisted hard enough to

spin him around. The recruiter's face thrust forward, inches from his.

"You did real good today. You competed against a hundred others and won enough money to make back your entry fees."

Clay tried to free his hand. The grip tightened even more. The man stepped forward and herded Clay off the path to the outhouse and into deep shadow.

"You said you had other things to do when I talked to you back in Bozeman. It was good seeing you out in the arena riding a nasty bronco and then winning when it came to the cattle. I want to hire you. Did then, do now."

"I wasn't interested then," Clay got out. "And I'm still not."

"Because you wanted to prove yourself coming here for the rodeo. I admire that. I do. Now you've done that, there's nothing stopping you from hiring on with my outfit. Your partner Lou's real happy since he signed up. We're getting ready to drive some cows to the coast. You got the skills we need to make it a quick trail."

"No."

Clay gasped as the taller man lifted. Clay's hand slipped away from the butt of his six-gun. He started to push the man away and found himself grabbed from behind. Two others had come up unseen. Each clamped viselike hands onto his arms and held him immobile. The dark man kept his face shoved within inches of Clay's.

"You might be a bit deaf after listening to all those people yelling and cheering today. I'm offering you a job. Good pay, too."

"No."

"You haven't taken a job with those two yahoos, have you? They're nothing but gaudy liars. They talk big but nothing they say is true."

"They're better at being a cowboy than I am. They proved it today. Let me go."

"You *have* signed on with them, haven't you? Now, I can't let you do that. I don't care if you refuse my offer, but if you do, all I'm letting you do is ride away. You're not going to work for them. Can't abide by that, no, sir." He reared back and drove his fist into Clay's belly.

The impact caused Clay to double over. He would have collapsed to the ground if the two behind him hadn't been holding him firmly. He got the idea that they'd practiced this, two holding a victim while their boss used his fists.

"You're going to find your horse right now, mount up and ride like the devil's nipping at your heels. Because he is." Two more short punches to Clay's breadbasket made him gag and then retch weakly. "Hold him up. I want to be sure he's got the message before he goes on his way."

Hands pulled Clay upright. He looked at a fist being waved in front of his face.

"One more, for the road." The recruiter reared back. Clay braced for the punch that would break his nose. It never came.

Clay felt himself be dropped as the sounds of a fight swept over him. Then he heard hammers being cocked. Clay rolled onto his side and fumbled out his own pistol. Finding a target defeated him. His vision was too blurred, both from the liquor and from his being used as a punching bag. The sound of feet running away gave him incentive to sit up. He pressed his back against the saloon's rickety wall as he tried to make heads or tails of everything happening.

"They have fled like the cowards they are."

Clay recognized Vasques' voice. He rubbed his eyes and focused on the two Hawaiians. They returned their sidearms to their holsters.

"You saved me from getting beat up even more," Clay said. "Thanks."

"Warnock roughed you up only because you were with us."

"Warnock? That's his name? I crossed trails with him back in Bozeman. He hired some of the hands from my last drive up from Colorado." Clay got to his feet and holstered his own hogleg. "He sure is anxious to hire a crew for his drive."

"His drive? He thinks to drive a herd to the coast?"

The two spoke rapidly, mixing Hawaiian, Spanish and English so that Clay caught the gist of what they said if not the full details.

"You obviously know him. He looks more like a gunman than a trail boss. Is he recruiting men for a gang of rustlers?"

"He is a liar and a thief," Vasques said.

Suárez added far more. Clay caught *pendejo* and *hijo de puta* among other insults comparing Warnock's ancestors to a variety of barnyard animals.

"I'm just a cowboy. I've never rustled a cow in my life. Does he think I can run a brand? What's he want from me?" Clay held his head to keep it from splitting apart. Then he rubbed his belly. After the day's battering during the rodeo, this beating only added to his physical misery. "I need another drink."

"José, fetch another bottle," Suárez said. He took Clay's arm and steered him away from the saloon. "We must find a place to sit and talk. Warnock does not want you. He wants to keep you from joining us. It is a pity you have blundered into this feud."

"What are you talking about?"

Clay let himself be maneuvered to a spot behind the livery stables. He sank down on a bale of hay and closed his eyes. The smells, the feel, everything now was right in his world. He slowly opened his eyes to Vasques holding out a half bottle.

He shook his head and regretted it. If he drank any more, he'd slosh whenever he moved. His head hurt something fierce, but by morning the hangover would be ten times worse. Vasques shrugged at the small rejection, then sampled the liquor. He passed the bottle to his partner. Suárez took a powerful jolt, wiped his lips and launched into his tale.

"There is bad blood between Warnock and the Barkers. Warnock wants the small ranch on the California coast, and Mr. Barker has refused to sell. It is a necessary part of supplying the main ranch in Hawaii."

"Back in Bozeman, Warnock said he was recruiting trail hands for a drive. Or it sounded that way when he hired on a friend of mine from the Rocking O."

"He is an evil man. He has no cattle to drive to California. We do. The Barkers do. All Warnock wants is to steal our breeding stock."

"More than that, Leo," broke in Vasques. "He wants to steal the cattle and hold them for ransom."

"Ransom?" Clay tried to follow what they told him. "Are the cattle that valuable?" To him a cow was a cow. Some fetched good money, maybe a hundred dollars a head, but ransoming a cow, even a prize bull, seemed crazy.

"They are needed to improve the herd, but you are right. We can always find others for breeding. He intends to steal the cattle, then return them in exchange for the California ranchland. The cattle are worth far more than the land."

"But giving up your property makes it harder to supply your ranch in Hawaii? Is that it?" Clay wondered if more than a land dispute was at stake.

"I know your thoughts," said Suárez. "Sell Warnock the land, find another patch not adjoining his ranch."

"That did occur to me."

"He intends to use the Barkers' dock to begin moving into Hawaii himself. He is a cutthroat. He must not gain a foothold on the island."

"What else is there? This isn't just about cattle or land. It sounds personal." Clay watched their expressions. He was right. And they weren't going to tell him. "Can't you go to the law?"

"He has done nothing that will please a judge enough to convict him," Vasques said. "What he did to you can be denied. It is your word against his, and he has men who will swear he had nothing to do with the beating."

"You'd testify that he did."

"Who will believe Hawaiians? We are not citizens. Our ancestors were never citizens. They left Oaxaca and never even passed through this country."

"I'd believe you," Clay said. "After all, you beat me in two events today."

Both Hawaiians laughed. Suárez held out the whiskey bottle again. This time Clay took it and tentatively sipped. The alcohol stung a split lip. He swished the liquor around and then spat. The burning went away after a second application.

"Will you step into this hornet's nest?" The two *paniolo* exchanged a quick glance. Both nodded at the same time. "We would hire you to ride with us, Clay."

Clay started to answer but the liquor tangled his tongue. His thoughts darted about like trout in a stream swollen with spring runoff. Riding with this pair would be an honor. There weren't many cowboys he'd ever met who bested him as easily as these two. He could learn from them, earn from them and see the ocean. He'd never seen that much water. Clay held down a belch and took another swig.

"We need to be sure he's not going to cause any more trouble. If he finds out I've signed on with your outfit, he's the kind to set up an ambush."

"He is a back shooter," Suárez said with a touch of bitterness.

Again Clay wondered what the real story was between the two ranches. Blood had been spilled—and there was something more. He knew it.

"Let's see what trouble we can cause for him," Clay said. "I'll hire on to ride with the two best Hawaiian cowboys in all of Wyoming!"

He heaved himself to his feet. For a moment he was giddy; then it passed. Seldom had he felt he was thinking this clearly. He had come to Hoback not knowing what lay in his future. With the rodeo behind him and because he had agreed to be a wrangler for the Barker Ranch, all uncertainty was gone.

"He will continue to hire cowboys," Vasques said. "He is collecting enough for an army. That tells much about his intentions."

"The men he was enlisting back in Bozeman, except for Lou, looked more like gunslicks than someone willing to ride night herd." He looked at the two and said, "That's what you want me to do, isn't it, take the least desirable jobs?"

"You are tedious enough with your talk-talk to put a man to sleep. That should work well with beeves." For a moment Suárez kept a straight face; then he broke out laughing and slapped Clay on the shoulder. "We live an easy life, one filled with joking. You are so serious, Forsythe."

"Clay. And there's one of the men I saw Warnock talking to in the saloon. I thought he had turned him down, but it looks like he's a new recruit."

Footsteps alerted them to someone's arrival, and Clay and the others pressed back against the wall, hidden in shadows cast by a quarter moon. Warnock and a man most notable for having no outstanding features came to the side door of the livery. The lights and gaiety up and down Hoback's main street—its only street—seemed a thousand miles away.

"You got the directions straight? Ride out and tell Ros that I signed you on."

"Ros?" The man yawned. "Got it, boss."

"Roskolnikov. He's from Russia. He talks funny English, but he's as tough as they come."

"What's he doing in California? Russia's a mighty far piece from there, ain't it?"

"He came over with Russian sealers and stayed," said Warnock. "You do as he tells you. If you cross him, you'll regret it." Warnock paused and added, "If you cross me, you'll be a buzzard's breakfast. Cross Ros and you'll end up even worse."

Clay bit down on his split lip when he saw how fast Warnock's draw was. His gun hand was hardly a blur as he filled his fist with the butt of his Peacemaker.

"There's no call for that," the new recruit said uneasily. "Pay me and I'll stay loyal. Cross me and being fast won't mean a thing."

Warnock took a step forward and swung his pistol. The barrel caught the man on the side of his head. He dropped to his knees, stunned.

"Never threaten me or even the buzzards will never find your carcass. You got that?"

The man climbed to shaky legs and supported himself against the stable wall. He rubbed his temple. In the faint moonlight a pure black smear showed on his fingers. Blood trickled down the side of the man's head.

"Got it . . . boss."

Warnock lowered the hammer on his six-gun, spun it around on the trigger guard and returned it smoothly to his holster. Without another word, he stalked off.

Suárez whispered, "We should tell him what he faces. This is only a sample of what Warnock will give to him."

Clay caught the *paniolo*'s arm and held him back.

"How long do you think he's going to put up with Warnock pushing him around? We've got a potential ally in his camp."

"It is as our new friend says, Leo," whispered Vasques. "Let this anger fester."

"He's useful in another way," said Clay. "You follow me in case I need help."

Before the Hawaiians could ask what he meant, he grabbed the bottle from Suárez's hand and barreled around the corner of the livery. He began singing a bawdy song.

Clay stopped and stared as if he had no idea anyone else was near. He hoisted the bottle and let the liquor slosh around.

"You want a pull of my whiskey?" He stepped closer with the bottle preceding him, clutched in his outstretched hand.

"Who're you?" the cowboy snapped.

"I just got hired by Warnock. Tole—told—me to ride on out and join the rest. Sure you don't want a drink?"

"He's really scrapin' the bottom of the barrel if he's takin' the likes of you on this little expedition."

"I can hold my own. I tole—told—him I was even up for a bit of rustling." Clay hiccuped loudly. To his surprise, it came easily. He had sampled more of the booze than he thought. It showed in how he walked and the way his belly felt. Worst of all, he realized how scatterbrained his spur-of-the-moment plan was, passing himself off as a new recruit.

"I'm going out there now."

"Kin—can—I ride along? Warnock gave me a map

but I lost it." Clay made a few tentative pats of his pockets as if hunting for the nonexistent map. "You want to share?" Clay held out the whiskey again.

This time the man took the bottle and knocked back a couple fingers from the contents. Then he threw the whiskey against the livery wall.

"You've had enough," the man said. "Saddle up and you'd better not fall behind. If you do, I'm leaving you." The man continued in a nasty tone. "I just got a gander at what Warnock's like if you get out of line."

"Staying in line, yes, sir, right in line," Clay assured his unsuspecting guide.

He hurried into the stable and found his horse. In the dark, saddling was more difficult than he expected. Or maybe his whiskey intake was responsible. Whatever it was, he had to ride hard to catch up with the man, who was already heading west out of town.

When he drew even with the other man, he asked, "If we're going to be partners, what do I call you?"

The man turned toward Clay and tilted his head back just a little to catch the faint moonlight. He sneered. "Sir. You call me sir."

"No need to get so testy. I was just asking to be hospitable."

Clay was relieved at not having to make small talk with the man, but if he learned a name, he might check with the marshal back in Hoback and see if the man's name and face showed up on a wanted poster. As dark as it was, Clay wasn't sure he would be able to identify the man, but a name would have gone a ways toward finding more about the type of men Warnock hired.

"Is that the camp? I see a couple fires." Clay inhaled deeply. "Cooking some beans from the smell. I could use a plate right about now."

The man raked his spurs along his horse's flanks and shot ahead. Clay followed more slowly, looking for a chance to stop entirely and decide what to do next. If he sneaked into camp, he might find out what Warnock was planning. The chance of him being recognized was small since the only hand likely to know him was Lanky Lou. Warnock and his two bully boys were still back in town.

The ride had cleared away the fog caused by the whiskey. As he considered the difficulties if he ran into Lou, he knew that was a bad idea no matter what happened. Lou was an honest sort and wouldn't understand why he ought to keep his old trail companion's identity a secret.

The man who'd led him to the camp galloped on. When Clay no longer heard the pounding hooves, he knew the man had arrived. He'd be asking around and presenting himself to Ros along with his story of being hired by Warnock.

Clay slowed and finally stopped a hundred yards away from the bivouac. He tried to get an idea as to how many men there were, but from this distance all he made out were silhouettes moving back and forth between him and the campfires.

He turned his horse's face to return to Hoback.

"Where you think you're going?" The voice was deep, resonant—and backed up with a double-barreled shotgun pointed straight at him.

CHAPTER FIVE

Clay Forsythe stared down the twin barrels, then hesitantly worked his gaze up to the man holding the shotgun. His assailant was as fearsome as he'd thought he would be. A giant of a man, his challenger looked ready to pull the double triggers just out of spite. At this range, even in the dark, he couldn't miss.

"I wandered off the road and got turned around. I saw that rider and thought I'd follow him and—" Clay saw his feeble excuse wasn't cutting it.

"Step down. Come closer." The man's thick accent warned Clay that this was Warnock's Russian ramrod, Roskolnikov.

"What are you doing out here in the middle of the night?" Taking the verbal attack to the giant was all Clay dared. Add a touch of confusion and a chance for escape might present itself. "You shouldn't wave that scattergun around like that, either. Folks might not take kindly to having it pointed at them."

"I do not care." The bass voice rumbled out contempt. "I do not shoot you on the horse. I can use another mount. I shoot you on the ground and not get blood on the saddle."

"You're one of those horse thieves I'm always hearing about!" Clay tried to sound surprised. He judged his chances of avoiding the buckshot and getting away. His odds were slim. Twenty-four double-ought pellets would turn him into a bloody mess and kill his horse, to boot. "You don't want to steal my horse. You—"

"Down!" The Russian snugged the stock into his shoulder as if he had to aim at this short range. All he needed to do was point the gun in Clay's general direction and pull both triggers to commit the murder.

"Whoa, I'm getting off just like you said. Don't shoot. This horse means the world to me. It's about the best cutting horse I ever rode. I'm just a cowhand hunting for a job." He rattled on senselessly, looking for the opening. It never came. The Russian was too focused.

Clay stepped down and stood close to his horse, hoping to make it hard for the man to shoot. If he wanted the horse badly enough, he might be a bit hesitant to injure a perfectly fine mount.

"Who are you? Why you come snooping in the night. You spy on us!"

Clay played a desperate card in the game of staying alive. He took a deep breath, then blurted out, "Warnock hired me. I rode out from Hoback with the other guy." He jerked his thumb over his shoulder in the direction of the camp.

"I saw him. If Warnock wants you, what is the password?"

Clay went light-headed at that. He hadn't considered Warnock might be so suspicious that he'd have secret signs or phrases needed to even enter the camp.

"The other fellow. He knows what it is. Warnock

said only one of us needed to know." Clay knew how
lame that sounded. It failed to satisfy his captor.

"You lie. And now you die!" He drew the stock even
tighter into his shoulder. Before he pulled the triggers,
a thwack sounded and he took a step forward. The barrels shifted from Clay to a spot on the ground.

Clay had never moved faster in his life. He vaulted
into the saddle and sent the horse straight for the
shotgun-wielding man. Both barrels discharged, filling
the air with a thunderous roar and foot-long flashes of
orange. Clay almost jumped from the saddle to bulldog the man. His instincts were good, but he didn't
have the ghost of a chance of overpowering the giant,
even with the shotgun chambers now empty.

As he rode the man down, he kicked out and grazed
the shaggy head. The man grunted and fell down in the
dirt, rubbing his forehead. Clay bent low over his
horse's neck and let the wind sail past as he rushed off
at full gallop.

A half mile down the trail heading back to town, he
slowed and then stopped to look around. Something
had distracted Warnock's foreman and kept him from
killing an intruder. Clay hadn't seen anything, couldn't
even guess how it was possible, but he knew Suárez
and Vasques had saved him.

If he'd had an ounce of sense, he'd have kept riding
into the night. Picked a direction at random and galloped away, never looking back. But they had saved
him somehow. Another thought chewed at his con-
science. He had agreed to ride with them and see their
trail drive through until they reached the coast. Abandoning a partner and breaking his word weren't done,
especially by Clayton Forsythe.

He turned back in the direction of Warnock's camp
but drew rein when two dark riders galloped toward
him. He reached for his six-shooter but left his gun in

its holster. Hitting anyone on horseback in the dark was nigh on impossible. If he started flinging lead all willy-nilly, he'd spook his horse and maybe hit a friend.

Clay sagged in relief when the two came closer. One waved and he recognized Suárez's voice.

"Ride! They are coming after us. That was Roskolnikov! The right-hand man for Warnock!"

"Where do we go?" Clay wheeled about, once more intending to reach Hoback and the safety it afforded. Losing himself in a crowd was the best way to hide. If necessary he could call out Warnock and put an end to this madness. After all that the rancher had done to him, settling accounts permanently became more reasonable by the instant.

"Not back. Go south. We must reach the pass leading west." Suárez sounded out of breath.

"That is where the herd is bedded down. They stopped until we won the rodeo." Vasques stood in his stirrups, waved his hat about over his head and let out a loud cry.

Clay looked behind them along the back trail. Such exuberance had its place, but not here, not with Warnock's ramrod chasing after them. The Russian looked to be a mean one, and only pure dumb luck had kept him from turning Clay into bloody mist.

"José," he called, hoping to calm down the *paniolo*, "what knocked Roskolnikov off-balance? He was ready to put me into a shallow grave."

"Thank Leo. He is expert with a slingshot. It was a difficult shot in the dark, but he has practiced since he was a small child."

"I'm glad he never outgrew his childhood. But then he didn't make a new slingshot. He had to have one with him. Why's that?"

"He calls it his hobby. Others whittle. He puts rocks

on top of others, then uses the slingshot to knock them off one by one."

"I've got a hobby of my own," Clay said, somewhat embarrassed to admit how he wasted time. "I find old bones on the prairie and carve them."

"What do you make?"

"All kinds of things. I'm about finished with a buffalo carved from a cow's thighbone. I've done bandanna slides and rings, and my best was a dog."

"Did it go *woof woof*? No? You must show me your skill. All I do is smoke and chew, but I am very good at both." Vasques pointed ahead. "There. Do you see? The road to the west."

"I haven't seen any of Warnock's men on our trail. That's more of a relief than getting back with your company."

Clay kept glancing behind, but the road stretched dark and empty. He doubted Warnock's men were the kind to rouse themselves and investigate gunshots in the night. By the time Ros could have hiked to camp and gathered his men, the chance of finding the intruders was small.

At least, Clay hoped the Russian thought that. Tracking in the dark was a special skill. He had done it a few times, riding along with flaring torches and looking for tracks and other spoor. The attempts had never been too successful, but he had learned how much skill was required. A former Russian seal hunter wasn't likely to possess such abilities.

Whether anyone in the camp had such expertise wasn't something Clay wanted to discover.

"You will not find it a relief, as you say, to reach the herd. We are shorthanded. You must take your turn riding night herd. We all work two jobs. More if necessary."

"What about you and Leo?"

Clay thought Vasques was joshing him. He had been through too much in the past couple days to spend another night immediately in the saddle, watching over cattle. Worse, these were special animals, ready for breeding. From his experience, such pure-breds were nervous creatures. That was saying something because a common beef cow lacked steady nerves at the best of times.

"Leo is trail boss. I am his sturdy right-hand man. More than this, I am scout to choose where the herd travels every day. I must get sleep to be up at dawn and blazing the trail. You would not want me to fall asleep performing such a duty, eh?"

Clay fell silent and rode along, lost in his grim thoughts that Vasques wasn't pulling his leg. So much for catching a night's sleep before hitting the trail again.

Two hours farther up the trail, they reached a dark, slowly moving mass of cattle. They rode into camp. Clay did a quick count and realized the Barker Ranch had begun a trail drive with only a half dozen men, with Suárez and Vasques slated to do other duties than ride herd.

"Stow your gear in the chuck wagon," Suárez said. He sagged a little, then straightened his shoulders as he assumed the duties of foreman. "You must ride for two hours this night. I am sorry, but those who are out now have even less sleep than you."

"José explained it to me," Clay said.

Even if he went back on his word and rode off right now, he owed both men his life. They had saved him from Ros. That counted for as much as giving his promise to work for the Barker spread.

He heaved his saddlebags into the back of the chuck wagon. There was no call to weigh down his horse while out tending the herd. Then a thought occurred to him.

"Wait a minute," he called to Suárez. He rummaged through the saddlebags and came out with a small figurine. Clay handed it up to his new trail boss. "Here's a souvenir of the Hoback rodeo."

Suárez dismounted, took it gingerly and moved it about on his palm until moonlight caused it to glow whitely. He grinned.

"It is a cow carved from bone! I recognize it!" He ran his fingers over the smooth surface.

"I did it," Clay said, "as my hobby rather than chew and smoke like José." This produced the appreciative laughter he had hoped for. "Since I won't be getting any break for a spell, I thought you should see what I can do with a knifepoint." He rummaged some more. "Here's one for José. It's not as detailed, but you can figure out what it is."

"A dog, yes," Suárez said, examining it alongside the cow in his hand. "You do fine work. Very detailed."

"Keep an eye out for any decent bones lying around on the trail. I'm looking to do a ring next. I don't know why, but it's something I've meant to do for a while."

"You can look all you like," Suárez said, "as you keep the dumb cattle in a herd. Go. Two hours." He craned his neck around and looked at the stars. "When that one touches the horizon, you can come back to camp for a few hours' sleep."

"That's Jupiter," Clay said. "I've spent too much time riding around in the dark not to figure out the constellations and planets."

"These stars look different here from in Hawaii. You will be an asset, *mi amigo*. Or should I say *paniolo*?" Suárez turned and made his way through the camp, agilely stepping over the sleeping cowboys as he examined the two figurines Clay had given him.

Trying not to move as if his feet had turned to lead and not quite succeeding, he mounted his horse and gave the gelding its head. They had ridden herd so many times, the horse knew instinctively what to do and where to go.

Clay touched the brim of his Stetson as he passed another cowboy heading for camp. There'd be time later to get to know those he rode with. If they were as competent and pleasant as Leo and José, he'd get along just fine with them.

As he rode along the far side of the herd, he felt rather than saw a few cattle stirring. Clay urged his gelding to a fast gait, occasionally bending over to swing his lariat at a stirring cow. Whatever made them uneasy was quickly taken care of by judicious use of the rope on their hindquarters. Without exception, all the ones he prodded returned to the center of the herd and settled down.

He kept riding, thinking the disturbance was due to a coyote sniffing around the edge of the herd. Coyotes weren't brave predators. They preferred smaller animals or something that had just died. He was more concerned that a mountain lion or a few timber wolves considered the beeves to be easy pickings. A quarter mile farther on, Clay pulled back on the reins and listened hard.

The usual night sounds came to him, reassuring in their sameness from so many other nights. But an occasional lowing alerted him that he was probably right about predators sizing up the Barker beeves. He slid his rifle from its sheath and rode faster now. The center of the commotion wasn't more than a couple hundred yards away.

He was so intent on the ground and low-slung, slinking forms that he failed to look up until it was almost too late. Clay saw distant motion. A man. Then the bullet and the report from the rifle came at the same instant. The slug passed so close, it caused him to jerk his head involuntarily. His hat went flying. That proved useful for him since he lifted his rifle and the Stetson didn't hinder his aim. He returned fire at the rider who had thought to ambush him.

In an instant lead sailed back and forth. Clay's horse sidestepped nervously, not liking the repeated gunfire, ruining his aim. Firing from horseback was hard at the best of times. The first round usually had to be the killing shot because of the nervous horse dancing about, but what was true for him went double for the other rider.

The cattle began protesting about such a noisy disturbance and moved about, considering what to do. The nervous cows bumped into the gunman's horse and spooked it. Clay tried to track the rider on the frightened horse, but his aim was off. He lowered his rifle just as his horse reared. He went flying and landed hard.

"Whoa, calm down," he called. The gelding continued to paw at the air. Its frightened neighs filled the still night—until the thud of heavy hooves signaled the herd winding up to stampede.

The beeves had made their decision: panic!

Clay scrambled to his feet and grabbed wildly for his horse's dangling reins. It spun and bucked and then lit out at a dead gallop. All he could do was watch it disappear into the night.

"I trained you better 'n that," he groused.

The horse was a perfect partner when it came to bulldogging or roping and throwing a calf. Then Clay realized losing his horse was the least of his problems. He twisted around and saw that the huge dark mass of cattle looked like an ocean, rising and falling restlessly. A wave started in the center and rolled outward, ending in the beeves closest to him.

For a moment he thought he was in luck, but like an

ocean storm, another wave came. This one was a tidal wave of bulk and hooves and snorting, angry critters. The bull closest to him lowered its head and charged.

If it had been a single charging bull, he might have avoided it. Somehow this bull had stolen leadership of the entire herd. Where it ran, the rest followed. Clay looked around frantically, then ran for all he was worth, choosing left as the most likely direction to save his hide. The bull veered after him, only to have the trailing cattle collide. The impact of a pair of cows against the bull's hindquarters broke its charge, giving Clay the chance to run even harder.

The respite was all too short. The bull regained its balance and came for him again.

"What'd I ever do to make you so mad?" Clay gasped out as he sprinted.

Motion infuriated bulls. Waving a cape like a matador caught its attention and forced it to charge where the torero wanted. But Clay wasn't any skilled bull-fighter, and he didn't have a cape. All he had were two feet and the impossible task of outrunning the bull.

Clinging to his rifle, he put his head down and ran hell-bent for leather. Within a few yards, he gasped. To anyone who might have overheard, he sounded like a steam engine straining up a steep grade. He had been through too much in the past couple days to hope to keep up this pace for very long. He slowed and imagined he felt the bull's hot breath on his neck. Half turning to look behind, he twisted his ankle and fell heavily.

Clay hit the ground and rolled to take cover behind a rock. A flying hoof grazed him and knocked him flat. Dazed, he looked up at the bull's belly as the animal vaulted over the rock and kept running. He knew one danger had passed but an entire herd remained, dutifully following their furiously snorting leader. A cow crashed into the rock and fell past him, making piteous sounds. It had broken a leg.

The rock was embedded in the sunbaked ground but repeated hoof blows broke it in two. Another assault would destroy what little shelter he got from it. He chanced a quick look up and went cold inside. All he saw was a solid heaving wall of bovine flesh speeding for him.

"Shut up, will you?" he growled at the thrashing cow with the busted leg.

Then he saw a way to survive. He swung his rifle around and fired into the cow's head. It kicked its legs straight, then died with a wet, gusty sigh.

"One of us is out of her misery," Clay said.

He grabbed for the cow, caught an ear and pulled himself up and over the carcass. Huddled behind the beefy bulk that gave more protection than he'd get from the rock.

The herd crashed past, hooves kicking at the dead animal. Clay had thought he was safe. Every passing cow or bull tore away a bit more of his once solid barrier against death. If the stampede lasted another minute, he'd be dead.

Clay had seen stampedes go on for days. He pressed closer to the cow's belly, closed his eyes and waited for the end.

CHAPTER SIX

G ET UP. STAND on your feet. You are too heavy for
me to lift by myself."

Clay felt hands tugging at his arms. He drew his legs
up even tighter into a ball and pressed his hands into
his face to protect himself from flying hooves. In the
distance, through the ringing in his ears, he heard a
voice ordering him to stand. He spread his fingers and
peered through. All he saw was darkness. Pulled this
way and that, he lowered his defenses and straightened. Every muscle in his body hurt. As pain lanced
into him, he thought bones had been broken.

"Leo? Are you dead, too? I never expected heaven
to be so . . . dark. It's like night here."

"I am not dead. You are not, either. Come on."
Suárez finally got a secure hold on Clay's arm and
dragged him upright.

It took some doing and a little wobbling around, but
Clay found his balance. He stretched and immediately
regretted it. Then he continued to get the kinks out of

his muscles. He felt better for it, but he knew the misery would return soon. It always did. He had ridden enough broncos in his day to know that the first pain faded, only to be replaced later with even more intense agony. He needed a few slugs of whiskey to numb himself, body and mind.

"Did you— You saved me!"

He looked around. The herd had run a hundred yards farther and then stopped. There was no accounting for a cow's fear. It went as suddenly as it came.

"You saved yourself." Suárez picked up Clay's rifle and handed it to him.

"There's almost some of it left." More than one hoof had crashed down on the stock and receiver. The barrel was bent at a crazy angle. Clay sighted along it and smiled. "If I want to shoot around corners, this is the perfect weapon." He threw it aside. No gunsmith, no matter how skilled, had a ghost of a chance of repairing it.

"You shot this one and hid behind it," Suárez said, kneeling to study the cow's skull. "Very clever."

"Very lucky," Clay said. "A bull almost gored me." He rubbed his face, then hunted for his hat. It was nowhere to be seen. "At first I thought wolves were after a quick meal, but when I saw somebody at the edge of the herd, I knew rustlers were at work. He shot at me and that started the herd running."

"We heard the shots and came. It is always the same. One shot, you kill a snake. Two means a fight. More than that means you are killing human snakes."

"I missed that owlhoot, but I did run him off before he had a chance to cut out a few dozen head and drive them off. My lead must have come close enough to put the fear of God in him."

"Where did you see this cattle thief?" Suárez put his fingers into his mouth and cut loose with a shrill whistle.

Clay winced. His hearing was returning. The thunder of cattle stampeding rivaled cannonade during a battle. Riders trotted over at Suárez's call. Clay reached for his six-shooter, but Suárez grabbed his wrist.

"José and another cowboy. Harrison is our best tracker. He finds lost cows quickly, and he can follow a snowflake through a blizzard."

"Mighty high praise," Clay said. He started to touch the brim of his hat when José Vasques trotted up, but his hand went to his forehead. He'd lost his hat and his rifle. Better to lose those than his own life.

"At least that is what he claims. I have never seen a snowflake, much less a blizzard."

"You should spend a winter in Wyoming sometime. It'll be different from anything you'll ever see in Hawaii."

Clay saw that the trail boss paid him no attention. He had walked to Vasques and was speaking in a low voice.

Drawing up beside Vasques was a rail-thin man with nervous gestures. His hands never rested, sliding up and down his reins and then rubbing on his thighs. As he turned, Clay got a better look at his face. Harrison had survived smallpox at some point in his life, and it had left his face looking like the surface of the moon.

Suárez spoke up now so all of them heard his plans. Most of what he said was in Hawaiian. Clay watched Harrison. The cowboy seemed to understand a few words. He went and stood by the man's horse.

"You're the best tracker in these parts. Or that's what Leo says."

"He exaggerates." Harrison wiped his lips, then ran his right hand up and down his left forearm. Watching him was like trying to follow a fish darting about in a stream. Always moving, never resting, he wore Clay out in a hurry.

"Can you find my horse? It lit out in that direction." Clay made a complete turn to figure out where the gelding had retreated.

"Done."

"What?" Clay stared up at the tracker. "What do you mean?"

"Found the horse. A gelding?"

Clay turned in the same direction Harrison faced. A grin came to his face. He had trained the horse better than he thought. It had abandoned him but was now returning. The gelding walked up, tossing its head about since the reins dragged and caught. When one rein tangled in a low bush, Clay went to pull it free. He patted the horse's neck, made certain it had gotten over its fright, then mounted.

"You all right?" Harrison rode over and watched Clay like a hawk. "You sound hurt bad. Leo said you was a mite woozy after gettin' stomped on."

"All banged up but nothing broken." Clay looked at his arms. The sleeves of his coat hung in tatters and blood oozed through. "I lost a fair amount of skin, but it's nothing new for me."

"Leo says you're good at breaking broncos. That's high praise. He don't say that 'bout many hands." Harrison shifted in the saddle, then snapped his reins and moved away.

Clay smiled at Harrison's compliment—or the praise passed along from Leo Suárez. As skillful a cowboy as the trail boss was, a tribute like that made Clay feel better. He rode around and saw that they had lost a half dozen head of cattle.

"This is a big loss," Vasques said, trotting alongside Clay. "These are more valuable as breeding stock than steaks. We paid a small fortune for each cow." He sighed. "That is wrong. It was not a small fortune. It was a big fortune."

"But worth it if you improve the line. You said the Barker Ranch was a hundred thirty thousand acres. That much land will graze a huge herd."

"The grass on the island is better than anywhere I have seen around us." Vasques made a sweeping motion with his hand. "These are good lands for cattle. For farming, not so much, but for ranching? *Maika'i*."

"That's *good*?"

"It is *bueno*, yes."

"I didn't have a whole lot of time to notice, but the cattle all carry a Circle K brand."

"King Kamehameha allowed Mr. Barker to use land on the northern end of the island near Waimea. The brand is a tribute to the king. Everyone calls it the Crown K brand."

Clay shook his head. It sounded odd to his ears that anyone mentioned a king. A friend of his down in Texas, a remittance man from London, always spoke of royalty, but whenever he did, it was about the queen. Being out West took a man away from politics back East but Colorado had just become a state. When he thought about leaders, it was always a president, not a king or queen.

Suárez rode over and said, "We go to find who started the stampede. They cost us many hundreds of dollars in lost stock."

"Harrison can track at night?" Clay bit his lip when he saw that tracking at night wasn't necessary. Dawn stirred on the horizon, peeking over the Tetons. He had lost track of time.

Suárez and Vasques looked at each other, but Vasques shook his head.

"Let us get to the tracking. The longer we wait, the farther they roam."

Clay rode with Vasques as Suárez and Harrison trotted ahead, hunting for the spot to begin.

"I'm still shook up from being caught like that in the stampede," he admitted when a stab of pain made him sit bolt upright in the saddle. "I won't hold you back. I promise."

"I know, *amigo*," Vasques said. "You are an honorable man. You will do well riding with us to the coast."

"I haven't given it much thought. What kind of work's out there after we deliver the cattle? Can I get a job working on the California ranch? At least for a season?"

"There are few cattle there. We ship everything to Hawaii and use the small ranch only as a shipping port."

"What do you do with the cattle raised in Hawaii? Don't you bring them back to California to sell?" Clay saw that both Suárez and Harrison had found a trail and begun the serious job of following it.

"We cannot raise enough head to supply our local needs. Ships crossing the Pacific in both directions buy much of our meat. Throughout the islands our beef is known as the best there is. If we double our herd, there is still no reason to ship back to California. And if we improve the quality, we can sell to royalty."

Clay pushed aside the notion of working for the California Barker Ranch. This drive was a rarity and definitely a one-way trip. He cut across the meadow and caught up with Suárez and Harrison. The nervous man made small fluttering motions with his hand, then pointed. Before Clay asked, Suárez explained.

"The men who started the stampede are not far ahead."

"Men? I only saw one. How many are there?"

"Harrison says two, but there might be many more if this is a gang of rustlers. They need as many as we do to move a herd."

"Not if they cut out only a few dozen head," Clay

said. "They don't have to steal the entire herd for rustling to be profitable."

"I know. Local ranchers would pay small amounts for such cattle as we have. It might even be possible to find an army post quartermaster who will pay much more for stolen cattle. Just because they wear a uniform does not mean they cannot be thieves."

From the way Suárez spat out the words, Clay suspected he had crossed some cavalry troopers more inclined to steal than to protect.

"There they are." Harrison put his heels to his horse and rocketed ahead.

His impulsive action took both Suárez and Clay by surprise, but Vasques paced their tracker.

"We'd better make sure those two don't get into more trouble than they can handle," Clay said.

He bent low and galloped after the others. Suárez trailed by several lengths. Clay almost slowed to let the trail boss catch up, then saw the men on the ground were reaching for their six-shooters. Vasques and Harrison would eat an ounce or two of lead unless the pair on foot were convinced to keep their six-guns in their holsters.

Clay called out and distracted the rustlers. This gave Vasques time to slip his pistol out and lay it across the saddle in front of him.

"What are you gents doing out here?" Clay called, further distracting them.

"We don't answer to you. You ain't the law." The taller of the men rested his hand on the butt of his six-shooter. His muscles twitched. He was a spring all wound up and ready to uncoil.

"We're not the law. That makes it easier for us to string up cattle thieves," Clay said.

By the time he joined Vasques and Harrison, Suárez made his presence known.

"Excuse my impulsive wrangler," Suárez said. "He is not calling you a cattle thief, though why you ride at the edge of my herd and cause a stampede is something I wish to know." Suárez drew his pistol and, like Vasques, rested it on the saddle in front of him, ready for use but not directly threatening the men.

"We don't know what you're talking about. We're just passing through and don't known nothing about no stampede." The man belligerently thrust out his chin as if daring his accusers to challenge him.

"Your tracks lead straight back to my herd," Suárez said. "Why is that?"

"You don't know what you're talking about. We've been here all night long, not roaming the countryside. We don't have any interest in your cattle."

"I know you two," Clay said. "I saw you in a Hoback saloon. You're both working for Warnock, aren't you?"

"I knew we shoulda took care of him when we had the chance," one said to the other.

His companion grunted assent. Both men went for their guns at the same instant.

Suárez and Vasques shifted their pistols fast, only needing to lift them and fire. The air filled with choking white gun smoke, hiding the men on the ground. As Clay knew from earlier shoot-outs, the only accurate round was the first one. Then rearing horses made accuracy impossible. He fired every time his gelding spun around and he faced the camp where the two men had taken cover in a shallow gully.

"Circle them. Get them in a cross fire!"

Clay's tactic wasn't as easily carried out as he'd hoped. The other three went away from him, leaving him alone to take fire from the gunmen. He bent low and guided his horse the best he could to get into the gully. He intended to catch the pair from the side.

His horse reared and threw him. Clay sailed through the air, but from all the broncos he had broken, he reacted fast like a cat. When he hit the ground, he was shaken a mite but not seriously injured. Better yet, he still clutched his six-gun. He rolled over and over, then came to his knees for a better shot.

· He faced one man. As calm as can be, he squeezed the trigger. The man showed surprise, looked down at his duster where red blossomed and spread, then fell forward.

"Give up. We won't hang you for rustling. We'll turn you over to the nearest marshal." Clay's promise fell on deaf ears. If anything, the remaining gunman sprayed more lead around. The bullet barrage drove Clay to fall flat on his face.

Then there was an ominous silence.

He thought the gunman had stopped firing to reload. Taking a chance, he scrambled forward, then froze. Both would-be rustlers sprawled on the ground, dead.

Suárez and Vasques exchanged grim smiles, then blew smoke from the muzzles of their six-shooters. It took only a few seconds before they began arguing over which of them had ended the man's life.

Clay advanced cautiously and looked closely at the dead bodies. He opened the gate on his gun and reloaded. He swallowed hard when he saw that he had tried to attack with an empty pistol. His hand shaking in reaction at the close call, he dropped the gun into his holster.

"It is good that you recognized them," Suárez said. "They are the two holding you for Warnock to punch you? I did not see them clearly enough to identify them."

"Neither did I," Clay said. "I was bluffing. How

many men can Warnock have riding with him that he trusts?"

"Bluffing, eh?" Vasques shook his head. "You are one lucky *kane*." He turned and walked away, leaving Clay with the bodies.

CHAPTER SEVEN

"WE CANNOT AFFORD to lose any more cattle," Leo Suárez insisted. "We must move on right away."

Clay shook his head slowly. He looked at the two dead men on the ground. Flies buzzed around their corpses and the plaintive demands of coyotes for a quick feast came from the nearby woods. The proper thing to do was bury them, then do as the Crown K trail boss wanted. Getting the herd to the coast was what he had been hired to do, but something gnawed away at his guts.

"You agree these men rode with Warnock?" He pointed to the bodies. "They won't bother us anymore, but what of the rest of the gang? I have to call it a gang since that seems to be the kind of men Warnock is recruiting. He wants your herd and won't stop until he steals it." Clay hesitated, then added, "And sees you both in a grave."

The expressions on the Hawaiians' faces confirmed

what he thought. This was about more than cattle. Something personal festered between the men.

"We can outride him. We can reach the California ranch before he can steal the cattle," Suárez said firmly, "or kill us."

"Time's against you. We can make ten miles a day. Maybe twenty if the land's good. With extra mounts, he can ride fifty. There's no way you can outrun him."

"Clay is right," spoke up Vasques. "These two found us. Was there a third who reported to Warnock? Or does our location die with them?"

"It doesn't matter," Clay said, "if Warnock knows or not. He will find us soon enough when they don't report back. The men back in his camp, the one commanded by his foreman, aren't that far away. He has plenty of gunmen ready to do his bidding."

"Perhaps they deserted," Suárez said, but the words lacked emotion. He didn't believe it for an instant.

"Let's take these two back to Hoback and turn them over to the marshal. It'll tell Warnock not to mess with us," Clay said, his passion for the plan rising. "It won't scare him off, but it might cause some of his new recruits to leave. Even if they stick around, the notion of losing their lives for a man like Warnock will be lodged in their heads. He can't be paying them enough to take a bullet."

"The herd. We must get on the trail," Suárez insisted.

"I'll take these two back to Hoback. You do what you must, and I'll catch up." Clay smiled crookedly as he said, "After all, like Warnock, I can travel faster on horseback than you can drive the cattle. I won't be more than a day or two behind you."

"You would still ride with us?" Vasques looked at Suárez, then back at Clay. "We cannot pay you so much money."

Clay realized he hadn't dickered over wages. That hardly mattered now that he had gotten himself involved in their trail drive and running blood feud. Warnock wasn't going to stop trying to kill him unless he rode far and fast.

He wasn't a coward to run from a fight, even one he hadn't started. And the two *paniolo* had shown themselves worthy of his friendship. Abandoning them wasn't something he would do. He had given his word.

"It'll be about a month to the coast? Pay me a hundred dollars when we get there."

Clay knew their answer when they huddled together and passed a wad of greenbacks back and forth. This was the prize money they had won at the rodeo.

"We will pay you fifty now and fifty then," Suárez said, holding out a fistful of scrip.

"Keep it until I get back from Hoback," he said. "But you can help me by finding these two owlhoots' horses and helping me hoist them up over their saddles."

The horses were hobbled some distance away. Clay saw how scrupulous the Hawaiians were about gathering the gear and strapping it to the horses. All they kept was the food. When they lashed the bodies across the saddles, Clay stepped up onto his gelding. The horse walked along, showing it was as tired as he was.

Clay gestured to bid Suárez and Vasques goodbye with a tip of his Stetson and again realized he had lost his hat. He'd have to buy a new one in town. After he decided that, his mind drifted. Keeping on the lookout for more of Warnock's men was paramount, but he approached exhaustion. Somehow he slept in the saddle as the stalwart horse kept on the road back to town.

It was turning chilly by the time he reached Hoback. The sun had sunk behind the Tetons a half hour earlier. He could have made better time, but rather than riding slowly straight here, he had rested his horse and taken short naps several times along the road. While he wasn't in top shape, he felt better. Except for the gnawing hunger and need for twelve hours' straight sleep and—

Clay snapped alert when the marshal strode up, thumbs hooked under his gun belt. The lawman looked him over, then went to examine the bodies. He made a shooing motion with his hand and finally said, "They sure do stink, don't they? Dead bodies. You responsible for them being like this?"

"You mean, dead? Yup, I'm responsible. I shot them, Marshal." Clay had gone over the story a hundred times on his way here. He launched into his speech and finished, "The way they attacked without any reason, I reckon they are—were—road agents out to steal whatever I was carrying."

"You have a wad of bills tucked into your vest pocket? I don't hear you tinkling coins like you were rich."

"You can never tell. These owlhoots rode up fast and opened fire. If nothing else, my horse and tack would be worth stealing."

"Looks worn to me," the marshal said, eyeing Clay's saddle. "The horse might be something special. I watched you at the rodeo. The horse's well trained."

"Maybe they saw that, too. But check your wanted posters. I'm willing to bet these two have rewards on their heads."

The marshal gestured for Clay to dismount. He eyed the pistol in his holster. Clay held his breath, waiting for the lawman to demand that he hand it over. With a shrug, the marshal went into the jailhouse. Over his shoulder he called, "Tie up the horses around back. I don't want the townsfolk complaining about me leaving bodies lying about again."

Clay did as he was ordered, but he made sure his six-shooter was riding easy when he entered the office. The marshal had settled into a chair behind a battered desk and hiked his feet onto it.

"Set yourself down and tell me all about how you happened to get the drop on two gents who look like real desperadoes. I musta missed a few details during your first recitation." He laced his fingers behind his head and lowered his eyelids as Clay began repeating his story.

Once, Clay thought the man had gone to sleep and stopped. The marshal's eyes popped open and he said, "That's all?"

"The truth doesn't get any more truthful if I say it once or a hundred times."

"Those gents followed you from town, do you think? I recollect seeing them around, but they weren't getting into trouble. If anything, they were spreading money around freely, looking for men to join a trail drive."

Clay almost blurted out Warnock's name but caught himself before he did. Showing more knowledge of Warnock and his henchmen wasn't clever. It made it look as if he knew them all and might have cut them down in some dispute. He had to smile just a little when he realized that was close to the truth. While Clay couldn't swear to it on a stack of Bibles, thinking on the matter he was pretty sure the two had held him behind the saloon while Warnock had whaled away on him.

Warnock was doing what he could to stop the Crown K herd from moving to California. That fact only clouded the situation.

"There anything more you want to tell me?" the marshal asked.

"Nope."

"Well, sir, I didn't find any of those two's faces on my wanted posters." The marshal glanced toward a stack on his desk. "But they're in no condition to suggest you murdered them, and you did go out of your way to fetch them back to town, so I have to accept your word for what happened."

"Let me flip through the posters. I might find something to make my good deed worthwhile."

Clay reached for the wanted posters but the marshal was quick. He dropped his feet to the floor, bent forward and had his six-gun out and lying on top of the stack in a flash. The message was clear. Clay wasn't to ask after any possible reward.

"I might need to hold you until the circuit judge swings back this way. Suspicious deaths require an inquest."

"A judge does that? Why not a coroner?"

"Hoback is a real small town. The judge is the coroner. Sometimes he acts as the undertaker, too. A versatile man, Judge Zane."

"If I say my business takes me away from town right away, then I can go?"

Clay fumed when the marshal moved the six-shooter on the pile of papers just a little bit more so the muzzle almost, but not quite, pointed in his direction.

They both jumped a foot when the jailhouse door slammed open against the wall. Suárez and Vasques pushed into the office.

"You find out who those *pendejos* are? How much is the reward?" Suárez squared off, his hand resting on the side of his holster.

Vasques moved quietly to separate himself by another few feet. Clay suspected they worked together well, both driving cattle and dealing with bothersome humans.

The marshal shifted his six-gun, then pulled it back

and slipped it into his holster. He glanced once at the wanted posters, then fixed his stare on the two Hawaiians. "You two have anything to do with *him* bringing in the road agents?"

"He rides with us," Vasques said.

The marshal looked toward Clay, only to realize Suárez had shifted farther away. If the marshal started to make a suspicious move, the *paniolo* had him in the cross fire. Seizing the opportunity while the lawman was occupied, Clay pulled the stack of wanted posters over and spread them out across the desk. He found the dead men's likenesses after leafing through only a half dozen posters. As he pushed them across to the marshal, he kept looking. He didn't find Warnock as he had expected, but then the rancher was from the coast. The gunmen he had hired were all locals.

Local gunfighters and robbers from the brief description of their crimes on the posters.

"Two fifty on each. That's five hundred in reward money, isn't it, José? Leo?" Clay spoke without his eyes leaving the marshal.

The man turned red in the face as his anger mounted; then he settled down. From the set of his jaw, he was coming up with another scheme.

"Five hundred," the marshal said, "but there's a two-hundred-dollar excise fee put on it by the city fathers."

"You expect to keep so much?" Vasques asked. His hand slid up and down along his holster's exterior.

"I do. And the horses and gear? The city'll claim them, too, but we'll use the proceeds to give them decent burials out on Mount Calvary."

Clay looked at the man askance.

"That's what we call the cemetery. They won't be buried in any of the good plots, mind you, but we'll see they get pine coffins and someone to say words over their grave. Unless you happen to know if they were Masons. That'd make the local lodge responsible for them."

"I doubt they were members," Clay said. "We'll take the hundred dollars apiece."

"Apiece? You including them in your reward?"

"We're partners. Partners share." Clay almost punched the lawman for his sour expression at that simple declaration.

"Let me get you the reward so you can be on your way. And you'll be back on the trail right away, won't you?" The marshal's tone told them this was an order and not a friendly question.

"We might find a saloon to have one for the trail," Clay said.

The marshal fumbled around in his center drawer, took out a tin box and opened it to flash a stack of greenbacks. He rapidly counted out one hundred in each of three piles. Then he returned the box to his drawer and reached under the desk. He set a half bottle of whiskey on the desk.

"With my compliments. There's no call to go to any of our drinking establishments." He put both hands on the desk, leaned forward and glared. "Now, get out of town before there's real trouble."

Clay considered the lawman's request—his order—and wondered what they might find if they ventured into a saloon. He passed the reward money to his partners, stuffed his own into a vest pocket and took the bottle.

"Much obliged, Marshal." He used the bottle to salute the man, who only stared at him with a coldness that chilled Clay's soul.

The trio left. Clay immediately handed the bottle to Suárez and said, "I'm not thirsty, just curious."

"He wanted us out of town in a powerful hurry," Suárez said. "The dead outlaws. He knew them?"

"Or who they rode for." Clay looked toward the nearest saloon, considering how hard it would be to find Warnock. *Not hard at all,* he guessed. He started to cross the street, but Suárez took his arm and swung him around.

"Let us return to the herd. I do not like leaving it," he said, lifting the bottle, "and it is a good thing not to drink if we have to shoot it out."

"If Warnock's here, he may have paid off the marshal," Clay said. "Cut the head off a snake and it dies. This can be our best chance of a peaceful drive to California."

"It will not die until sundown. We must wait for the day to pass and then sunset," said Vasques. "But Leo is right. We left the herd with Harrison. He has only three others to keep the cattle safe."

Clay wanted to root out Warnock, but Suárez was his boss. And the more he considered the matter, the less confidence he had in Harrison. The man's nerves were always on the breaking point. Such men made poor decisions when faced with thorny problems.

They rode steadily. The clouds cleared, giving them a road map in the sky. The moon wouldn't rise for hours yet, but the brilliant diamond-bright stars lit the road as well as if they carried torches. Clay trusted his horse and allowed it free rein. More than once he dozed off, only to be awakened by the Hawaiians demanding that he settle an argument. They rattled on, more to keep him awake than to work out any disagreements. Before he knew it, Suárez pointed.

"There. Campfires. We must decide who rides night herd." He looked at Clay and said, more to Vasques than to Clay, "He has done much today. Let him sleep until dawn."

"He can cook breakfast. I am afraid I will poison everyone if I fix one more meal."

Clay listened with half an ear. It suited him to fix chuck if they let him sleep. All it'd take for him was to tumble to the ground and wrap a blanket around himself, and he would be snoring in minutes. Clay started drifting off while still in the saddle, only to come completely awake when Suárez let out a cry of pure anger.

"What is it?" Clay looked around, a hand on his six-shooter.

"The herd! It is gone!"

"So is our entire crew," Vasques said. "Where have they gone?"

"Where have they gone with our herd!" Suárez circled the camp. "There is no sign of a fight."

Clay dropped to the ground and looked closer at the camp. Fires guttered, but iron tripods holding coffee-pots were missing. The men's bedrolls were gone as were their belongings—and their horses. All the horses.

"They packed up and drove the herd that way," Clay said.

It was hard to hide where a hundred head of cattle went across grassy mountain meadows. He stood numbly staring into the darkness as if he might see the missing herd.

Nothing. Absolutely nothing.

CHAPTER EIGHT

"THEY WON'T BE hard to track," Clay said. "But not right now. I need sleep. I won't be any good to you if I can't focus my eyes."

"You will not come with us to find the stolen cattle?" Leo Suárez thrust his chin out belligerently and looked as if he was going to throw down on Clay.

"I'll ride to the ends of the earth to find the herd," Clay said, "after I get some sleep. Everything's a blur. I can hardly see. If you go, I'll catch up."

"I am in need of sleep, too," Vasques said. "He is right about following the tracks. Even blind I can do it, but not if I fall asleep."

Suárez jerked his horse this way and that and finally came to a decision. With ill grace, he dismounted and stepped closer to one of the guttering campfires. He kicked a few dried sticks on it.

"At first light. We will find the cattle and do anything we must to reclaim them." He rested his hand on his pistol. "Anything."

"Agreed," Clay said.

He had already taken the saddle from his horse and laid the blanket on the ground. He unfurled his bedroll, then made sure to tether his horse securely. Even the remuda was gone. Whoever had taken the cattle had cleared out with everything: supplies, chuck wagon and extra horses. He wanted to think the best but only one answer came to whatever question he posed to himself. Everything being gone this way meant it had all been stolen by Harrison and the rest of the cowboys entrusted with guarding the herd. Such betrayal tore at his gut. He couldn't imagine how it affected Suárez and Vasques.

By the time Clay stretched out near the fire, he heard José Vasques already snoring softly. Suárez continued to grumble for another minute or two before sitting by the fire. He rested his head on his drawn-up knees and let out a long, shaky sigh. Clay closed his eyes. He didn't want to see Suárez in such emotional pain. For a short while, he tried to make sense of what had happened. Missing herd. Lost. Horses run off. Entire crew dead. What had happened?

Betrayal. That fit the facts better than any other explanation.

The next thing he knew, the sun warmed his face. He stirred, considered rolling over to get more sleep, then heard both Hawaiians tending their horses. They were raring to go. He owed it to them to ride alongside and watch their backs. Whatever had happened here was going to end in gunfire. He knew there couldn't be a peaceable solution to an entire herd of expensive breeding stock disappearing in the middle of the night.

Clay stretched, yawned and sat up. Suárez mounted and looked down at him impatiently. Without so much as a *good morning*, Clay gathered his gear, made sure his horse had enough water, filled his own canteen and then prepared for the hunt. It was going to be a deadly day.

As he had predicted the night before, tracking a herd of a hundred cattle was easy enough for any greenhorn. The three of them had no trouble following the cut-up turf across the broad mountain meadow and into woods. Even here, with leaves and pine needles carpeting the ground, they had no trouble working through the trees and keeping on the trail.

"We're gaining on them," Clay said around noon. "The more they try to go through wooded areas, the quicker we catch up."

"A road," Vasques said, pointing. "It must lead to a ranch. A heavy wagon has come this way recently."

Clay rode a ways down the road, then returned. The direction was apparent where the cattle had been driven. They cut off the road and rode another mile before coming to a fenced-in pasture.

"There they are," Suárez said. "All of them. Does your count match mine?"

"It does," Vasques said, his head bobbing as he ticked off one cow after another in a mental inventory. "How did they get here? I don't see any sign of the rest of our trail hands."

"You won't, either," Clay said. "See that game trail leading north? Two men rode there. Another three went on farther west. After leaving the herd in the pasture, they split up."

"Five worthless pieces of . . ." Suárez rode away, muttering to himself in Hawaiian.

Clay understood the tone if not the words. He was thinking the same thing of Harrison and the others. They had rustled the cattle.

"If we cut the fence here, we can drive the cattle west as we intended. We have come too far south, but

angling that way will put us on the right path again,"
Vasques said.

Clay rode to the fence, stretched down and shoved
his boot against a post. It wobbled back and forth.
Then he stopped before it was dislodged and brought
down this section of fence. An angry voice from behind him bellowed a warning loud and clear.

"We shoot varmints tearing down T Bar T fences.
Any reason I shouldn't blow you to hell and gone, you
miserable yellow-bellied rustler?"

Clay heard the hammer cock. He settled back and
turned in the saddle to a man florid with fury and
pointing a Winchester directly at him.

"Those aren't your cattle," Clay said. "It's mighty
nice of you to pen them up for us so we can be on
our way."

"I bought 'em at a good price. From where I stand,
it's you who's the rustler."

"They all carry the Crown K brand. Not yours."

"Not yet. But that don't mean they aren't T Bar T
beeves. I got the bill of sale to prove it." The man
moved closer as if he didn't have a clear enough shot
from where he stood.

"You bought stolen cows. Whoever it was selling
them wasn't the owner."

"I got a bill of sale. That's all the legal paper I need.
Now you ride on out and I'll forget you tried to steal T
Bar T cattle." The man edged closer. His finger tightened on the trigger. At this range he wasn't going to
miss, but Clay refused to back down.

"Was it a nervous fellow who sold them to you?
Twitching all the time? By the name of Harrison? He
wasn't anything more than a wrangler and wasn't
owner. The cattle belong to the Barker Ranch."

"Never heard of it."

"It's a big spread in Hawaii." Clay chanced a quick

look around. Suárez rode in from one direction and Vasques from another. They had the rifleman dead to rights, only the Hawaiians could never stop that first bullet from taking Clay out of the saddle.

"Never heard of the ranch or this Hawaii. I'm done jawing. You got to the count of three to hightail it. One—"

"Two," called out Suárez. He had his six-gun leveled.

"Three," said Vasques. He had unlimbered his rifle and sighted in on the irate rancher.

"Three of you varmints? I expected as much. Which tree do you want to swing from?"

Clay expected some sign that the rancher was giving up. When he saw no hint of surrender, Clay knew he, Suárez and Vasques were in big trouble. He blinked. In that quick moment, a half dozen ranch hands stood from where they had hidden in ditches and gullies. Whoever shot first had the advantage, but Clay saw that the Crown K riders were the ultimate losers in any gunfight. They were outnumbered two to one.

"Three to one," the rancher said as if reading his mind. "We outnumber you three to one."

More cowboys appeared like spring flowers sprouting up from the fertile ground.

"Those cattle are not yours!" Suárez rode over. "They belong to Mr. Barker."

"This owlhoot already said something like that. You're wrong. You the ramrod?" The rancher held out a slip of paper. "The bill of sale saying whoever owned these beeves before, they belong to me now."

Suárez bent low and grabbed the paper. Clay saw the dark fury mount in the man's swarthy face. He tossed the sheet back angrily and turned to Vasques. He rattled off a short string of Hawaiian, then said to Clay, "Harrison. He signed it. The shaking hand betrays him even if he signed it with King Barker's name."

"We can take you to court," Clay said. "You have to prove you bought them fair and square."

"Go on, do it. By the time the worthless judge gets around to listening, the cattle will be on their way to a Chicago slaughterhouse. I got standing contracts with a couple of them." He turned and snapped at two of his men who had come to stand by their boss. He cuffed one and kicked the other. "Get these varmints off my land. Now. Chase 'em off now!" He directed another kick at his cowboy.

Clay saw the look of pure hatred boiling up from the hand, but the man rubbed his butt where a dusty boot print remained and fired in the air. Startled, Clay jumped and almost went for his six-shooter. He stopped himself in time to keep from getting filled with lead.

"Leo, José, let's go. We can talk this over when we get away from here."

"Don't show your ugly faces here again. I swear I will string you up and laugh as I'm doing it. The T Bar T's got plenty of sturdy trees for the chore, and I'll give my boys new ropes to wrap around your thieving necks!" He shoved a couple more of his ranch hands out of the way as he stormed off.

Silently Clay led his partners from the fenced-in pasture. When they were out of earshot, he said, "An unpleasant fellow."

"How could he not know the cattle were stolen?" raged Suárez.

"He's not stupid," Clay said. "He knew and never felt any remorse. He's as much a rustler as Harrison and the others."

"Ten dollars a head. That is all Harrison asked!" Suárez was sputtering mad.

"Ten!" Vasques looked as if he had been punched in

the belly. "But the bulls cost five hundred! And the cows were two hundred."

"Whatever he paid was pure gravy for Harrison and the others. They collected a thousand dollars and each got a couple hundred as their share. That's half what you offered me for a full month of work driving the cattle to the coast and I thought that was a princely sum." Clay worked over all the things they could do.

"We will run them down and get back the money," Vasques said, seething. "Then we will cut out their lying tongues and—"

"Forget them, José. Let them go. The important thing is recovering the cattle from the T Bar T pasture."

Clay felt as forsaken as his friends did angry. He had plenty of money. He wasn't out anything if they didn't get the herd to the California ranch. He'd been promised a hundred dollars, but he had made that much turning over the two outlaws to the Hoback marshal.

Suárez and Vasques carried equal amounts of money in their pockets. No matter what Barker intended to pay them, they weren't going to starve. If anything, they probably had more from the rodeo and the bounty than from promised wages for completing the drive. Money wasn't a concern for any of them.

Pride was. Clay felt as bad about Harrison rustling the Crown K herd as if those smelly, cantankerous beeves were his own property. He had hired on to deliver the cattle, and by all that was holy, he would. He told Suárez that.

"You are not leaving us? You do not have a dog in this fight, as they say," Suárez declared.

"The hell I don't. I'm taking this as a personal insult. As much as I'd like to see Harrison in jail, I'll be satisfied knowing *he* is out the money he forked over for the cattle." Clay jerked his thumb over his shoulder in the direction of the larcenous rancher.

"What is your plan, Clay?" Suárez looked at him hard. "You have a way to get our cattle back?"

"I don't have one right now, but I will by the time it's sundown."

Both Suárez and Vasques rode closer and heartily slapped him on the back. He smiled grimly. Now he had to think of something that would recover the cattle and not get the three of them killed.

T HERE IS ONLY one guard on the herd. He is too confident that we will slink away," said Leo Suárez. With surprising speed, he whipped out his six-gun, did a border shift, then tossed it back into his right hand. In the darkness, he grinned broadly.

"Gunplay's not going to be necessary," Clay said. "I can sneak up on the cowboy and get the drop on him. He'll be hog-tied before he knows it."

"You are good with the lariat," Vasques said. He paced back and forth before saying, "When do we make our move? I am anxious to be done with this. Although we only recover Mr. Barker's herd, it feels like rustling."

"If the guard's asleep, that makes it easier. He won't even see me."

"The rancher will know who is responsible."

"We won't leave any evidence that'll stand up in court," Clay said, but he knew Suárez was right.

Harrison and the other rustlers were long gone. They had no reason to sneak back and steal a herd they'd sold for, to them, good money. The T Bar T owner wouldn't have any more trouble tracking Clay and his companions than they'd had finding this meadow. A moving herd of cattle left tracks no one could erase.

"We must put as many miles between us and this ranch as possible. He will come after us." Suárez sounded grim and continued to twirl his six-shooter.

"We get the cows, start them for the pass at Alpine and then get into Idaho. With only three of us, it's going to be hard."

Clay considered all the diversions they could cause. Sadly, he kept returning to the answer. Nothing was going to keep the rancher from pursuing the herd. There wasn't any distraction they could conjure up that'd derail him.

"Idaho Falls," mumbled Suárez. "We must get there. Then we will be safe."

Clay wondered at that. What was magical about Idaho Falls? He had heard about the gold rush there, but otherwise nothing suggested they'd be rolling in clover. From there it was still a ways to the northern California coast Barker Ranch. He started to ask; then other questions popped up requiring immediate answers.

"Can we reach Alpine before dawn? I haven't had much luck herding in the dark." Neither of the Hawaiians answered. He rambled on, talking more to himself to get details straight in his head. "There aren't that many cattle to move, not like in a big drive. Three men can do it. It's going to be hard, but we can do it. I know we can." Clay repeated such sentiments over and over to convince himself this harebrained scheme wouldn't get them hanged as cattle thieves.

"Can we go now?" Vasques asked. "Waiting makes me more nervous than being shot at."

Clay understood. The longer they waited, the more problems they thought up. If lead started flying, that focused their attention on one thing only. And once they recovered the cattle, it would take all their expertise to keep them moving. Five more men would be useful for a herd this size, but that was out of the question.

"Let's go. Back me up," Clay said.

He mounted. The trio rode in silence to the spot they had chosen to break through the fence and drive off the pricey cattle.

Clay dismounted, went to a fence post and leaned against it hard. He yanked it back and forth a few times. It had rotted below the surface and broke off. Two more posts quickly followed, Suárez on one and Vasques on the other. Clay silently signaled them to mount and get ready with his horse. An hour's scouting just before midnight had revealed the spot where the guard had built a small fire to stay warm. He wouldn't stray far from here and had no reason to worry about the cattle breaking out of the herd. They were penned in a pasture.

Steps quick and lariat swinging in his grip, he went to the edge of a small wooded area and peered through the trees. The guard's fire danced warmly. The smell of boiling coffee made his nostrils flare. He regretted now that they hadn't eaten before coming to take back the Crown K herd. Once they hit the trail, there'd be scant time to chow down. At least the cattle had had their fill of luscious knee-high grass and plenty of water before starting the desperate travel.

The undergrowth was sparse. Clay walked without undue crackling and snapping from fallen limbs or dried leaves. He came within a few yards of the fire and hunted for the guard. He tightened his hands into fists as frustration hit him like a physical blow. The guard was nowhere to be seen. Having the man ride night herd had never entered his mind. Why bother if the fence around the area was secure?

Clay stepped forward, then froze. A horse nickered to his right. If the guard was tending the cattle, he was doing it on foot. That made no sense. Before he had a chance to investigate, he heard a loud sigh and someone walking back to camp from the other direction.

The guard buttoned his fly. He had been off relieving himself. All of Clay's earlier reconnaissance had been accurate. Jumping the gun had almost betrayed him. He had let Vasques' anxiety spook him.

The guard sank onto a stump and poured himself a cup of coffee. Clay moved around, formed a loop and spun it a couple times over his head. The whistle of the rope through the air caused the guard to perk up like a prairie dog leaving his burrow. When the loop tightened around the cowboy's upper arms, he shot to his feet, dropped his cup and foolishly tried to run.

Clay jerked on the rope and brought the man up short.

"Don't struggle," Clay said.

He kept the rope taut and worked his way hand over hand to where the guard lay on his back, fighting to get free. Using his skills. Clay lashed the man's feet together with the other end of the rope. He had him hogtied as securely as any calf in a roping contest.

"You're gonna take back your cattle?" The man stopped struggling and stared up from the ground.

"Reckon so." Clay stepped back, then turned cold inside when another voice came from the heavy shadows.

"Move an inch and I'll ventilate you, you danged cattle thief!"

Firelight danced off the bore of the rifle pointed squarely at him. Caught, Clay slowly raised his hands.

CHAPTER NINE

W HERE DID YOU come from?" Clay felt stupid asking the obvious question. The T Bar T owner
had posted two sentries, and Clay had missed the one
hiding in the woods.

"You suppose we ought to string him up, Fred?"
The man edged around and gave the bound cowboy a
hard kick in the ribs. "Should I save Mr. Neill the trouble and string you up, too? Or will you be happy with
another lashing?" The man laughed harshly.

"Get me out of the ropes," Fred said. He rocked
back and forth but couldn't get free from Clay's careful
hog-tying.

"I don't think so. If I drag you back to the bunkhouse, do you think Mr. Neill will give me a bonus?
Maybe he'll just not pay you and let me have your due."

Clay listened to the byplay in wonder. He locked eyes
with Fred and mouthed, *I'm sorry.* And he meant it.

Fred kicked and jerked about and finally got his feet
free. From there it took another few seconds to loosen

the lariat around his upper arms. He coiled the rope
and held it in his left hand. With his right he ran out a
loop and spun it around a couple times.

"You enjoy tormenting me, don't you, Hastings?"

"That's *Mr.* Hastings. I'm gonna be the foreman.
You wait and see."

Hastings spun around, his finger tightening on the
trigger as Clay tried to make his move. His hand went
for his six-shooter, but he stopped halfway to the holster. He wasn't fast enough to beat a bullet. From the
look in Hastings' squinty eyes, he should have made
the effort since he was going to catch a bullet in the gut
no matter what he did. Better to cash in fighting than
to be killed in cold blood.

"Hanging's too good for you. I'll cut you down and
let the coyotes eat you if your putrid flesh don't make
'em too sick."

Clay vowed to go for his pistol. Before he had a
chance to slap leather, the cowboy's feet were yanked
out from under him. He landed facedown on the
ground. As he sputtered to get dirt from his mouth, the
lasso lashed out again, this time dropping around his
neck. He dropped his rifle and grabbed at the hemp
rope with both hands as the noose strangled him.

"Think I should fasten this end to his saddle horn
and send his horse back to the bunkhouse?" Fred put
a boot in the middle of Hastings' back and tugged with
both hands on the rope around the man's neck. "Maybe
I should just toss the end over a limb and see if he dies
before my grip gives out holding this end of the rope."
He reared back. Hastings turned bright red, gagged
and then passed out. "The way I'm feelin' right now, I
can hold on to the rope for a powerful long time. While
it's something I ain't seen with my own eyes, I've heard
it takes less than a minute for a man to choke to death
if his neck's not broke by a fall."

Fred kept up the pressure for a second longer, then released his hold. A quick jerk loosened the rope from around Hastings' abraded neck. Slowly drawing it in, Fred formed a loop and held it out to Clay.

"This here rope's yours. Do with him what you will, but getting his blood on it ain't worth the effort."

"You and Hastings aren't partners," Clay said. "I get that. But your rifle's over there and I have my pistol right here." He patted his holster. "What are you telling me?"

"Take back your damned cattle. Neill stole them and knew it. When that nervous cowboy rode up, there wasn't a soul among us that didn't see him for a rustler. Neill jumped on it because he's cheap." Fred sneered. "Cheap and crooked. He hasn't paid me in close to a month, and I'm not the only one. He can peel off a thousand dollars in greenbacks and not blink an eye, but he won't pay me twenty 'cuz he claims he don't have it."

"Why not?" Clay used the rope to tie Hastings to a thick-boled tree. "If he had the money to pay cash for stolen cattle, he has money for his hands."

"He charges us for room and board. Somehow, it always comes out to a dollar more than we're owed."

"He runs a company store. Is that it?"

"I heard about them mining companies and how they keep the miners in debt the same way. Yeah, that's what Mr. Randolph J. Neill of the T Bar T Ranch does." Fred spat.

Clay cinched the rope a bit tighter around Hastings, then picked up Fred's rifle from where it leaned against another tree. He balanced it for a moment, then studied the cowboy standing forlornly by the fire. He looked like a man whose execution was inevitable. He waited for the firing squad.

"Here," Clay said. He tossed Fred his rifle.

The cowboy fielded it easily and held it in both

hands. He looked from the weapon to Hastings and then to Clay. His expression changed again. With carefully spoken words, he asked, "You need help moving them cows? I know the countryside as good as any man in these here parts."

"That'd be appreciated, but you don't have to. You're going to be in plenty of hot water."

Clay looked pointedly at Hastings. Once the man reached his boss, every man on the ranch would come after them with blood in their eyes.

Or would they? Clay wondered at Fred offering to help recover the cattle. He had volunteered his services out of the clear blue. Only it wasn't entirely unexpected if Hastings and Neill had treated him like dirt ever since he hired on at the T Bar T. Fred might not have been the only one among the hands carrying a grudge.

"You thinking on driving the herd south? If you intend to keep going west, you need to cross the mountain pass at Alpine."

"That's what we were intending." Clay felt more comfortable letting Fred join up because he and Suárez agreed on the best trail west.

"If we make good time, we can be there by sunup." Fred began breaking camp. He paused, then added Hastings' rifle to his own gear. "Never leave a gun behind that can be used against you. My old man taught me that." He snorted and shook his head. "The one time he didn't follow his own advice, it got him shot in the back."

Without another word he disappeared into the dark and came back with two horses.

"Mine," he said, patting one horse's neck. "The other is Hastings', but you be careful trying to ride her. He's mistreated her like he does everyone else."

As if to emphasize the claim, the horse reared and

lashed out with two deadly front hooves. Fred side-stepped and jerked on the bridle, bringing the mare under control.

"You need to fetch your partners?" Fred swung into the saddle and fastened Hastings' horse behind him.

"They're likely already working the herd," Clay said.

He trotted after Fred, then urged his horse to a quicker gait to arrive before Fred. Having Suárez or Vasques take a shot at their new trail hand wouldn't do.

He reached the herd and found Suárez already using his lariat to whip the reluctant animals into motion.

"All went well?" Suárez asked. He looked past Clay as Fred rode up.

Before the trail boss went for his six-gun, Clay explained the situation. "We have an ally. I hadn't expected to recruit a new hand, but we have."

Suárez hesitated, then asked, "Will you vouch for him?"

Clay nodded.

"Then let us move cattle this night!"

Suárez went back to applying the rope to the rumps of the nearest cattle, looking for one of them to become the leader. When none did, he lashed his lariat down and took out his slingshot. Suárez found a small pebble in a vest pocket, stood in his stirrups and found a bull at the edge of the herd. He let fly. The bull roared and began running. The others followed him.

Suárez blew a quick kiss to his slingshot and said, "The trick is more than finding the right leader. It's hitting him in the rump not too hard to make him mad but hard enough to get him moving."

"I'll keep that in mind," Clay said, grinning.

Before Suárez replied, Fred said, "This is taking too long." He gave Suárez a quick once-over. "Should I?" He held up his rifle, muzzle aimed into the night sky.

"He's got the right idea," Clay said. "It'll take four of us too long to start them moving if we keep doing it like that." He pointed to the slingshot Suárez held.

Suárez sighed and nodded. "The bull has already chosen to sleep again rather than lead the others from the meadow. How quickly they become accustomed to a pasture." He tucked the slingshot away and settled down in the saddle, ready to ride. "The fence is pulled down over yonder," Suárez said to Fred, suggesting the direction.

The cowboy rode a dozen yards to a spot, putting the herd between him and the broken fence. Even knowing it was coming, Clay flinched when Fred fired his rifle.

The beeves let out frightened cries and began to stampede. It took all the skill of the four riders to direct the rampaging cattle toward the gap in the fence. Even then, they missed by a few yards. The bull that had taken the lead once more cared nothing that the fence was in his path. Frightened but accepting that he chose the direction, the two tons of beef and mean crashed into the wire and ripped out two more posts. The bull rushed into the night trailing barbed wire.

Clay took a deep breath, then rode to one side of the moving mass of beef. Keeping them headed out of the pasture was easy. Turning them onto the road once they escaped their pen was a different matter. The four of them worked back and forth to entice the leader to charge blindly after them. When Clay galloped ahead, he felt his horse beginning to flag. The bull neared, snorting and tossing his head with the massive horns turned to silver in the rising moon. They had been polled but still presented a problem. A man on the wrong end of such ferocious long horns would have no chance. Worse, any horse veering too close might be ripped open.

A dying horse under him meant the rider would be

tossed under the crashing hooves. Clay had seen one man trampled in all his time on the trail. It had been a terrible, painful and slow death. If a horse was severely injured, a bullet to the head put it out of its misery. He wished someone had done that for the cowboy. It had taken him almost a day to finally die.

That memory faded as he raced through the night and was replaced with more recent ones of cowering behind a cow he'd killed as those deadly hooves sought to turn him to bloody pulp. Clay's heart hammered and fear rose, but he knew this was no time to turn cautious.

He lowered his head and bent forward, putting his weight onto his gelding's front shoulders. This eased some of the strain of galloping along. The night air cut at his face and whipped back his lank hair. If he hadn't been riding for his life, the exhilaration would have been something to brag on around a campfire.

All he really wanted now was to be able to tell tall tales of outdistancing the stampede.

He flinched again when someone behind the cattle fired again. Clay tried to twist around to see who was responsible. He hoped it was their new cowpuncher and not any of the T Bar T ranch hands. Dealing with mindless cattle was increasingly hard. Dodging lead aimed to kill him subtracted from his chances for surviving the night.

Clay's horse began to tire. He veered away, hoping the leading bull would continue down the road. The ferocious juggernaut followed him like a baby duckling after its mama. Cursing didn't make his horse run faster or the bull any slower. But he noticed the rougher terrain caused the heavy bull to wobble back and forth. Keeping its balance became harder. Then the frightened, angry animal simply stopped. Clay quickly outdistanced the herd.

When he saw this, he drew back on the reins and let his horse come to a halt. The herd had decided stampeding wasn't as good as grazing on a new field of knee-high grass alongside the road. Clay wheeled about and walked his horse back to where the other three cowboys already huddled together. Suárez gestured while Vasques sat quietly as he usually did. Fred argued. Being the tie-breaking vote wasn't a role Clay relished, but they had no time to let the recaptured herd simply munch away. Neill would find out about their theft and bring the wrath of God down on them.

He ran his fingers under his bandanna and around his grimy neck. A hemp necktie wasn't anything he looked forward to wearing.

"Due south, I'm telling you. Don't go back to the road you were gonna take," Fred insisted. "This is a shorter route to Alpine where you can get through the pass into Idaho. That's where you want to go, isn't it? Idaho?"

"They will be waiting for us in Idaho Falls," Vasques said to Suárez so softly, Clay almost missed it. He started to ask who they were meeting there, but Suárez loudly protested.

"In the dark we will become lost!"

"Leo, the sooner we get out of Wyoming, the sooner we can find a tiny bit more safety," he said. "Fred here's helped us so far. He knows the countryside better than any of us."

Clay saw Suárez chewing on that.

"Why do you help us?" Suárez finally asked. "You have betrayed your employer."

"He owns purty near all the land around here, so there's no one else to work for. It'll be winter in another six weeks, maybe less. Probably less this year from the signs. The woolly caterpillars are extra fuzzy right now. Moving on and finding a way to survive in this country is hard when the weather turns bad. I was going to stay until spring, then sneak away."

"You'd leave behind a pile of debt," Clay put in.

He quickly explained how Neill charged his men for room and board in excess of what he paid them. If they didn't come up with extra money to pay off that debt, he kept them indentured.

"So you were willing to rob your employer in the spring but chose to do it now by helping us regain our herd?" Suárez frowned.

"You're making him out to be a thief, Leo. What his boss is doing isn't right. It's close to slavery, and maybe there's no *close* to it. Some folks would call it outright slavery." Clay felt getting his dander up now was necessary. This had to be settled and quick.

"Will you ride with us to the coast?" Suárez scowled even more. "We have little money to pay you."

Before Fred answered, Clay cut in, "I'll pony up a hundred dollars. That's what they promised me."

"But, Clay, you will not earn anything, not if you give what you make to him!" Suárez was taken aback.

"This has to be settled now. I've got enough money riding in my jeans from turning in Warnock's men and a few dollars left after the rodeo. All I want is to clear out now!"

"He understands what'll happen if we dawdle," Fred said. "Why not get moving, then argue later?"

"But we quarrel over the best route." Suárez looked set in his ways.

"Vote," Clay said in as commanding a voice as he could. "I vote we take the route Fred says is shortest."

"My route," Fred said, sticking up one hand.

"The road from Hoback going south," Suárez said. Then he sat straighter. "I am trail boss. There is no voting. Besides, why should *he* get a vote?" He stared at Fred.

"He's a paid hand, that's why," said Clay. "Just like me."

José Vasques cleared his throat. "I have yet to cast my vote."

All three of them looked at him.

"Our new *amigo*, Fred, risks his life for us. I vote for his road."

"But I am trail boss!" Suárez puffed up. "Then you no longer want me to lead you?"

"That's something else we can discuss," Clay said. "Ride scout, Fred. Lead the way while we get the herd moving again. They've rested a mite and have gobbled up plenty of grass to last them for another couple hours."

Fred trotted off, then turned directly south.

Clay waited for Suárez to protest losing control of the Crown K herd. Instead, he silently rode to the far side of the dark mass of cattle and began urging them to move.

South.

Clay started to thank Vasques, but the other man turned and trotted away to work the other side of the herd, leaving Clay to ride behind, eating their dust and enduring a view that never changed as the cattle flicked their tails about.

He wasn't sure he had done the right thing, wresting command from Leo Suárez the way he had. After all, he was a Johnny-come-lately and these weren't his cattle. Worse than this, he had no real interest in seeing the herd reach the coast and, eventually, Hawaii, but he felt obligated. He liked the Hawaiians and owed them for saving his life.

Sticking it to Neill entered into it, too. From all Fred had told him, the rancher deserved whatever he got in way of retribution.

CHAPTER TEN

CLAY WAS ABOUT at the end of his endurance—and afraid that would soon mean at the end of a rope. Neill and at least a half dozen of his ranch hands narrowed the distance between them. "We won't make it," he gasped out.

Just after dawn Fred had spotted them on the Barker drovers' back trail. The herd moved along slowly, and nothing they did made the cattle speed up. Clay realized it didn't matter now. They were near the spot where the trail split, part going due south and the other crossing the mountains through the pass just north of Alpine. Escaping from Wyoming into Idaho wasn't possible before Neill caught up with them.

Even if they had reached Idaho Territory, the rancher wasn't inclined to stop. He wasn't the law. He wasn't a sheriff limited to a single county or a marshal seldom venturing beyond the boundary of the town paying his salary. He was more like a Federal marshal

ranging wherever he wanted, enforcing the law at the
point of a gun.

Clay drew his six-shooter and checked to be sure it
was loaded. Satisfied, he yanked the rifle taken from
Hastings from its scabbard and saw that he could put
in a few more rounds. He did so as he rode, then returned the long gun to its resting place under his knee.
The next time it came out, he'd be fighting for his life.

"We need to find a place to make a stand," Suárez
said, "if you agree."

His bitter tone told the tale. Clay wished he hadn't
usurped the man's position as trail boss. Somehow,
though, being in charge turned him more stubborn. He
was an interloper on this trail drive, but he was no
stranger to service and duty. It was his responsibility to
see the cattle reached the Pacific coast.

Clay almost laughed out loud when he wondered if
he ought to ask for more money to go with the added
responsibility. The hundred dollars Suárez had offered
him was more than fair for a trail boss. It was close to
three times what any reasonable man expected riding
herd. But Clay felt more than responsibility to the
Barkers. He had never met any of the family. He had
never even heard of the Crown K brand, and certainly
the notion of Hawaiian cowboys had been as far from
his mind as volcanic eruptions or crazy nuts covered
with bristly brown hair and edible interiors and milk.
Those sounded like stories to tell around the campfire,
yet when Vasques had described Hawaii and mentioned Mauna Loa and coconuts, he had sounded
sincere.

That was either the mark of a very good liar or
someone telling the truth. Clay found himself wondering which it was in Vasques' case. He almost hoped all
the tall tales were true. It wasn't right for a man to have

an imagination able to conjure up such wild images to tell around the campfire.

"Fred knows the road. Have him and Vasques keep the herd moving. You hang behind, and if Neill and his men get through me, you can take them on. Keep the herd moving." Clay knew he was signing his own death warrant. He hoped the sacrifice would be good enough to let the others get away.

"That is not a good idea, Forsythe. You stand no chance of slowing them, not alone. I do not, either," said Suárez. "We stand together or we fall one by one."

"Where've I heard that before?" In spite of being a foreigner, Suárez knew human nature. Clay nodded in agreement. Suárez had thought it through and he hadn't. "Let the herd graze down by that stream. When they stampede from the gunfire, they'll head in the direction we want."

"It will take a day to round them up," Vasques said.

"I hope so" was all Clay said.

Their chances against Neill's crew were slim. Having to re-form the herd meant they'd won the fight. They were outnumbered more than two to one. As he thought about the numbers, he looked at Fred. The cowboy nervously shifted in the saddle.

Clay rode to him and said, "You ought to hightail it. This isn't your fight. Neill's going to be especially vicious if he catches you. Us, he might hang if he doesn't gun us down where we stand. You betraying him means special torture."

Fred blinked as Clay spoke. His mouth opened, then snapped shut. He chewed on his lower lip for a moment, then said, "You're the first boss I ever had who put me ahead of his own best interest."

"It's our fight, not yours." Clay wondered why he thought that way. This was Suárez and Vasques' fight, not his. Not really. He and Fred could reach Alpine in an hour and be safe there.

That idea died as quickly as it came to him. He was in this with the Hawaiians and not because he somehow found himself tagged with being the trail boss.

"Make it my fight, too," Fred said. He cocked his head to one side. The thunder of approaching hooves warned of the fight to come. "I gotta wonder how many of them boys with Neill think the same way I do."

"Hastings didn't," Clay said.

"He's a snake in the grass. He's the first one I'd think of if somebody broke into the henhouse and sucked the eggs."

"But you think others might throw in with us?" Clay's brain began to churn, the wheels in his head spinning wildly. "How do we ask them to switch sides?"

"Neill's not going to let us mosey on over and ask, that's for sure," Fred said.

"Why not? You and the Hawaiians back me up."

Clay had thought up some crazy schemes. Another, crazier one wasn't amiss if it gave them even a slight chance of riding away without a dozen bullets in the gut.

Clay tried not to shake as he wheeled his horse around and rode back toward the approaching T Bar T riders. A spot in the trail gave him a small advantage, being on a small rise above the oncoming men as well as affording the trio behind him a chance to lay down supporting fire. He sat astride his horse and tried not to surrender to his emotions and quake like an aspen leaf. The cowboys he faced slowed and finally halted. Only their boss advanced. Twenty yards off, Neill dismounted. Clay hopped to the ground to conduct the negotiation.

The set to the rancher's shoulders showed he wanted

a fight, maybe more than he did his cattle back. That warned Clay about Neill losing his control over his men and how this confrontation was intended to win it back.

Neill started walking. The closer Neill got, the steadier Clay's nerves became. By the time the rancher shouted at him, his hand was firm and the tremors in his gut were distant memories.

"You got nerve, stealing my cows," Neill bellowed.

"You bought stolen beeves. They belong to the Barker Ranch. The Crown K brand shows that."

Clay shifted slightly to rest his hand on the saddle horn. This fight wasn't going to go to the one who cleared leather fastest. The best marksman would win the day.

"Don't matter to me. I paid good money for them. They're mine and you stole them."

"Let's go on into Alpine and see if they've got a judge who can decide the matter. The brand shows they aren't yours."

"I've got a bill of sale!" Neill waved the sheet around over his head.

"It doesn't mean anything if it's fake."

"You had to steal the cattle. There's no question about that. You assaulted my foreman to get them. Get up here, you coward."

Neill motioned Hastings forward to stand in a spot beside him. Hastings' choleric expression told Clay that being called a coward in front of the other riders didn't sit well with him. Clay had to play on Neill's thoughtless insults being a sore point with the rest of the men.

"It seems like you don't hold your men in too high esteem. They look like decent wranglers to me, hard-working and honest. They have to know how you got the cattle. Maybe they realize you used their pay to buy stolen beeves."

"They work for me! Don't go trying to seduce them with your lying ways." Neill rested his hand on his six-shooter. "You got one chance and this is it. Ride away. Leave the herd for my cowboys to drive back, and I'll let you go as much as the notion rankles."

"What are the chances of that?" Clay asked Fred so that everyone heard.

"Razor-thin. You can't believe a word he says." Fred spoke loudly enough for his words to carry to the men who used to ride with him. "I'm proud to say I quit and joined a decent outfit. These men keep their word and don't charge for food."

"If any of you T Bar T riders want to join the Crown K drive, come on over and we'll talk pay. A month's work to get the herd to the Pacific Coast. That's better work than you'll ever see on the T Bar T. Nobody's going to rag on you, either."

"I'm getting paid a hundred dollars," Fred said.

Clay ground his teeth together. If more than a couple of Neill's men thought they'd get that much for a month's work, the Barkers would be bankrupt. On the other hand, making such a generous offer now avoided shooting it out with Neill.

The rancher realized what was eating at his men when a pair of them began arguing about the offer. Neill whipped out his pistol and opened fire.

For an instant Clay stood frozen. That saved his life. Neill and his cowboys were terrible shots. If Clay had tried dodging, he might have run into a bullet. As it was, more than one slug whizzed perilously close. One parted his hair just above his right ear, but didn't break skin. The rest went wild. He half turned and realized he was in more danger from behind than from the T Bar T ranch hands. Suárez fired almost at him. Vasques sprayed lead all around, and Fred fired with some hesitation. Clay didn't fault him for that. He was shooting at men he'd worked alongside. From the sound of it, none could be counted as a friend, but the bond forged driving cattle on the range endured.

Clay kept spinning and then threw himself level with the ground. He landed hard enough to knock the wind out of his lungs for an instant. Kicking and thrashing about, he wiggled to safety behind a large rock. Lead splashed against the far side of the boulder, showing Neill was homing in on him as a primary target. Clay pressed his back against the cold rock for a moment, then drew his six-shooter, cocked it and chanced a quick peek around the side.

He had his choice of a half dozen targets. The other drovers stood their ground, firing from the spot they'd occupied when their boss opened fire. Clay felt a little guilty. This was like dynamiting fish in a pond. He got off three quick shots and wounded two of the cowboys. They yelped and danced around. Neither wound was serious, but he let them know they weren't safe standing out in the open the way they were.

Vasques popped up and used his rifle. The more accurate weapon took out a cowboy. Then he laid down covering fire so that Clay had a chance to retreat to safer ground.

"We don't want to shoot it out with you, Neill," Clay yelled once he had crouched behind an even larger rock near José Vasques. "You don't have any claim to those cows."

Both Suárez and Vasques popped up before the words were finally out of his mouth. They instinctively knew how Neill would respond. And he didn't disappoint them.

The rancher let out a bull roar and charged. They hit Neill three times before the madness was erased by pain, and he fell kicking to the ground.

Clay stood and rested his gun hand on the top of the

rock, waiting. He wanted to see what Hastings did. The foreman either came to rescue his boss or he ran. If it was the former, Clay was ready for him.

He shook his head when he realized Hastings had hunkered down and left his boss exposed to the Crown K fire. It provided mute witness to what he suspected about the foreman. When he saw the ranch hands slipping away one by one, that confirmed everything Fred had told him about how Neill treated his men. Clay had seen the man's rudeness in dealing with his crew. He treated them like inferiors rather than skilled drovers deserving his respect.

"Cover me," Clay said.

He slipped away. Vasques protested, then did as Clay asked. His rifle barked out one shot after another, holding the T Bar T fighters at bay.

Clay heard a stone turn behind him. He whirled around, gun leveled. He relaxed when he saw that Fred came along.

"I want to be there," Fred said. "I worked for him long enough to hate him so much, my soul withered up and blew away."

"We're not looking to kill him, just chase off his wranglers."

Clay wasn't sure Fred shared his plan, but there wasn't time to argue. Gunfire intensified. None of the bullets came their way since they had flanked the spot where Neill lay moaning in a puddle of his own blood. He tried to stanch the flow from a chest wound with one hand even as he fired his six-shooter with the other. Neither proved very effective.

Clay motioned for Fred to hang back, but the man wasn't having any of it. Clay had to rush to keep up as Fred raced around and came up on the T Bar T men from behind.

"Drop the guns, boys. There's nothing I'd like to do more than to—"

Clay silenced him.

"You heard him. Lose the hoglegs. Now!" He fired once into the air to emphasize his orders. The cowboys did as he commanded. "Where's Hastings?" Clay did a quick count and came up one short.

"Don't know." The one speaking looked at the ground and mumbled like a schoolboy caught throwing spitballs in class.

"You've got two choices. The first is to mount up and ride out."

"You know what the second is," cut in Fred.

Clay had started to offer any of the cowboys a spot riding with the Crown K herd, but Fred changed the second choice from hiring on to dying then and there. From the way the men glowered now, chasing them off might have been safer. He walked around and kicked their six-shooters away.

"What's it going to be?" Clay was almost bowled over as the men raced for their horses. In seconds all that remained to show they'd ever shot it out on the Wyoming terrain was a billowing dust cloud.

"None of them's going back to the bunkhouse," Fred said with grim satisfaction. "They wouldn't risk their lives for Neill. They surely won't risk having him put them to the lash for not standing with him."

"Is that good enough for you?"

Clay saw how Fred kept glancing toward where Neill still fired sporadically. The rancher had weakened from blood loss but still fought on. If he didn't get his wounds patched up quick, he was going to die. Fred's expression warned Clay that that was exactly what he wanted if he couldn't put a bullet into Neill himself.

"They're all losers. Let them ruin the T Bar T."

"Stay here," Clay said.

He caught movement out of the corner of his eye. A bush rustled and then stopped. He trained his six-gun on the clump of greenery but saved his ammunition. He knew a baited trap when he saw one.

Walking gingerly to avoid making a sound, he entered a maze of rocks. Stepping over the vegetation to keep from alerting his attacker, he came up behind Hastings. The foreman sat on his haunches, gripping his pistol in both hands. He stared so intently at the brush that had moved that Clay wondered for a moment if some other critter poked about there. Then he saw how Hastings had taken off his gun belt and thrust a branch through the buckle. Tugging now and then on the leather belt caused the bush to rustle.

"I wouldn't turn around—from here I can put a bullet smack through the back of your head."

Clay almost triggered a round. If he had fired, Hastings' only response would have been to spin and try to kill his attacker. As it was, he knew Clay had the drop on him, but not exactly from where.

"You coward. You gotta shoot a man in the back. Ain't that right? Let me turn around. We can have this out face-to-face like real men."

"You don't know the meaning of that," Clay snapped. "You're the one that ran like a scalded dog when the lead started flying." He stepped over some of the vegetation and got into position for an even better shot if he needed to take it. "Lift those hands sky-high. Now!"

Hastings' dirty hands shot up.

"You're not going to believe it, but I'm saving your crow-bait life. Fred wanted to lay you out in the sun, riddled with holes."

"That—"

"Shut up."

Clay moved close enough to shove Hastings with his left hand. The man responded as Clay had suspected, trying to whip around and grapple. He found himself staring down the barrel of Clay's gun. Taking any satisfaction in watching how Hastings turned pasty white in fear was beneath him. But Clay gloated just the same. A little.

"Start walking. You're going to be a hero, like it or not."

He marched the foreman back to where the cowboys had all scattered to the four winds. Clay motioned for Fred to keep Hastings covered so he could survey the battlefield. Neill muttered feeble curses. Whether he had run out of ammo or had become too weak to use his six-shooter wasn't something that mattered much to Clay. He turned back to the T Bar T foreman.

"Go on out there and tend to your boss before he bleeds to death."

"I ain't—" Hastings turned even paler when both Fred and Clay thrust their six-guns into his face.

"He might be running dry on bullets. Or he can be playing possum and waiting for a better shot. Whichever it is, he's bleeding something fierce. Patch him up. Then get the hell out of here. The cattle belong to the Crown K Ranch, and there's nothing you or Neill can do about that."

Hastings let them prod him into motion. He shuffled toward Neill, then called out to his boss to let him know he was coming to save him. When Neill rolled onto his back and pointed his gun at his foreman, death was in the air. Then the hammer fell on a spent cartridge.

"Let's go," Clay said to Fred. "They can work it out themselves."

"They deserve each other," Fred said, "but putting a bullet into their rotten hearts would have felt good."

"Getting back on the trail and leaving them far behind will feel better."

Clay was right.

CHAPTER ELEVEN

"FOUR IS NOT enough," Leo Suárez complained. "We are spread too thin. A single mistake and we lose the herd."

Clay looked up from his plate of beans and a biscuit that would have been better used in Suárez's slingshot than for sustenance. Things hadn't changed much after wresting the herd from Neill, but one thing happened that suited Clay just fine. Suárez had quietly regained his position as trail boss. It had happened over the span of a week, with the Hawaiian falling back into the job and Clay letting him. Clay had never wanted the job even if he had the skill for it.

He had to agree about part of the trail boss' complaint. They needed a cook more than they did another wrangler. Each of them took care of his own horse. A proper trail drive had dozens of horses—and that many men. The distance they covered every day depended more on how tired their mounts became rather than having anything to do with the herd.

"There doesn't seem to be much danger," Clay opined.

"You have never followed this trail," Suárez said. "You cannot know what lies ahead."

"Never having been this way before's not the problem, is it? You're grousing because José is such a lousy cook." Clay looked around. José was out on night herd, so Clay could voice his complaint without offending the cowboy. With so few of them tending the cattle, Suárez was right about losing even one of them. "Fred should take a turn fixing chuck, too. It wouldn't kill him. And now that we got through the pass into Idaho, there's no call for him to be our only scout. He doesn't know the countryside any better than we do."

Clay hated cooking and the only thing worse than José's thrown-together plates of mismatched items was his own chuck. Fred might not have been an improvement but he wasn't likely worse than Clay or José when it came to poisoning themselves.

"You have never followed this trail," Suárez said again. It had been a simple statement the first time he asked Clay. Now it became a lament.

"All my work's been farther east and a ways south. Colorado, Texas. When the Rocking O drove up to Bozeman, that was the farthest north I'd ever been."

He used the last morsel of a doughy biscuit to sop up the juice from the beans. José needed to make them with less liquid, but then Suárez complained when he turned out a mess of beans that had to be chipped off the plate with a knife.

"Fred is a good scout. He chooses our route well," Suárez said. "In exchange for that, he can skip being cook."

"You're no great shakes yourself as a cook," Clay pointed out. "Let's not squabble over this. We have food and the trail's not going to stretch a thousand miles. We're within two or three weeks of getting to the coast."

"We risk valuable breeding stock," Suárez said.

Clay scraped off his plate, took Suárez's and rubbed some sand on it to scour away any food stuck to the bottom. A few swipes with a rag completed the cleaning chore. He made packing up their supplies take longer than it should to give Suárez a chance to calm down. By the rotation, Suárez was due to fix breakfast. Clay would clean the utensils again, then fix lunch and dinner while the others took care of the housekeeping.

He preferred tending the cattle. They might get moody or even downright ornery, but he understood them. People were something different. Suárez was moody and grew more sulfurous the longer they rode. José kept to himself, and Fred? Clay had had little to do with the new recruit after the shoot-out with Neill and the other T Bar T cowboys. He wondered if Fred thought he had betrayed him by not murdering the rancher and his foreman.

"Get ready for a hard day tomorrow," Suárez said. "We can get close to Idaho Falls if we do not pamper the cattle."

"You're the one who said they're valuable enough to be coddled. Do we have to be there by any specific time?"

"No," Suárez said curtly. He offered nothing more in way of explanation.

Clay stretched out and stared into the night sky, tracing patterns and finding constellations. His favorite, the one that looked like a desert scorpion, crawled across the southern sky. He found the bright red star and wondered if the scorpion looked back at him in wonder. A shooting star occupied him for a moment;

then his eyelids drooped and the day's work took its toll on him.

A NOTHER MILE," FRED said. "There's a meadow that's about perfect for grazing. Are you sure you don't want me scouting farther toward town? We've been on the trail only a couple hours."

"We rest the cattle," Suárez said.

The way he spoke caught Clay's attention. Suárez wasn't willing to argue over the matter.

"Yesterday we about drove ourselves into the ground to cover extra miles, and now you want to rest? If we get closer to town—"

"Idaho Falls," Fred cut in.

"If we find somewhere within spitting distance of Idaho Falls, we can take turns hitting the saloons. My whistle is in serious need of wetting," Clay said. He kept his tone light and bantering, but Suárez wasn't having any of it.

"We do as I say." He tapped his spurs against his horse's sides and galloped off.

"How far from town is this pasture?"

Clay watched Suárez as he circled the herd, counting to be sure they hadn't lost any strays along the trail. With a hundred head it was easy enough to count. He had learned to glance over the sea of beef and instinctively know if any of the expensive animals had wandered away.

"Several miles. Call it an hour's ride. Why doesn't he want us going into town? He's not one of them there teetotalers, is he? I heard passels of women in the big cities are wanting more than the vote. They want to keep men from drinking."

"Temperance leagues," Clay said. "That's what they call them. Suffragists and temperance leagues. The

Wyoming legislature already let women vote. They're the first in the country, and now the women're feeling their oats about drinking."

"Let 'em vote all they want," Fred said, "just as long as nobody keeps me from a shot of rye whiskey."

Clay agreed. It made sense that the no-drinking edict was enforced while they were on the trail. Having a drunken cowboy trying to work a herd was downright suicidal—or homicidal. A single mistake or a stampede, and men died.

But they deserved to cut loose in town. More than the comradeship involved, the booze eased the aches and pains of being in the saddle for long hours, sleeping on hard ground and simply living on the trail.

"If we speed things up, it might give us a chance to sneak off into town one by one," Fred said. "He can't watch us all around the clock, and if we cover for one another . . ."

Clay nodded. If the cattle found easy grazing and sweet water, they wouldn't be inclined to cause much trouble. A couple of the men could guard the entire herd, let one cowboy tend to cooking and chores, and the fourth one could go into town, even if only for a few hours. He looked at Fred and wondered if a few hours would be enough. Fred might take it into his head to really tie one on. They hadn't traveled together long enough to really know.

For his part, as good as he knew the taste of whiskey was, finding a café that served decent food was more enticing. His belly rumbled constantly and not from lack of food. The quality mattered more than he had appreciated. A tiny smile came to his lips as he remembered the trail drive from Colorado to Bozeman. The Rocking O cook had been better than they deserved—or than he appreciated until now. He wondered if he was cursed since their cook had died of a snakebite right after they hit the trail and forced cowpunchers to double as cooks then, too.

Clay's thoughts turned to Lanky Lou Larson and how he was doing. Larson's signing on with Warnock meant Clay and his old trail partner would cross paths eventually. It was hard to believe their reunion might be more deadly than a simple howdy, but the prospect loomed.

Just before midday Fred galloped back with the news that he'd located a perfect stopping spot for the herd. Clay watched Suárez's expression change from worried to delighted. When they drove the cattle into the meadow, Suárez was beside himself with glee.

"This is the spot. Check the area for any place cows might wander."

"Why should they?" Clay asked. "There's grass here and a small pond for them to drink from. For a critter, this is paradise."

"We should rest here a few days. They will eat the grass in the center and move outward."

"Why stick around so long?" Clay asked. "We need the rest more than the herd, and a day will suit all of us just fine."

"Do as I say," Suárez said, his tone suddenly frosty. "Ride the edges and see if there are bogs the cows might mire themselves in. The area does not have rustlers—that we know of. Go. Go!"

Clay did as he was told. If he had to imagine a more perfect pasture for the herd, he would have failed. Fred had done a good job of scouting this out. After making a circuit and finding nothing to endanger the cattle, he returned to where José had started the midday meal. Even the burned smell made Clay's mouth water. They ate and Suárez scheduled their patrol.

They lazed about until the sun began to sink behind the trees along the western perimeter. Fred grew restive, wanting to ride into town, but it was a full hour away. Clay turned in early but kept an eye on Suárez. When the trail boss saddled his horse, Clay talked to Fred and got him to agree to take back-to-back stints riding night herd. Then he mounted and followed Suárez.

He thought he knew where the man was riding, and he wasn't wrong. Suárez made good time reaching the town. Clay bent low and stared at the signpost at the edge of town: Idaho Falls. Suárez had talked about coming here, but only as a brief stop along the trail to the coast. Clay urged his mare to a faster gait and quickly spotted Suárez.

"Well, that's one thing I was wrong about," he said to himself. His horse twisted around and fixed a big brown eye on him, waiting for an explanation. "I thought he'd make a beeline for a saloon. Where is he heading?"

Clay dropped to the ground, tethered his horse and rushed forward on foot in time to see Suárez duck into the Wells Fargo office. He waited a few minutes, growing more impatient when Suárez didn't immediately come out. Just as he was sure the man was going to camp out in the office, Suárez exited, vaulted into his saddle and rode away.

Again Clay expected him to find a saloon. Instead, Suárez retraced his route through town and looked as if he was heading back to the pasture and the herd. He had ridden a long way for only a few minutes in the Wells Fargo office.

Torn between racing back so Suárez wouldn't know he'd followed him into town and wondering about the trail boss' mission, Clay decided in favor of scratching the curiosity bump. He stepped into the office and looked around. No one was in the outer office. Clay took a deep breath and started to leave but a pungent odor caused him to cough. Using his sleeve he swiped his nose as it began to drip.

"That happens to a lot of folks," a disembodied voice said. Clay reached for his gun and had it half out of the holster, then let it drop back when a small man wearing spectacles stood up from behind the counter.

"Why were you hiding back there?"

"Hiding? 'Twarnt doin' nuthin' of the sort." He motioned Clay closer.

The only clutter on the well-polished oak counter was a pad of blank sheets and a pencil. Behind the counter stretched a different world. Dozens of heavy glass jars filled with yellow liquid had thick rods shoved into them. Wire ran everywhere. Stacked boxes formed a knee-high maze, but a low desk with a chair answered Clay's questions. The telegraph key had been nailed down to the desktop to keep it from dancing away as the telegrapher worked frantically on it. Or so Clay guessed. It might have been nailed down to keep it from being stolen.

"Wait a second. Got a new message comin' in."

The man dropped into the low chair, pushed his glasses up on his nose and touched the sharpened tip of a lead pencil to his tongue to prepare for transcription. Quick, sure moves filled half a sheet of paper with the translated message. He sent a quick few dots and dashes when the incoming message stopped, then leaned back.

"That's Sonny Lee on the other end. I do declare, that man's the fastest key in all the West. Takes every bit of my skill to keep up with him on the receivin' end, and there's no way nohow I can match his transmission speed. How he ever learned to work so fast is a mystery, for certain sure. Now, what can I do you for, mister?"

"The smell? From the batteries?"

"Sulfuric acid. Lead. Gets a bit close in here from

time to time, but you get used to it. I have, and that's all that matters. You want to send a 'gram?"

"My boss was just here," he said.

Clay saw no reason to pretend he had drifted into town independent of Leo Suárez. Two strangers coming here in the span of a few minutes was more likely to create a stir than admitting they knew each other.

"Sent a 'gram," the telegrapher said carefully. He took off his spectacles and polished them using his coattail.

"He told me to check to be sure the recipient was right."

"Did he, now?" The telegrapher's mood changed. Getting more information from him was going to be hard because Clay had done something to arouse the man's misgivings.

"His name's Leo Suárez. He might have sent it to the wrong man."

"I don't ask the name of whoever's sendin'. Who's on the receivin' end's all that matters to me. The telegram's been sent, so if it went to the wrong party, that's too bad."

"Let me ease his mind," Clay said, floundering about. "Where was it sent?"

"Have your boss come ask himself. I remember his looks. Drover from the cut of his clothes." The telegrapher gave Clay a once-over and nodded. "If I was a bettin' man, I'd peg you as a drover, too. That don't mean you really work for him."

"Reckon not. I'll report back that you weren't all that cooperative."

"No, sir, you report back that I respect his privacy. If he comes in, I'll be happy to talk over the matter with him, and if he sent the 'gram astray, I'll be more 'n happy to send another one. For an additional fee, of course." The man grinned, pleased with himself.

The key rattled out new code. The telegrapher turned his back on Clay, just until he settled into his chair. That didn't provide much time, but Clay used it to good advantage to slip the pad of telegram forms off the counter. Where the telegrapher couldn't see, he tore off the top blank and dropped the rest to the floor, as if they'd blown off.

He waved goodbye and left the office. Idaho Falls was a progressive place with a half dozen gas lamps to light the main street. Clay held up the blank sheet, trying to read the impressions made when Suárez pressed down to write his message.

Clay swore under his breath. The page was smooth. Almost smooth. He wasn't able to make out the faint indentations. He started to fetch his horse; then an idea came to him. A quick look around assured him nobody paid him any attention. With a running jump, he caught the gas-lamp post halfway up. Feet kicking and hands grabbing, he pulled himself up to the glass chimney. Soot collected around the base. With a quick swipe he captured a finger's worth.

Dropping back to the ground, he rubbed the soot over the sheet. Clay sagged in defeat. Nothing on the sheet popped out as soot covered most of it.

Nothing but part of the message. "What's this mean?" he muttered to himself. He held it up again and read, *Pacific Star*. He had no idea, but it wasn't anything Suárez had ever mentioned, even in passing.

CHAPTER TWELVE

CLAY RODE LIKE the wind all the way back to where they had bedded down the herd. He hit the ground running, stumbled and almost tripped over José, who was working to pile up dried wood to fix breakfast and avoid the chore in the morning. They all wanted to sleep an extra few minutes.

"You are in quite a hurry. Fred still rides herd." Vasques studied the stars as thin clouds danced around them. "You have another hour before he wants you to relieve him."

Clay heaved a sigh of relief. He had made good time from Idaho Falls. A quick look around their small camp assured him he had beaten Suárez back. The trail boss had no reason to hurry. If anything he wanted to keep his horse fresh and would walk it the entire way back. Clay looked guiltily at his gelding. He should have tended to the animal, but all he did was take off the saddle and let the tuckered-out horse graze on a patch of succulent grass. While it should have been cur-

ried, all his own aches and pains from the do-or-die
ride back needed tending more.

He stretched out and moaned softly as his muscles
knotted and his joints swelled.

"You need a shot of medicine?"

Vasques held out their lone bottle of whiskey. They
all kept it strictly for medicinal use. More than once,
cuts had been bathed in the fiery potion and kept from
becoming infected. As much as Clay wanted a taste, he
knew that making "just one exception" opened the
door for another and another. Better to keep trail dis-
cipline and endure the twinges bedeviling him.

"I'm all right," he said. "I need to take my mind off
the way my back is kinking up."

He fished around in his saddlebags and found his
thin-bladed whittling knife and a piece of bone. Deft
moves cut out the marrow. Turning it over and over in
his palm gave him a better idea of what to carve.

"You use your knife well. The tiny dog you gave me
has details I missed at first."

"You've been looking at it?"

Clay puffed up with pride. The carved figures he
had given both Hawaiians weren't his best work, but
they had taken hours of idle time to make. Every piece
coming under his knife showed increasing skill.

"What do you make now?"

"It's a rib from the cow that saved my hide during
the stampede," he said. "The shape speaks to me and
says it ought to be a ring."

"Like a bull wears in its nose?" Vasques laughed at
this. "You will look good wearing a bone ring in your
nose."

"For my finger," Clay said. "There's a powerful lot
of carving ahead. I intend to use a design I saw over in
Denver. An Irishman had a backpack embroidered
with a pattern like a knot: a twisty, turny, special kind

of knot. A Celtic knot he called it. I spent a fair amount of time studying it." Clay burrowed a bit deeper with the knife tip and reamed out part of the softer interior. "If I remember it aright and can do the carving properly, the knot will look like a curled-up snake all around the outside."

"You should use a Hawaiian pattern. No one out West has seen such fine designs."

"Me included. I'd need to see one before I can copy it. You have anything for me to study?"

"We left Hawaii in a big hurry. The purchase of the cattle was done between banks, so we needed to come drive them to the coast. Mr. Barker heard of the rodeo and suggested that Leo and I try our skills."

"You certainly tried 'em out on me," Clay said. "You both beat me all hollow."

"Perhaps we should have worried more about hiring a trail crew, but showing off our skills tempted us. Leo thought it was good to show others who they might work with. Our efforts foundered, like a ship on a coral reef."

"What happened?"

José snorted in disgust. "Warnock began hiring the best and left us with men who drank or who had the gleam of a rustler in their eyes. That is obvious now." He snorted again and shook his head. "Harrison surprised us. Leo did not see the thieving seed growing in his soul. I barely spoke with him after I hired the others. They were as bad."

"Harrison might have talked them into joining him." Clay doubted that. Harrison had been too nervous to do much convincing. The entire crew had larceny in their hearts.

"But I blame Warnock. He offers more than any drover can ignore. We are lucky he did not send his men to work for us. They would have stolen the herd for Warnock. Getting the beeves back then, well, Harrison was an inept crook. Warnock would have dozens of guns to back his claims of ownership." Vasques turned dark eyes on Clay. "Why did you not accept his employment?"

"I saw the men he hired in Bozeman. One from the Rocking O was a good enough fellow."

He thought of Lou riding with Warnock and men with low-slung pistols and a hint of murder twisting their lips. That wasn't the kind of man Lou was, but the money had lured him. Clay had to admit the money had sounded good to him, too.

And that was the problem. It was too good to be entirely honest earnings. The men Warnock paid to ride with him weren't the kind he expected to watch his back, not like José and Leo. Even Fred had shown himself to be trustworthy.

"They will try to steal our cattle," Vasques said angrily. "I am sure of that. He will have trouble running the Crown K brand, but if he kills us, he might not try. Who in this country has ever seen a Pacific Star?"

Clay's knife slipped and he nicked himself. He stared hard at Vasques. "What'd you say?"

"The Crown K is a difficult brand to turn into another. Why is that so strange a thing to say? The Barkers long ago worried over such a thing. Even in Hawaii we have rustlers."

"Not that," Clay said. "What's this Pacific Star?"

He pressed his hand over the vest pocket where he had tucked the sheet from the telegraph office. All he had been able to make out on it was *Pacific Star*.

"That is Warnock's ranch. The brand is a large star with a P in the center. The Star P, as they call it, is a difficult one to run also. Many nights Leo and I scratched brands in the dirt to run Warnock's." He looked sad. "No matter how inventive we became, there was no single brand to change it into something else. I came closest, but it took two different irons. What cow tolerates that?"

"Pacific Star," Clay muttered.

Carefully pulling the sheet from his pocket, he held it up to the firelight. The dancing flames caused the portion where soot had rubbed into the indentations to almost shout at him.

Pacific Star.

Suárez had sent a telegram to someone on Warnock's ranch. That was the only explanation. Clay's belly twisted and turned, and he felt as if he had stepped off a high cliff and fallen endlessly. Suárez had betrayed the Barkers.

He jumped a foot when the steady clop-clop of an approaching horse echoed across the meadow. Leo Suárez was returning from town. Clay hastily crammed the paper into his pocket. He had no idea what to do. Confronting the trail boss would get him nowhere. Suárez would deny it. If Clay spoke privately with Vasques, he might find himself in an even worse situation. Vasques and Suárez were lifelong friends. Whatever Suárez schemed to do, Vasques must know.

But why keep it secret? Fred wouldn't care as long as it wasn't Randolph Neill they dealt with. Clay's vocal complaints about Warnock might have been responsible for Suárez and Vasques not coming out and telling him they intended to turn the herd over to Warnock. But why bother spinning such a tall tale about the owner of the Pacific Star Ranch? Clay had no loyalty to the Barkers.

All that Warnock had done, beating Clay up and trying to kill him, guaranteed he'd never go along with any double cross on the part of the Hawaiians. Valuing his skill as a cowboy so highly they felt the need to hoodwink him made no sense.

More than once since he had signed on, both men had spoken of Warnock with real contempt. Were they laying a false trail? Why bother if they worked for him? Or was Suárez the only one and José Vasques was being duped?

None of it made a lick of sense. Duping Clay got them nowhere. Send him on his way if they wanted Warnock to take the herd.

"How long have you and Leo been partners?" Clay had to ask. Jumping to conclusions was easy enough. He assumed they had been friends for years, working the whole time on the Crown K.

"I can't remember," Vasques said. "Most of my life. Thirty years? My father and his grandfather come from the same town. We grew up together on the Barker Ranch."

Vasques heaved to his feet and went to speak with Suárez. They walked some distance from the fire, leaving Clay to his dark thoughts. Until he figured out more, he had to string along with the trail drive, but having Warnock pop up suddenly wasn't going to surprise him. What he needed to guard against was getting shot out of the saddle to make Warnock taking the herd look like rustlers.

Clay held his head as if it would explode. The headache built until he wanted to scream—or rummage about and find the whiskey Vasques kept for medicinal purposes. Fixing the way his head filled with throbbing pain counted as purely medicinal. But he didn't. There had to be some explanation. What it could be danced just beyond his grasp.

He lay back and dozed, only to come awake when Fred shook him.

"Your turn. This is a decent pasture for our four-legged friends. They nibble a bit, then sleep, wake up and do it all over again. One bull hasn't moved twenty feet from where he staked out his territory when we got here."

"Thanks," Clay said.

He rubbed his eyes and looked around their camp. Both Hawaiians huddled under their blankets, sound asleep.

It took longer to saddle his horse than he'd expected. His horse complained how he had neglected the simplest of currying, although the animal had found plenty of grass to eat. Clay led it to the lake and pushed through a few cattle washing down their constant meal with some of the sweet water. Dropping to one knee, he cupped his hands and sampled it. When he had his fill, he popped the cork on his canteen and filled it.

The watch went slowly as he tried to make sense of Suárez's behavior. He returned to camp, thinking it was the trail boss' turn to ride herd. His heart pounded faster when he saw that Suárez had left camp. Fred stretched and made tiny snuffling noises to get himself awake. José Vasques still slept. Fred motioned him over.

"Leo asked me to take his watch. José's got breakfast in a few hours unless you want to do it."

"Why should I? I hate cooking."

"You're not much good at it," Fred said, "but you're better than him." He glanced toward Vasques.

"Where's Suárez?"

Fred shrugged, heaved his saddle to his shoulder and went to prepare his horse.

Clay waited for him to vanish into the darkened meadow before climbing back into the saddle. He aimed his horse toward town. That was the only direction that made sense.

No matter how he pushed his horse, the gelding stubbornly refused to rush. Both rider and horse were tired, but curiosity burned bright in Clay's breast and gave him energy. The horse knew only exhaustion after making a trip into town earlier, then walking about on night herd for three hours. Returning to town was punishment.

Clay dozed as he headed for Idaho Falls. He didn't know how big a start Suárez had on him, but he was past caring if he ran into the man along the way. Overwork had a way of cutting through politeness.

A fitful breeze kicked up at daybreak. Clay turned up his collar to keep the chill fingers from creeping down his neck. By the time the sun poked up over the horizon, he rode once more into Idaho Falls. This time the saloons were quiet. The town stretched and stirred from its slumber. A few diligent entrepreneurs prepared for another day. A shopkeeper swept the boardwalk in front of his mercantile. Bakers put out racks of freshly prepared bread for customers. One urchin staggered under a load of several dozen loaves, heading for the restaurant in the middle of town.

Clay's belly rumbled at the fragrant aroma. He had a few dollars. Buying a loaf or two for breakfast would go a ways toward making José's cooking bearable. He might even find some butter to go with it. Or jam.

His mind snapped back to the reason he had come to town. Suárez slammed the door to the Wells Fargo office behind him, kicked at a hitching post, then vaulted into the saddle and galloped off. Clay didn't have to be a mind reader to know his boss hadn't received the news he had expected.

Stepping down from horseback, he hesitated before going into the telegraph office. He composed himself and worked on a new story before walking in as bold as brass.

The telegrapher peered at him through his spectacles. The man's eyes were bloodshot. He might have been up all night listening to the clacking key nailed to his desk.

"What is it?"

"I'm supposed to meet my boss here. Leo Suárez."

"Suárez, eh? He stormed out a few minutes ago. I don't know how you missed him." The man pushed his glasses up and spat out, "He's one unpleasant fellow if I do say so."

"Once his dander's up, he can be," Clay said. "What set him off? Bad news from the telegram he sent?"

"Bad news? Not a bit of it. No news. He didn't get a reply. They always blame it on me as if I control when answers come in. All I can do is decipher the Morse code. I don't invent it, though heaven knows I should. That would have made him happier."

"That's a good idea, inventing an answer. What would it be, do you think?" Clay fished around.

"What are you saying?" The telegrapher leaned on the counter and glared.

"You had to send the telegram. To Pacific Star Ranch, right? What reply would smooth my boss' ruffled feathers?"

"How should I know? And if you want to pump me for information, you're out of luck. Go ask your boss what he said. Now excuse me. I'm busy dealing with *real* work."

He turned away and fiddled with the nearest vat of smelly yellow acid, reconnecting wires and grunting with effort as he moved the lead poles around. Clay wondered if the telegrapher accomplished anything other than ignoring him by trying to look busy.

"I can give you a hand. That answer might come in, and I'd be here to take it to Suárez."

"Clear out. I don't need your help. If he wants the 'gram, he can pick it up himself. That's the way it works here. Go!"

Clay backed out of the Wells Fargo office and turned his face to the warmth of the rising sun. He closed his eyes and let its warmth soothe him. Try as he might, he had no idea what was going on. Only suspicions, and they were dark ones with Leo and Warnock being in cahoots. If he had a lick of sense, he'd ride south and let the double-dealing come to a boil without him.

If he had any sense. If . . .

He mounted and started back to the meadow.

CHAPTER THIRTEEN

Unlike on most trail drives, whatever meat they ate had to be hunted. Clay hadn't had a chance to take a potshot or two at rabbits and deer because they kept their distance. When the herd being moved numbered in the hundreds if not thousands, killing and butchering one to feed the trail hands was common. All too often a cow broke a leg or ran into some other danger and had to be put down. That made for steaks and stew for a week. These beeves were too precious for that. Clay thought the Hawaiians treated the cattle better than the men driving them.

Suárez swore a steady string of curses in English, Spanish and Hawaiian when Fred suggested putting just one heifer into the fire. The trail boss made it clear that the hundred head were sacrosanct.

"I've heard the other Indians, the ones from India, worship cows," Clay said. "The Crown K cattle are expensive, but just one—"

He had dropped the idea when Vasques joined his partner in cussing a blue streak. They were both committed to each and every bull and heifer reaching the coast untouched. From what Clay had heard about the cost of the beeves, he didn't blame them. The problem he had was who ended up with the cattle.

Barker or Warnock?

He shoveled in whatever Vasques had whipped up for breakfast. Some of the food carried a mysterious texture and the aroma wasn't too pleasant. Trying to figure out what he had thrown in with the oatmeal was a fool's errand. It tasted fine for a change and filled the hollow in Clay's belly. He finished his plate of the sticky, almost solid lump. He stared at Suárez so hard, the man felt the inspection and looked up.

"What is it, Clay?"

"The cattle are fed and watered. When do we hit the trail? It's still a ways to the coast."

Suárez tried not to look uncomfortable as he answered. If anything, he was too nonchalant when he said, "Let us stay another day or two. This is a pleasant spot. We need the rest, and pushing the horses too hard is not a good thing."

"We can walk the horses and not wear them down. The cattle aren't running along at breakneck speed, after all," Clay prodded the trail boss. He suspected Suárez wanted to stay near Idaho Falls until the answer to his telegram arrived.

"There's nothing wrong with taking it easy for a few days," Fred said. "It'll give us a chance to get into town and spend some of our earnings."

He eyed Clay. While Fred said nothing, Clay hadn't made any secret of his last trip into Idaho Falls, at least to the man who had to cover for him. What Fred thought Clay had done that had to be hidden from Suárez hardly mattered, as long as he held his tongue.

"What do you think, Leo? Can we go into Idaho Falls and sample their whiskey? Just a drop or two?"

Clay continued to push Suárez, and he felt guilty about it. Just a little. Then he thought on it and all guilt disappeared. What business did Suárez have with Warnock that he sent a telegram to the man's ranch? Clay had taken an immense dislike to the Pacific Star owner and his henchmen. He rubbed his gut where he had caught a few punches. The bruises had long since healed, but the memory lingered and would for a long time.

"It might be possible if there remain in camp enough wranglers to handle the herd. One at a time? We might do that." Suárez seemed to be thinking out loud.

Clay heard the undercurrent of the trail boss making sure nobody spied on him when he waited in town for the telegram. More than the possible telegram being answered, Clay saw another obvious reason for Suárez coming up with this idea. He wanted three men on the herd at all times. That kept two of them from carousing in town together and getting into trouble. Having the law come down on them attracted unwanted attention to the herd.

When the entire trail gang numbered only four, losing even one to a week in jail would be disastrous. If two were locked up in the calaboose, the herd wouldn't go anywhere.

Clay's suspicious mind churned out even more reasons. Was Suárez worried about Warnock finding them? Or not finding them? The unanswered telegram still gnawed away at Clay's trust of the trail boss.

"I must scout the area," Suárez said.

He sent Fred out to circle the herd in one direction and Clay in the other. Vasques again had drawn the short straw and stayed in camp to prepare the evening meal.

Clay and Fred exchanged looks. After Suárez rode away, Fred said, "I've been doing a decent job scouting. Why's he all het up to do my job when I've already done it?"

"Stay with the herd. I'll find out," Clay said. Before Fred objected, Clay found Suárez's tracks and set out following them.

When it became obvious Suárez was heading for town, Clay veered away and cut across country. He felt confident in reaching Idaho Falls before the trail boss since he had hunted out shortcuts over the last couple days. Suárez preferred to stay on the road, but Clay cut several miles off the trip. Even so, he discovered that Suárez had beaten him to town. The man was in a special hurry this morning.

Clay considered confronting Suárez, then chose to watch and wait as he had before. Something today stirred the Hawaiian up to the point he paced to and fro in front of the Wells Fargo station. That impatience finally drove Suárez back inside. Even from his vantage point down the street, Clay heard the heated exchange between Suárez and the telegrapher. The words were indistinct, but the tone was obvious. Suárez wasn't happy about something.

No telegram? There wasn't any reply. That explained Suárez's choler.

Clay moved into the shadow cast by a tumbledown wall to keep from being seen as Suárez boiled from the Wells Fargo office. The telegrapher trailed him, arms windmilling about as if he tried to point out something at either end of the street. Suárez wasn't having any of it. He shoved his face so close, he must have fogged the smaller man's glasses. They argued until Suárez ran out of steam and stepped away. The telegrapher whirled about and stalked back into the Wells Fargo office.

Suárez looked in both directions, threw up his hands in defeat and stormed off. Clay tried to make sense of it. The Wells Fargo agent had no control over telegrams coming into his office. That showed how anxious Suárez was.

Clay stepped out into the street and watched Suárez duck into a saloon. His own mouth was as dry as the Sonoran Desert, but Clay faded back into the shadows and waited. Something must happen at the Wells Fargo office eventually. When it did, he wanted to see what had gotten Suárez so het up.

He sank down, using the wall to support himself. Still days and days shy on sleep, he closed his eyes. *Just for a minute,* he told himself. Sunlight on his face woke him. He blinked and shielded his eyes. For a moment he tried to figure out what happened; then he realized he had been asleep so long, the sun had erased the shadow hiding him.

Clay hunched over when the trail boss left the saloon, as if this kept him from being seen by anyone looking in his direction. But Leo Suárez was too intent on returning to the Wells Fargo office to notice anything around him. Working his way farther down the alley until he barely had a view of the office door across the street, Clay had only seconds to wait until Suárez came out once more. The man's anger boiled until Clay imagined he felt the hot waves coming after him. Again Suárez took refuge in the same gin mill he had sought out earlier. His unsteady gait showed he had sampled a fair amount of the beer offered by the saloon proprietor.

Getting to his feet proved harder than Clay had expected. His knees were stiff. He bent over and stretched the cramped muscles until they quit trying to hog-tie him. His lookout had accomplished nothing. Whatever Suárez expected in the telegram wasn't worth spying on him any longer. Clay brushed off some dust and stepped into the street. He jumped to keep from being run over as a stagecoach drew up in front of the Wells Fargo office.

With legs still stiff, he started to retrieve his horse and ride back to take his turn at guarding the herd. Glancing one last time toward the telegraph station, he froze as if a polar wind had blown down from the north months early. Clay stared as the most beautiful woman he had ever laid eyes on stepped down from the stage. She was covered in dust from the trip, but that did nothing to take away from her elegance and, somehow, her dignity. How anyone remained so composed after being bounced around inside a stagecoach was something Clay decided he could think on later. Right now he wanted nothing more than to stare.

She was tall, as tall as he was and dressed in a gingham skirt almost uniformly brown from dust. Pulled around her shoulders was a shawl with a dark blue blouse beneath. A neat hat perched at a jaunty angle on her head, holding hair so blond it looked as if it glowed with its own inner light in the sun. A few quick, dainty taps warned her it'd take more to pound the trail from her clothes. She let out a sigh of resignation at the realization she would be dusty for a spell longer.

Then she turned and looked straight at him. Eyes so green they reminded him of spring exploding in the mountains fixed on him. Her bow-shaped red lips curled slightly in an inviting grin. Dimples graced her cheeks and deepened with her smile. That smile was just for him.

Clay's paralysis passed. He stepped into the street to go offer his services. A lady like this must have a couple trunks, maybe more, requiring a strong back and a helping hand to move. Three steps toward this vision were all he took.

She turned and reached out to a man descending from the coach. Taller than the lady by several inches, he had the look of royalty. Or what Clay thought of as royalty. Somehow the man's frock coat had escaped the worst of the travel. There weren't even wrinkles to be seen. He settled a shining black silk top hat on his head and used an ebony cane to balance as he stepped closer to her. She spoke softly, then reached out and brushed off his shoulders, straightened both lapels and adjusted his crimson cravat so that a headlight diamond caught the sun and dazzled Clay.

The only thing that ran through Clay's head was this was how a wife treated her husband. She wanted him to be as presentable as she was, and he had to do it through clothing while her beauty made her the center of attention no matter how mussed from travel she was.

He backed away and watched the pair. The man needed the silver-headed cane for more than decoration. He leaned heavily on it. Something had injured his right leg. The woman moved with assurance, ordering the driver and the shotgun messenger about to take the luggage from the stagecoach boot.

The Wells Fargo agent bustled out and ignored the stage crew. He shook the man's hand as if he pumped water from a balky well. The woman came to her husband's aid. Clay almost laughed at the agent's reaction. He dropped the man's hand and accepted the woman's. She shook his hand as vigorously as he had her husband's. The agent reluctantly loosed her hand and bent slightly, bowing from the waist, arm extending in a sweeping grand gesture to invite them into the office.

The couple linked arms as if they couldn't get enough of each other. Clay understood the man's sentiment, wanting to stay as close to the lady as possible. It took him a few seconds, but he reluctantly admitted they made a fine couple. The man wasn't as handsome as his wife was pretty, but at any barn dance, he would have turned female heads and set them to gossiping. Clay had never been to the Union Club in San Francisco but these two looked as if they would fit in perfectly among high society, with railroad and banking and mining millionaires. They carried themselves like . . . royalty.

Clay backpedaled fast, stepping onto the boardwalk when he caught motion out of the corner of his eye. Leo Suárez rushed forth. He pushed past the driver and never slowed to apologize for his rudeness. That alone told Clay something was in the wind. Suárez was always a gentleman and polite.

Suárez stopped in the office door, took off his hat and waited. Clay couldn't see what went on inside the Wells Fargo depot, but the trail boss never budged. After almost a minute, he turned and went to the stagecoach. He picked up two large carpetbags set on the boardwalk and nothing more. Clay had expected trunks laden with clothing. Or perhaps they had been left in the boot for the stagecoach employees to move later.

He caught his breath again as the woman exited. She waited, extended her arm, looped it through her husband's and helped him along since he moved with a slight limp. They walked along, as regal as you please, Suárez trailing them with the two bags.

With nothing more to see, and the image of the woman burning in his memory, Clay stepped up into the saddle and rode slowly back to the Crown K herd. He'd have to work double shifts to make up the time he'd taken. But that was all right with him. He had plenty to think about.

CHAPTER FOURTEEN

F RED SNIFFED THE air like a bloodhound, then shook his head as he regarded Clay closely.

"I don't catch the faintest whiff of booze. What did you do in town?" Then his face brightened. "You'll have to tell me all about her."

Clayton Forsythe recoiled. "How'd you know about her?" Then he realized he was having a different conversation from the one Fred intended. "It's not like that. I didn't find a cathouse. I just . . . walked around town," he finished lamely.

"What's her name?"

Clay blurted his reply before he realized he should have kept his own counsel in this matter. "I don't know. Look, get on out of here. I'll take your next two shifts. Don't get into too much trouble."

"You want to keep her all for yourself, eh? That's not very friendly of you. I reckon I'll find a filly of mine own and . . ."

Clay had no call to listen to any more of the man's

wild flight of fancy. Fred laughed at Clay's discomfort and turned his horse toward Idaho Falls. He touched the brim of his hat and rode off at a gallop. That reminded Clay that he needed a new hat. The sun pounded down on his head something fierce, but every time he'd been in town, distractions kept him from finding a haberdashery and choosing a new Stetson. With money burning a hole in his pocket, he could afford a decent one and not some floppy-brimmed felt hat that would fall to pieces in a drenching rain or a straw hat unable to withstand the rigors of a decent wind.

He circled the herd, distracted by the memory of the woman who had arrived in Idaho Falls. After a full circuit, he frowned. Something was wrong. Riding through the middle of the contented herd, he counted.

"Three short. Where'd you go, you lamebrained animals?" Paying attention to his job now, he got halfway around the herd again before he saw tracks leading from the meadow. The strays had worked their way into a wooded area he had scouted before Suárez decided to stay here so long.

Clay zigzagged through the increasingly dense thicket, hunting for the errant cattle. He found two of them grazing on grass nowhere near as succulent as that in the meadow.

"Forbidden fruit is always sweeter, isn't it?" Clay said softly.

They paid him no attention as he rode up, checked the Crown K brands, just in case some other rancher's stock had escaped, and started hunting for the third cow. This one had been more determined to cause him trouble and had gotten mired down in a bog.

The lowing sounded so pitiful, Clay decided to pull the animal free before taking the other two back to the herd.

"Let's see how good your roping really is, cowboy,"

he said to himself. Then he called out to the cow, "You keep your head still. You hear? You're complicating my life plenty enough, wandering away like you did."

The cow looked up at him with big brown eyes. Clay missed the first cast because the cow jerked its head at the last instant. Clay drew the lariat back and circled the bog, coming at his target from behind to hide his approach. His rope whistled through the air. The loop fell neatly around a now frightened cow. He rode back to face the victim. A couple turns around his saddle horn told his gelding to begin backing up. Slowly the cow pulled free from the sucking bog, but at the last instant, it balked and was once more caught.

"More leverage," Clay said, more to his horse than to the cow. He circled a tree, then had his horse back up again, this time with hindquarters toward the cow. Inch by inch the gelding retreated. The rope around the tree trunk caused the sapling to bend with the strain. Just when Clay thought the pressure would yank the tree out by its roots, the cow popped free. It let out a mournful moan and tried to run off.

Clay kept the rope around its neck until they rejoined the other two, more passive cows. A quick wrist flip loosened the rope. He pulled it away, coiled the hemp length and then used the free end to whack bovine butts until they reluctantly retraced the trail to the herd. Seeing the others and listening to a bull snort and stomp and bellow convinced the runaways they were once more home.

Clay waited until dusk to hunt for Vasques. José was to take the next shift; then Clay had to return for both Fred's and his own. By daylight he'd be falling asleep in the saddle, but it had been worth the trip into Idaho Falls. The lovely woman's image still burned in his brain, but so did Suárez greeting her and her husband. Something went on that the trail boss wasn't sharing.

Clay dismounted and tended his horse, making his way wearily toward the campfire, where Vasques had left a pot of coffee dangling over the coals. Clay poked the embers and added more wood to build the fire. He wanted coffee that was more than lukewarm. As he stirred the fire, waiting for the coffee to reach a decent drinking temperature, approaching horses made him pop up and look around. He slipped the leather thong off his six-gun's hammer to free it in the holster. Visitors after sundown meant trouble.

As the three riders neared to where he recognized them, he stared in surprise. Suárez waved while the other two trotted alongside.

"Clay, are the others out on night herd already?" Suárez dismounted, then took the bridle of the woman's horse.

Clay found himself tongue-tied as he stood only a few feet from the woman who had gotten off the stagecoach that afternoon. Their eyes locked. Clay felt as if he had stepped off a cliff. Then Suárez broke the spell.

"Help Mr. Barker down, will you? He's got a bad leg."

"I can get down just fine, Leo. I'm not an invalid." The handsome man who had accompanied the woman used both hands to lift his right leg across the saddle, then hopped down. He took a step and caught himself, using his cane to keep from taking a tumble. "Back home, I use a buckboard to get around, but there weren't any for hire in town."

"Mr. Barker?" Clay's voice almost broke. "You're the owner of the Crown K?"

"I am. You must be Clayton Forsythe. Leo's sung your praises. You gave him a run for the top prize money at the rodeo, to hear him tell it."

"He finished third in two of the events, Mr. Barker," Suárez piped up.

Clay shook the man's hand. To his surprise, this wasn't

the hand of a man used to sitting behind a desk and signing papers. The calluses showed Barker put in hard work.

"And this is Sarah," Barker said, introducing the woman. He shifted his cane as he reached out and took her hand.

Clay felt a touch of envy at the way they held hands. "Pleased to meet you, Mrs. Barker," he said.

She started to say something but Suárez interrupted.

"Pour them some of that coffee, Clay, if it will not poison them."

"I'm all right," Sarah Barker said. "I know what terrible potions drovers fix."

"José brewed it," Clay said. "José Vasques."

"Of course he did," she said, laughing. "That means I made a wise decision turning down a cup. Many's the time I've choked down his coffee. He is a terrible cook!"

"We can agree on that," Clay said.

He looked guiltily at Suárez, wondering if Vasques would take offense when Suárez told him of the conversation. There wasn't any hint that the trail boss even heard the exchange. He busied himself with the Barkers' horses.

"You can build the fire up a little higher if you would," Mr. Barker said. "I need to keep my leg warmer than I'd like. Otherwise, it gets so stiff, I can barely bend the knee."

"King, you shouldn't have come out. The hotel in town was perfectly adequate." Sarah sank beside him on the ground, paying no attention to how she dirtied her skirts.

"I couldn't leave you to do all the work, my dear." He squeezed her hand again, then lifted it and kissed the back.

Clay brightened when pieces of the puzzle fell together. "King Barker? That's why the brand is the Crown K, isn't it?"

"I'm second generation. King Barker Sr. was my father. He established the ranch around Waimea." King
Barker edged toward the fire and turned so it cast its
radiance along his right side.

"I wondered if it might be homage to King Kamehameha since he deeded the land over to you."

"You're well versed in Hawaiian history, Mr. Forsythe. How'd that come about? Have you been to the
islands?" Sarah Barker's interest seemed genuine. She
fixed him with her brilliant green eyes until he felt like
a schoolboy unprepared for a big test.

"All I know's what Leo and José have told me. And
call me Clay. Everyone does."

"Everyone?" Sarah smiled.

"Well, my friends."

Clay found himself getting tongue-tied again. He became aware of King Barker watching him closely. Or
maybe the man was protective of his wife when it came
to randy trail hands. He had every right to be, especially
if he had a hint of what thoughts ran through Clay's head.

Clay found himself blushing.

"There's José returning. It's time for me to be sure
no more of the cattle wander off."

Clay felt the need to escape from the discomfort he
felt being so near to Sarah Barker. If he kept talking,
he'd say something to embarrass himself or maybe get
King Barker mad enough to fire him.

If Barker reached that point, Leo Suárez would be
going for his six-gun. Clay saw how Suárez worshipped
his boss and his wife.

"Have some of the herd taken it into their skulls to
desert?" asked Sarah.

"This afternoon. Early evening, really. I— Never
mind. I rounded them up and they're back in the herd.
Mrs. Barker. Sir."

Clay reached up to touch the brim of a hat he wasn't

wearing. It made it seem as if he saluted them. This caused him even more chagrin. Only José Vasques greeting the Barkers saved Clay from further humiliation.

He started to saddle his horse when Sarah called out to him, "Mr. Forsythe. Clay! It's not necessary to—"

"Don't let the herd go untended," Suárez ordered.

Clay muttered assent to the trail boss, saddled and rode away, relieved at escaping the social disaster of meeting his employer and his wife.

The cool night wrapped around Clay and evaporated the sweat that had formed on his face. By firelight he must have looked like he had been dipped in diamonds. That was further mortification he didn't need. There wasn't any call to feel bad if Sarah Barker thought him nothing but a rodeo clown. She was married and his employment ended when they reached the coast. All he had to do was avoid her and keep their conversation at a minimum when they were together. On a trail drive with so few hands, that shouldn't be too difficult.

"Keep riding, keep tending the beeves, keep out of camp," he warned himself.

His gut clenched when he wondered if the Barkers were going to ride with them all the way to California. What worried him about that wasn't clear. Did they know their trusted employee Suárez sent telegrams to Warnock? Clay's stomach knotted even more when he thought about Sarah Barker. He pushed unacceptable thoughts about her from his mind. He was a hired hand, nothing more. He owed them nothing.

And there wasn't any reason for him to expect anything more than his wages from the Barkers.

He forced his attention back to the herd when he saw the south end of a northbound cow disappearing into the dark. Another two tried to follow. Clay chased them back to the herd, then headed after the last errant animal. This was the same section where he had driven the three cattle earlier. Something here called to the bovine sense of adventure—or hunger.

Walking his horse slowly into the forest gave him a chill. The night dropped a wet, cold blanket of dread all around him. He started cursing the wandering cow. If he had been on a normal trail drive, he would have ignored the stray. One missing from among so many in the herd didn't matter too much. A hundred dollars, nothing more. But this drive changed all that calculation. The amount paid for this one purebred cow was several times what he was earning for a month on the trail—and his pay was three times what any other rancher paid for his expertise.

Clay leaned down low, trying to find any hint of hoofprints on the forest floor. Leaves and other detritus hid the trail. He stepped down and led his gelding. Staying closer to the ground let him examine brush and the branches on low-growing shrubs. For several minutes he worried he was never going to find the trail; then he found freshly broken limbs as if a big animal had passed recently.

He dropped to his knees and brushed away some compost. A smile came to his lips. His instincts had proved good. A distinct hoofprint showed in the damp earth. On hands and knees Clay edged forward and found three more. Coming to his knees, he oriented himself so he peered along the line established by the prints.

"There you are," he said.

A dark shape ahead rustled the undergrowth. He stood, ready to retrieve the wayward cow. His horse suddenly let out a frightened whinny and reared. Clay clung to the reins.

The horse backed away, yanking his arm painfully and driving him to his knees again. He landed on a rock. The shock lanced up from his kneecap and thigh into his body. For an instant, the world went white with pain. The reins slipped from his fingers. A wild grab as the horse raced away only landed him facedown on the ground.

"What's with you?" He tried to stand and found that his leg refused to support him. He sat on a fallen log and rubbed away the pain. Then he looked up into a pair of feral red eyes.

Behind those eyes lay ears sleekly pinned back with hunting fervor. Gray fur moved into plain sight. It wasn't the biggest wolf he had ever seen, but it looked to be the meanest. A snarl revealed wicked white fangs. Moving slowly, Clay drew his six-gun. His hand shook just a little as he aimed, cocked the pistol and fired.

Everything happened at the same instant. The wolf leaped just as Clay let loose. The bullet entered the wolf's mouth and blew out the back of its skull, but that didn't stop its forward motion. The heavy predator crashed into him. Clay fell backward with the wolf atop him. A heave moved it off him.

"That was a close call," he muttered. Then he looked up and saw a ring of eyes. Some flashed silver. Another pair was yellow. And two others were as fiery red as the wolf he'd just shot.

An entire pack ringed him and moved slowly toward him. He heard low, guttural growls, but they came for him in an eerie silence that scared him more than if they'd growled and howled and made all the sounds he associated with wolves. But these weren't lovelorn and baying at the moon. These were deadly hunters. Deadly, *hungry* killers.

Another wolf rushed for him. He fired and missed, but the bullet sang close enough to make the wolf veer away and retreat. Two others tested him from different directions. Clay realized this was how they hunted. Ever closer, never quite attacking full out until enough of them got near enough to jump him. Then the entire pack would surge in for the kill.

He fired again. This produced a howl of pure anguish. He had wounded one, but the remainder of the pack pressed their attack.

"I've got a few shots left," he cried out.

Clay swung to a small wolf trying to leap on him. He pulled the trigger. The instant he drew back, he knew the mechanism had jammed. The wolf launched itself toward him.

Unable to fire, he did the only thing he could. He swung the six-shooter as hard as he could. The barrel connected with the wolf's head and sent it tumbling. It hit hard, got to its feet and slunk away. As it did, he tried to unjam the six-shooter. Even with frantic strength fueled by stark terror, he wasn't able to draw the hammer back and rotate the cylinder. Whatever had caused the jam now mocked him with a broken mechanism.

He shoved the pistol back into his holster and fumbled around. He found the thin-bladed knife he used for carving bone trinkets. It felt pitifully small in his grip. Clay tried to stand to force the wolves to attack a bigger target. His leg gave way, and he collapsed to one knee.

The wolf on his right let out a snarl. A quick glance behind him showed another making a silent attack. One distracted him while the other came for him. He slashed about with the pitiful little knife, vowing to go down fighting. He'd killed one and wounded another. His goal was to take at least one more with him before the pack dined on his flesh.

Clay swung the blade in a wide circle that did nothing to stop the ever-tightening ring of fur and fangs around him.

CHAPTER FIFTEEN

CLAY STABBED AT an exposed furred belly as the wolf leaped. The weight carried him back and drove him to the ground. He tried to twist the knife around in the wolf's gut, but his arm was pinned to the ground, half under his body. He looked up into fangs and a face boiling hatred for him. The wolf snapped, missed Clay's neck, then started to bite again when a loud report echoed through the still forest.

As suddenly as the wolf had attacked, it left. Clay felt dampness on his hand. Blood. He let out a cry, thinking it was his blood. Then he saw the wolf stretched out a few feet away. The bullet had taken the animal's life with a clean through-and-through shot just above the front legs. Pushing around, he forced himself to hands and knees, then heaved to his feet. His leg threatened to give way under him, but he braced himself against a stump to keep his balance. Once a momentary dizziness passed, he hobbled about on his good leg, brandishing the knife.

Two more wolves came for him. Two more shots in rapid succession ended their attack, amid howls that signaled their deaths. He waved his whittling knife about in a circle to hold off any further attack, but the remainder of the pack edged away, then turned tail and vanished into the forest as silently as they had come.

"You guys came at the right time. Another minute and I'd have been dinner." He twisted around and sank to the stump, rubbing his injured knee. "Could one of you fetch my horse? It abandoned me when the wolves attacked."

Clay wiped sweat from his eyes and saw the dark shape of his gelding being led to him, but none of the cowboys held the reins.

"Where are the . . . ?" Clay's words trailed off when he saw Sarah Barker still holding a six-shooter in her right hand.

"Where are Leo and José? Back at camp, I think. Fred's out riding night herd. Since he couldn't find you, I told him I'd track you down."

"You shot them?" Clay looked around. Three wolves, three shots.

"Of course I did. Why'd you stop shooting? I heard a couple reports, then nothing."

"My gun jammed. Serves me right for not taking better care of it. We've been working double shifts, and sleeping always seemed a better use of time than oiling my gun."

"Understandable," Sarah said. She handed him the reins. "But if I hadn't found you, well, the one wolf you shot before your gun misfired would have been the only lupine casualty."

"That was mighty fancy shooting. In the dark, to boot. You must practice a lot on wolves in Hawaii."

"There aren't any there. The number one predator

is the cat." Sarah came around and poked at the wolves' carcasses.

"Cats? You mean, cougars?"

"I mean house cats. Feral cats. The little bastards are everywhere. They jumped overboard when sailing ships docked in the eighteen thirties. They're good for taking care of the rats, which we have roaming in packs, but they've found they can kill a mule deer." Sarah crouched down and lifted the large wolf that Clay had shot. "You got this one good. A shame you ruined its head."

"Why?"

"The skin looks better with the head still attached."

"You want to skin them?" Clay wasn't sure what to say to that. This beautiful woman shouldn't have been thinking about a messy pursuit like skinning dead animals.

"Of course I do. You have anything bigger than that?" She pointed to the whittling knife he still clutched in his hand. "Never mind. Let me have it."

He silently handed the short-bladed knife over. He watched as she judged what to do, then applied the tip and expertly peeled back the skin. Sarah looked up and said, "If your leg's not hurt too bad, go find the cow you came after."

"How'd you know that's why I came into the woods?"

"Why else? Besides, I saw the tracks. Yours, too. It wasn't hard to figure out why you were here. Then I heard the shots and came running."

"You saved my life. I owe you."

"The pelts will be payment enough," she said, completing the skinning of the first wolf. She laid out the skin and went to the next of the wolves she had shot. "This will look good hanging on my study wall."

"Mr. Barker won't object?"

Sarah laughed. Clay wished he could listen to that musical sound all night long.

"King used to be quite a hunter himself before he hurt his leg." She eyed Clay. In the dark her green eyes gleamed like those of one of the wolves. "You're not going to pull up lame, too, are you? From what Leo says, you're quite a bronc rider. It'd be a shame if you had to give that up."

"Roping and bulldogging are also things I do pretty well." Clay blushed when he realized how he was bragging on himself.

He blushed even more when Sarah said, "I know. Leo told me." She finished with the second wolf and laid the smaller pelt atop the first. "Two down, one to go." She wiped the knife off on a leaf, then asked, "You're able to walk, aren't you? Or do you need help mounting?"

"I'll be fine, thanks," Clay said.

Somehow, admitting to any infirmity seemed wrong. She was his boss—or his boss' wife. It wasn't right being injured when there was work to be done.

He took a tentative step, then another and ignored the pain until it faded to a dull ache. Somewhere off in the forest, he heard a cow mooing plaintively. Walking faster helped his leg. The pack had missed an easy kill in favor of attacking him. Letting the hungry wolves circle the cow was out of the question now. Clay bent, found a fallen limb just the right height to use as a walking stick and crashed through the brush to find the cow had tangled itself in ropy vines and couldn't pull free.

The cow stopped kicking and tugging when Clay approached. Big brown eyes sized him up, as if considering how best to create complete chaos. A snort and a toss of the head showed that determination. The cow began pawing the ground like a bull preparing to charge.

"Settle down now," Clay said, advancing cautiously. "Don't go giving me another bum leg by kicking me."

Clay used the walking stick to pry loose some of the

vines, then left a couple strands around the cow's neck. Using the vine as he would a rope, he led the complaining animal back to where he had left Sarah Barker. The way the cow balked told him it smelled wolf blood. He pulled harder on the vine leash and ended up leading the cow around the slaughter.

"Can you bring me my horse, Mrs. Barker? I want to keep from having to chase down this cow again."

She looked up, distracted from her gory chore of skinning the last wolf, tossed her head to get a blond strand from her eyes and shouted, "What's that?"

"Please fetch my horse. I need to get a real rope around this wayward's neck."

"All right." She wiped the knife off by thrusting it into the damp earth and returned it by expertly tossing it to stick in a tree next to Clay. "Thanks for the use of the knife. It was a tad small, but it served my purpose." She retreated in the direction of the meadow, the darkness swallowing her within a few yards.

Clay sighed. Coming or going she cut a fine figure. He pulled the knife from the tree trunk and shoved it into the sheath at his waist. The wolf pelts were stacked next to the last carcass. The bright flash of white bone drew his attention. Sarah's bullet had broken the wolf's spine and left behind a piece of backbone. He pulled the vertebra from the bloody body and examined it. It was a perfect ring. Clay tucked it into his vest pocket to devote his full attention to the cow trying to break free of the vine rope.

"Settle down, you stubborn—"

He clamped his mouth shut when he heard Sarah returning. It wouldn't do to be cussing in front of her. That wasn't done in front of the boss' wife.

She led his gelding along with her own mount to where Clay struggled with the increasingly restive heifer.

"Here's your lariat." Sarah tossed the looped rope to him.

With a deft twist, he dropped the loop over a straining bovine neck and then secured the other end to his saddle horn.

"You look like you've done that before."

Sarah graced him with a mischievous smile. She slung the bloody wolf pelts over her saddlebags and secured them with strips of rawhide. Neither of the horses was pleased with this cargo because of the coppery blood smell, but she handled them expertly.

"Thank you," Clay said, taking the reins.

A quick flex of his right leg convinced him he would be able to mount without taking a tumble. He positioned his left boot in the stirrup and pulled up hard. His injured right leg almost didn't clear the horse's rump as he swung around, but he had ridden bucking broncos enough to know how to shift his weight to keep astride. He was proud that he hadn't appeared too badly injured or, worse, looked like a fool by falling off his own horse.

"You managed that well," Sarah said, laughing. "I won't think less of you because you banged up your leg. It happened in the service of recovering a stray. That counts for a lot."

"That's big of you," Clay said, trying to keep the resentment out of his tone.

He wanted to make a good impression. Hobbling around wasn't the way to do it. Failing to look like a top rodeo rider certainly wasn't, either.

Sarah led the way from the woods. He trailed behind, occasionally tugging on the rope to keep the contrary critter moving. When they reached the herd, he shook the rope free. His prisoner mooed loudly, then sauntered back to nudge another cow out of the way to graze at a patch of grass.

"People are like that sometimes," Sarah said. She let Clay catch up to ride alongside. "Cantankerous and perverse just because it makes them feel like they have control over their lives."

"None of the herd knows what's ahead for them," Clay said.

"Not a one," she agreed. "Do you?" Sarah looked at him.

He tried to read her expression but couldn't. "I'm not going to Hawaii, but from what Leo and José tell me, it is something like paradise. All the cattle will have to do is bask in the sun, graze and, uh . . ."

Everything he said was inappropriate. His pa had told him, *When you're in a hole, the first thing you do is to stop digging.* Clay shut his yap and fell silent. Better to stay quiet and have Sarah wonder if he was a fool than to yammer on and have her know that he was.

"There's no 'something like,'" she said, a longing coming to her voice. "It is a paradise. The weather's moderate, the grass is lush and the ocean is spectacular."

"I prefer the mountains. I worked in Texas, where it's as flat as a . . . It's flat. I drifted north to Colorado and found myself staring at the Rockies because they were so . . . spectacular."

"We've got mountains," she said. "And volcanoes. You should see an erupting volcano. It lights up the night, and rivers of fire flow down to the ocean. Huge steam geysers rise as new islands are formed. Destruction and creation, all from one event." She shivered just a little, and Clay doubted it was from the chill wind blowing off the Tetons. She missed her home. "And there are fish like you've never seen in all your born days. Tasty fish. And fruit you can't imagine."

"José was telling me about coconuts," he said. "It sounded like he was feeding me a lie to see if I'd believe it."

"I don't even know what he told you, but it was true."

"It sounds like you're trying to sell me on Hawaii."

"Am I succeeding?"

Before Clay answered, King Barker called out. He hobbled from camp, leaning more heavily on his cane than ever.

"Sarah! There you are. Where'd you go?" King Barker stopped to brace himself against Sarah's horse. He stared at the wolf pelts and shook his head. "You shot them?"

"They made such good sport. Mr. Forsythe deserves the real credit for rescuing one of the cattle from the pack."

"Pack? A wolf pack attacked you?" King Barker stepped back and stared at her with dark disapproval. "You shouldn't endanger yourself like that."

"Oh, King, darling, Mr. Forsythe was the only one in danger. He hurt himself." She motioned for Suárez to come over. "Leo, can you see that he's patched up properly. He did such a fine job and getting his leg infected isn't any fitting reward." Sarah graced Clay with a bright smile. "Thank you for your help. You saved the Crown K a considerable amount of money by rescuing our property."

Sarah hopped to the ground and took King Barker by the arm. She spoke quietly with him as they returned to camp.

"She is unharmed?" Suárez demanded.

"I twisted my knee," Clay said. "Thanks for caring."

"She is your boss."

"She saved me, not the other way around. My gun jammed and the wolves were ready to invite me to dinner as the main course."

Clay gingerly slid his leg over the cantle, hesitated to be sure he was up for the impact, then dropped to the ground. He winced, then composed himself and turned to face the trail boss.

"José rides herd now. You rest. I will take over after he finishes." Suárez looked after the Barkers, then back at Clay. "She was not hurt?"

"Even the wolf pack learned not to tangle with her. She's a crack shot and pretty good with a knife, too."

"Knife?"

Clay laughed it off to Suárez's displeasure.

"Are we leaving in the morning?" Clay asked as he led his horse off to the rope corral. He had to tend the steady mount before curling up for a little sleep himself.

"One more day, Mr. Barker tells me."

Clay started to ask if both Barkers were riding with the herd, then held back the question. He'd find out soon enough. Before having Sarah Barker pull his fat from the fire, he'd thought a woman that lovely had to be a hothouse flower. His fingers lightly brushed over his whittling knife. It hadn't been designed to carve up a carcass, yet she had made do. She was a dead shot and able to use what was at hand to get what she wanted.

He wondered if that desire to use what was at hand extended to her husband. The way she cooled King off after he and Sarah rode back to camp suggested that was so. Clay finished tending his horse and limped to where his bedroll had been stashed. He dropped his saddle, arranged his blanket and stretched out. His knee throbbed if he stayed on his side, so he lay flat on his back.

Sleep eluded him. His mind raced, turning over how close he had come to dying. And how Sarah Barker had rescued him when things looked darkest. Fumbling in his vest pocket, he found the wolf vertebra and looked through the middle, centering on a bright star. It took him a few seconds to realize he was ringing the morning star with the wolf bone.

He unsheathed his whittling knife and applied the point to the middle of the bone, reaming out enough to smooth the inside. The vertebra faded in his sight as he imagined the finished product. He blinked, then applied the tip to the outer ring to begin shaping it.

It distracted him enough from his leg so that he eventually drifted off to sleep.

CHAPTER SIXTEEN

WORKING THE KNIFE tip across the bone produced grooves and ridges and even the beginning of a wolf head so tiny, it required all his attention to carve. Clay turned the spine bone around and around, then blew away the dust from a new cut. He started to expand the figure when the sun blinded him. He blinked and realized he hadn't gotten much sleep at all, only napping fitfully, and a new day had to be filled with tending the herd and all the other tasks of a trail drive.

He moaned as he moved his leg. The swelling caused the pants leg to press hard against his skin. Bending the knee was almost impossible. He rolled over, then levered himself up, hopping on his left leg. He sheathed his knife rather than use it the first way that came to mind. Cutting away his pants leg would ruin the only decent pair of jeans he owned and did nothing to ease his agony.

Suárez worked to start breakfast. From the look of it, everyone'd have to be satisfied with a plate of oatmeal. Fred still snored from his bedroll. That meant José was with the herd. Some distance away a tarp had been slung between two bushes to give the Barkers privacy as they slept.

A quick glance at the sky warned Clay that a storm moved down from the high country. This time of year, it might carry a few snowflakes. They needed to move the herd soon.

Clay waved to Suárez to let him know he was going to take a bath over in the lake a few hundred yards away. Suárez nodded, but Clay thought it was reaction to the boiling oatmeal lumps in the Dutch oven rather than acknowledgment for his hired hand's absence from camp.

Clay took a deep breath, then started toward the lake. The herd had settled at the west side. They should have brought them around to spend the night on the east side since tracking strays would have been easier without a forest filled with wolves. The rocky stretch to the east held no appeal at all for a cow.

Every step he took loosened his leg a bit more, but it still ached when he got to the shoreline. The lake stretched for a quarter mile straight ahead, with rocky terrain giving a modicum of privacy on either side, not that this mattered. All he wanted to do was soak his leg until it felt better.

Pulling off his boots proved harder than he'd thought, especially his right one. The swelling from his knee reached all the way down to his ankle. A huge sigh of relief gusted from his lips when he finally yanked that boot off. His left one followed easily enough. He inched forward and sat on a moss-slippery rock.

He let out a cry of sheer release when he pushed his right leg underwater. The water was cold. The shock brought him entirely awake. It was as if he had slept the night away and readied himself for another full day

of work instead of merely dozing. The cold water eased
the swelling. He leaned back so he could stare at the
clouds gathering overhead. The dark underbellies did
more than hint at rain—or snow. Such clouds formed
all the time over the Rocking O ranch just before vio-
lent, if short-lived, storms rolled down from the Front
Range.

He closed his eyes, wondering how the ranch fared.
Not well, he guessed. It might be worth his time to return in the spring after he saw the Crown K herd to the
coast and found a job to get him through the next few
months. If Henry Oakes' son, Sullivan, spent the winter drinking and carousing, the ranch might be for sale
at a bargain price. Clay wouldn't have the money to
buy such a good spread, even if he saved every penny
he earned, but he was a slick talker when the occasion
rose. Finding investors for the ranch wouldn't be too
hard. Convincing a banker or another investor that he
was the man to run the Rocking O would be hard, but
it wasn't impossible. If Vic Reedy was willing, the two
of them might team up as co-owners.

From the way Vic had taken to life in Bozeman,
buying him out after a season ending in another trail
drive to Montana wouldn't be too hard. Not at all.

Clay liked the idea of owning a ranch in Colorado.
Or anywhere, for that matter. The way his leg ached
now warned him his bronco-busting days were coming
to an end. Another injury or two and he'd be hobbling
around on a cane like King Barker.

The steady clop-clop of an approaching horse made
him come alert. He tried to sit up but his leg betrayed
him. It felt better and the swelling had gone down after
Clay dunked his leg in the cold lake, but a twinge
through his thigh made movement painful.

He stopped trying to sit up when he heard a lilting
voice singing "Oh My Darling, Clementine." Clay shut

his eyes and listened to Sarah's rendition. She was out
for a morning ride. Fantasies filled his head; then he
jerked upright when he heard a loud splash.

Clay's incautious movement on the moss-slippery
rock caused him to slide waist-deep into the lake. He
yanked off his gun belt and stared at the pistol. There
wasn't anything the water could do to it that hadn't
already been done. He hadn't tinkered with it to find
why it had jammed. A little water wasn't going to make
the damage any worse. Twisting around, he tossed his
belt onto dry land. As he looked to his right, he saw her.

Sarah Barker had stripped down to her underwear
and stood, like him, up over her hips in the cold water.
He swallowed when he saw how the water plastered
her skimpy under things against her body. The sight
made him blush, but he couldn't turn and look away.
This was wrong to covet another man's wife, but Clay
couldn't help himself.

She washed out her trail clothing, getting off the
dried wolf blood. Rubbing the cloth, one layer against
another, wasn't working. She turned to beat the clothes
against a rock. As she did, she bent over and gave Clay
a still more revealing look at her.

Frozen, Clay stared. He knew what he should do.
Stop gawking was at the top of that list, but he was unable to force himself even to close his eyes. His heart
hammered until he was certain she heard it. Sarah went
on washing her clothes, unaware she had an audience.
When she was satisfied with her washing, she laid her
clothes out on a rock to dry in the new day's warmth.
She climbed from the lake. Every move showed off a
different aspect of her almost naked beauty. Sarah
stood on the shore, threw back her head and let her
lustrous blond hair fall down her back. She squeezed
out the water, then daintily stepped onto the largest
rock and stretched out like a lithe cat to sun herself.

Her legs moved about, then strained against the damp cloth clinging to her body like a second skin.

"She brought down three wolves with a handgun and did it in the dark," Clay whispered. "She saved my life. I can't repay her like this." Even putting that sentiment to voice, Clay found it hard to pull himself away.

Inch by inch he crept to dry land. He flopped down when he could and tried to catch his breath. The urge to simply stand and peer over the rock between them was almost more than he could resist. But he pulled on his boots. His knee had shrunk to a more normal size, and the right boot slipped over his foot easily now. He stood, grabbed his gun belt and began walking back to camp. Exercising immense willpower, he didn't once look back to catch a final sight of Sarah stretched out on the rock like some rare sunbathing lizard.

In camp Suárez called to him, "You are late for chuck. I have some left for you." He held out a frying pan with a slice of meat still sizzling hot.

"You fixed something more than oatmeal," Clay said in amazement. Then he realized it hadn't been for him, José or Fred. The boss was in camp now.

The boss and his wife.

A thousand thoughts buzzed in his head like he had poked a wasp's nest. He sank down and ate. Suárez added a piece of hardtack to what must have been salt pork he had fried up.

Clay ate mechanically, then said, "I quit."

"Of course you do. There is nothing more. Fred was very hungry this morning and ate most of it. Like a pig, José ate most of the oatmeal."

"That's not what I mean. I'm quitting the drive."

Suárez stared at him. The frying pan hung from nerveless fingers. He noticed how he was dribbling hot grease on his own boots and lifted the pan, then dropped it in the dirt next to the campfire.

"You cannot quit. You will give up all you have earned."

"I don't care. I'm riding on. Now. With the Barkers, you've got enough help to drive the herd. The cattle are theirs, after all."

Images of King Barker whaling away on him with his cane made Clay cringe. He'd be lucky if that was all that happened if Barker caught even a hint of how Clay felt about his wife. Sarah could shoot the pips off a deuce. All it'd take for them to fly into a rage over what he thought was to look at him.

Guilt was written all over his face. He blushed, thinking of how he had felt gaping at her while she washed her clothes.

"Why do you want to quit? This is not like you, Clay." Suárez came around and towered over him, as if intimidation would force him to stay. "You do not quit."

"I'm sorry, Leo. You don't know how much."

"You did not win the top prizes at the rodeo, but you showed great courage. You fought hard for what you won."

Clay got to his feet and tried to leave. Suárez grabbed him by the shoulder and spun him around.

"The wolves? You are leaving because of the wolves? They were fierce killers. You think being frightened of such beasts makes you less a man?"

"Yeah, that's it. I can't face you and . . . the Barkers." He jerked free and went to collect his gear.

Suárez kicked dirt on the campfire and came after him.

"You have seen Mr. Barker. He is in no condition to work on the drive. His leg—"

"He gets around just fine. He has her to help him."

Clay found it impossible to even say Sarah's name. His words jumbled in his throat because of her.

"I will get him to convince you to stay!"

"No need to try." Clay carried his saddle and other tack to the corral and was ready to ride in a few minutes. He mounted and looked down on the trail boss. "I'm sorry, Leo. I wish I— Never mind."

He put his heels to the gelding's flanks and trotted off. As he turned west, he saw Sarah returning. She was dressed in clean, dry trail clothes. She waved. He turned away, pretending he did not see her. Suárez yelled to her. Clay imagined what the scene looked like.

The trail boss implored Sarah to stop his top hand from leaving. What would she say? Do? Clay hoped she shrugged off the request and went back to the tent where her husband still snored away the morning. Wranglers were a dime a dozen, especially now at the end of the drive season. They were close enough to Idaho Falls to ask around and find a replacement before they hit the trail again.

"You can ride the worst bronco that ever bucked," he told himself as he rode a little faster, "but you can't keep yourself from thinking bad thoughts about your boss' wife."

Clay argued with himself as he rode. Continuing to the coast was only another couple weeks off. Less if they finally got the herd moving and kept to a schedule. Suárez had camped near Idaho Falls because the Barkers were arriving.

Cold fingers clutched at his belly when he remembered how he had spied on Suárez and saw where the telegram had been sent. Pacific Star. Warnock's ranch. Suárez was secretly working for the Barkers' sworn enemy. Clay slowed and started to return to warn them. He came to a complete halt and considered what that meant. He had to face Sarah and her husband. Would King Barker believe a word of it? There wasn't any way Clay could hide what he felt for the man's woman.

He had thought he was in love once or twice, but the feelings had been nothing like he had for Sarah. That confused him and made him doubt his own feelings. He hardly knew her.

"I don't know her at all," he said aloud, arguing with himself. "What a fool I am! I'm like a lovesick heifer mooning after her. For no reason. She saved my life, but she's not the first one."

He grumbled a little. Sarah was the first woman to save his life, and no one else had done it in such a spectacular fashion. But his feelings went beyond this. The way she moved, the way she looked at the world, it all appealed to him too much—way too much because she was married to another man.

How they acted together haunted Clay. Sarah hung on King's arm and exchanged whispers with him constantly. Clay had to wonder if he had injured his leg so she would hang on his arm like that. Clay shook off the notion. Limping around wasn't the way to win her love.

There wasn't any way he ever could. Riding away before he started something that ended in a big row— or worse—was the smart thing to do. It wrenched at his heart, but she didn't feel the way toward him that he did for her. How could she? He had never believed in love at first sight before. Why should she?

"She's too sensible for that, wanting a cowboy when she has a rich rancher who owns half of Hawaii."

He felt like a coward running away, but it was best for everyone. If he failed to warn the Barkers about their trail boss and his telegram, that wasn't anywhere near as bad as the trouble he'd cause by staying. Deep down Clay knew what he felt was real, rock-solid. Putting as much distance between him and Sarah saved her from heartache. Or even outright hatred for him.

A tap on his gelding's flanks sped up his escape. He hadn't been thinking straight or he would have picked a different direction to travel. The herd was headed in this direction. Clay considered cutting off the road and going in a new direction. South? Utah? Arizona? He'd never been to Arizona. Prescott claimed to have put on the first rodeo. He didn't know about that, but it gave a destination other than the limitless horizon.

He started south, then decided to stay on the westerly road until he came to a southbound trail. Easier travel now meant he crossed more miles.

Away from Sarah.

Away from the woman he suspected he loved—and who couldn't ever love him.

"She doesn't have any reason to. She has a husband."

"Who might that be?" The voice came out of nowhere.

For an instant Clay thought he was talking to himself. Then he realized a man up in the rocks to his right had overheard and answered.

"Sorry, mister. I was thinking out loud." Clay frowned. Something about the man looked familiar. "Have a good day."

He started to touch the brim of his hat and remembered for the dozenth time he hadn't replaced the one he'd lost. Memory of that caused him to look more closely at the man in the rocks.

He rested his rifle in the crook of his left arm. The smirk on his face warned Clay this hadn't been a casual encounter. He bent low and snapped his reins. His gelding rocketed forward at a full gallop.

"Where you going, Forsythe? You running away?" the man shouted after him, confirming his suspicion. They had crossed paths before.

Clay bent even lower over his horse's neck. How had the road agent known his name?

He sawed at the reins to get the horse off the road. Three men blocked the path ahead, all with rifles lev-

eled at him. The road agents had chosen their spot
well. Boulders lined the road here, making it necessary
to slow and work his way through a tortuous maze if he
hoped to evade them. A glance behind confirmed what
he feared. Three more bandits blocked a retreat, including the man who had called to him from the rocks.
He was trapped in the jaws of a vise.

In spite of the danger, he left the road. His gelding
struggled to press through the close-spaced rocks.
Clay hunted for a spot to make a stand when a bullet
sang past his head. He ducked. His horse reared. No
amount of bronco busting could save him from taking
a tumble. He crashed to the ground and lay there
stunned. He reached out feebly. His rifle rode in the
saddle sheath—and the horse backed away to return to
the road, leaving him without a long gun.

He pushed himself to his feet and drew his six-
shooter. The instant he tried to cock it, he remembered. Not only had it been soaked in the lake, but he
had also never repaired it after it had jammed.

"Get back or I'll shoot!"

Mocking laughter greeted his bluff. Then he felt as
if he stepped off a high cliff. Downhill, Warnock held
his horse's reins in one hand and a six-shooter in the
other.

"I said you'd rue the day you crossed me. That day's
come, Forsythe. Drop the gun or get shot full of lead."

Clay looked around and saw a half dozen men in the
rocks above him, all with their guns trained on him.
He dropped his broken pistol and raised his hands.

He'd stood a better chance against the hungry wolf
pack.

CHAPTER SEVENTEEN

"THAT WAS ABOUT the dumbest thing I ever saw," Warnock said. "What do you think will happen now? You had a chance to shoot it out, maybe take one or two of us with you to the grave. Not now. Now you're going to end up drawing flies in the hot sun without any of us joining you."

Clay realized that. If he had started a gunfight, he'd have died instantly because his pistol was a worthless hunk of steel. While he was likely to still die, he would survive another few minutes. Warnock might get careless. Or the Pacific Star owner might believe a bit of tall-tale spinning.

"You're not going to hurt Suárez and the rest of them on the drive," he called to Warnock. "Kill me and it won't matter to them one whit."

"Why's that? You were their champion, the rodeo star they hired away from me." Warnock passed the reins to one of his henchmen. He made his way through the rocks until he stood a few feet from Clay, towering over him. The rancher glanced down at the fallen six-gun and laughed. "I don't even have to pick it up to see why you gave up so easy. That gun'd blow up in your hand. What? It won't?"

Warnock scooped it up and examined it. His belly laugh echoed through the mountains. "Boys, take a look at what he was going to use to fill us full of lead." Warnock tossed Clay's gun high into the air.

A cowboy halfway down the hillside caught it awkwardly, then tried to spin the cylinder. He joined his boss with his raucous laughter. "This here gun's all froze up. He was bluffin'!"

"You were bluffing," Warnock said, taking some pleasure in that. "I have to give you credit for having the stones to do that. Why are you out on the trail with a gun not even useful enough to drive nails?"

"I quit. I left the drive a couple days ago."

"You didn't quit. You're scouting the trail, aren't you? How far east of here are they?"

"I locked horns with Suárez and couldn't stand him bossing me around like he did. They went north. I came west."

Warnock looked at the cloudy sky and shook his head slowly. "Telling lies like that, I'm surprised you don't get hit by lightning. That's what happens when you tell a whopper. If you're here, the herd's not more than a day east of here." Warnock stared hard at Clay.

Clay had never been good at poker. Each time he was dealt a good hand, everyone at the table read his expression. It was worse when he tried to bluff. Dropping his hand faceup on the table and pointing would have been less revealing than the twitches around his eyes, the way his mouth turned to cotton, how he chewed at his lower lip. Warnock read all that and knew the truth—even if the part about actually leaving the Barker drive was true.

"Phillips, Carson, take this lying skunk down to the river and get rid of him."

"You want his mangy carcass poisoning the fish, boss?"

"Toss him in when you're done playing with him," Warnock said. "That way you don't have to dig a grave." He smiled. The wicked grin made Clay shiver. "The fish might feed off him, just like the great white sharks do at the P Star docks."

With that, Warnock turned his back on Clay and marched off. His two henchmen drew their six-shooters and aimed them at Clay's head.

"Shoot him here, Phillips?" asked the one on the left. He sounded nervous about killing a man in cold blood. His partner didn't.

"Not here. We'd have to drag his body a mile or so. Besides, the boss said we could have some fun with him before we killed him." Phillips cocked his pistol, then pulled the trigger.

Clay ducked, even if he couldn't dodge a bullet at this range. He fell to his knees, then looked up. The hammer had fallen on a spent cartridge.

Phillips cocked his Colt again fast. "This time there's a live round in the chamber. Want to call me out on that?"

Clay had no reason not to. He dug his toes into the rocky ground and launched himself. The six-gun's report deafened him. Lead drove past his head and took a tiny chunk out of the earlobe as it passed. The sharp pain caused him to yelp in pain.

This brought the biggest response from Carson. He whooped and hollered and danced around.

"This is fun. Can I try shootin' off his other ear?"

"Not here. Down by the river," Phillips said. "We can get him to dance a jig for us or lose a toe. Might be he's got a nice voice. He can sing for his life."

"You think he knows any real bawdy songs? I'd like to hear him warble some."

"Think he can still sing with an ounce of lead in his lungs?" Phillips aimed at Clay's chest and started to fire. At the last instant, he relaxed. "Get a move on, you. We're headin' down to the river. The three of us. But only two of us'll ride away. What do you think of that?"

Phillips did the taunting, and Carson proved the more cautious of the pair. He cut off lengths of rope from a lariat and secured Clay's hands behind his back. With a double turn, he looped the rest of the rope around his prisoner's neck. No matter what Clay tried now, he was sure to fail. Carson didn't quite drag him all the way down the slope to the road, but Clay had more cuts and scrapes than when he'd taken refuge in the rocks. What proved worse, every time Carson tugged on the rope, it cut off his air.

The two gunmen mounted and rode due south across rugged terrain. It took every ounce of Clay's concentration and balance not to be knocked to the ground and dragged along by his neck behind them.

"We can take our sweet time tormentin' him," Phillips said. "The boss and the rest are goin' huntin' for the herd. It might take them the better part of the day to even find the trail."

"Why so long? Even you can find tracks left by a herd of cattle." Carson chuckled.

This set off a verbal argument between the two men as to which of them was a better trailsman. Clay had no interest in who won. He tried to loosen the rope around his wrists. All he accomplished was abrading his skin and soaking the strands with his own blood.

Wild escape schemes raced through his mind. Fall and let them drag him so he could rub the ropes against sharp rocks. In his dazed condition he knew that was suicidal. These two wouldn't slow down. They might not even notice until his head popped off. Even if he got lucky, his captors kept too quick a pace for him to take time to cut the ropes. Clay doggedly worked his wrists back and forth and concentrated on not falling.

Before long this became increasingly difficult. His right leg swelled up again from the abuse of stumbling over the rough terrain. Just when he was about to give up and let the men drag him to death, they reached the river.

"Any spot you want your body thrown in? It's your funeral, after all," Phillips said.

"There's a sturdy-lookin' limb stickin' out over the river," Carson said, pointing. As he did, he tightened the rope and forced Clay to his knees. "We can use it as a gallows tree."

"The branch looks dead," Phillips said. "We wouldn't want him to kick all around and struggle and almost choke, then have the limb break off. He'd land in the river and might not die."

"We can tie his feet together. Ain't no way he'll swim around like that. And how about we find another limb, string him up and use him for target practice? I bet he'd swing back and forth enough times to make it interestin' again for us. It's been a spell since we done anything like that."

"That oak looks study enough to hold him," Phillips said. "What'll we bet on? First to hit him from twenty yards?"

"The bullet what kills him loses," Carson said.

The whole time they conjured up increasingly outrageous ways of killing him, Clay held his breath. His hands were numb, but he noticed something they had overlooked. Once Warnock had disarmed him, he and his men never thought Clay would have another weapon. Twisting until his shoulder felt like it would dislocate, he stretched around and closed his fingers on his sheathed whittling knife. It had been hidden under his coat.

"You ever see how the Apaches torture their prisoners?" Phillips pointed to a small mound a few yards away from the river. "They stake 'em out on an ant hill and let the bugs chew away their flesh."

"I heard tell how they'd cut the eyelids off. Staring up into the sun'll make a man blind in a few minutes."

"Blind, feelin' ants chewin' away at your skin. Maybe we can prop his mouth open and let the ants get down into his guts."

"I like that notion," Carson said. "The ants can devour him from the inside out."

"And," said Phillips with too much glee, "from the outside in, too."

"It'd be better if we had a way of enticing them, but I don't have any honey." Carson pretended to poke through his saddlebags, only to come up empty-handed.

"I don't, either, but why waste it? Honey on biscuits, mm-umm, good." Phillips paid Clay no attention as he looked around for other possible ways of killing his prisoner. "You gotta agree to that, don't you? You wouldn't want us to waste something valuable like honey on your worthless hide. We can come up with something else. Those don't look like the right kind of ants, anyway."

Clay slid the knife from its sheath. He tried not to drop it, but his numbed fingers lost hold. The knife fell to the ground. To keep Warnock's men from seeing the weapon, he fell on it and twisted around. All he accomplished was tearing his vest so that it flopped in tatters.

"I think our friend's gettin' antsy," Phillips joked.

"Leave him be. He can stew out in the sun a spell.

Look what I found in my saddlebags." Carson pulled out a pint bottle sloshing with amber fluid. "We can reflect on how best to make the boss proud of us."

"He does like it when we show initiative," Phillips said.

"Yeah, but not Ros. I swear, that Russki is about the most hidebound, muleheaded man ever to set sail from— Where does he say?"

"Kamchatka, wherever that is," Phillips said. "Hand me that bottle, 'less you're plannin' on hoggin' it all for yourself."

They dismounted and walked toward the shade from the trees offering the sturdiest branches. Testing them, they made lewd observations about what happened to a man who got hanged.

Carson had left the rope around Clay's throat secured to his pommel. The horse dragged him a few more feet. Clay panicked. The knife was left behind in the dirt. The silver blade gleamed in the sun. If either of his captors saw it, his only chance to get free would be lost.

Phillips and Carson sank down, using the oak tree for support. They passed the bottle back and forth. With so little in the bottle, they'd polish off the whiskey in a few minutes. Clay worked more frantically, but the ropes refused to budge. He rolled onto his side. A sharp pain drove into his ribs.

"The ring," he whispered. "In my vest pocket."

"Ain't that touchin'?" asked Phillips. "He's sayin' a prayer."

"I'll drink to that." Carson took another pull.

Phillips grabbed the bottle and started a minor scuffle.

Tugging at the strip of his vest, Clay pulled the pocket with his carving around. His fingers were too numb to drag it out, but he finally thrust his index fin-

ger through the circle of bone. Having just begun
working to carve it, he had left sharp edges on the wolf
vertebra. Tensing and relaxing moved the bone across
his ropes. It felt like an eternity, but when the rope
parted, it took all his willpower not to cry out in relief.

His hands began to burn as circulation returned.
Wiggling his fingers helped. He looked back a couple
yards at his whittling knife. The sun had moved
so that the blade no longer reflected toward him. Getting the double loop of rope from around his neck
without the two cowboys seeing wasn't likely. Moving
slowly, he worked his hand around and began sawing
at the rope with the bone ring. Seeing what he was doing only inches from his face made the chore easier.

Just as the final strand parted, Carson and Phillips
finished the last of their booze.

"Set the bottle on yonder stump," Phillips said.
"Whoever hits it first gets to decide how to take care of
him." He jerked his thumb over his shoulder in Clay's
direction.

"You won't have a stinking chance," Carson said.

The way he walked showed the liquor had affected
him. Clay hoped it ruined both men's marksmanship.

He saw how wrong that was. Carson and Phillips
stood side by side, slapped leather, drew and fired.
From where he lay, Clay couldn't tell which of the gunmen hit the bottle. Maybe both had at the same time.
He remembered why he hadn't signed on with Warnock back in Bozeman. The men Warnock had hired
there all looked like gunfighters. These two were quick
and accurate, even half drunk.

He tugged at the severed end of the rope, pulling it
along to maintain the fiction that it still wrapped
around his throat. Inch by inch he slid back in the dirt
until he was once more lying on the knife.

Just in time.

Both Carson and Phillips strutted over. Clay clung to the end of the rope with one hand and gripped his knife in the other, keeping it hidden under his body.

"We decided. We're gonna string you up on tippy-toe and wait to see how long before your legs get all tired and you hang yourself." Phillips reached down.

Carson saw what his partner didn't.

"The rope's been cut!" He went for his iron.

Clay erupted straight up, the tip of the knife finding Phillips' chest. The tip bounced off a rib, then sank hilt deep into the man's heart. As Phillips jerked about in death, Clay caught him up in a bear hug and heaved with all his strength. He lifted the gunman off the ground just enough to move the lifeless body between himself and Carson.

Carson's bullet crashed into his partner. Clay leaned forward and slammed Phillips against Carson's gun hand. The two went down in a heap. Seeing he had one chance only, Clay snarled and leaped like the wolves had when they attacked him. Carson batted the knife out of the way.

The knife was out of play, but the bone ring still on Clay's finger slashed across the man's throat, sending out a geyser of hot blood. Clay flinched in spite of himself. If Clay hadn't been lucky for once, Carson would have gunned him down. Instead, the gunman dropped his six-shooter and grabbed at his severed throat with both hands. Clay stood and watched the man bleed to death.

He felt no triumph, in spite of besting the two men who had intended to torture and kill him. Clay stared at the bodies. Warnock had told them to dump his body in the river. Clay did the same for the pair after he plucked their six-shooters from the dirt and a low-slung holster. He had lost his gun back where Warnock had captured him. In all likelihood, the gun was a complete loss. Even a good gunsmith wasn't going to repair it easily.

Clay drew the six-shooter he had taken from Phillips a few times, getting the feel of it. The Colt found a good home in his holster. Carson's gun he tucked into his waistband. Then he removed the bone ring and put it back into the vest pocket. A quick cleaning of the knife by sticking it into the dirt removed all but a spot or two of blood. He returned it to its sheath.

Then he saw his predicament. The men's horses had run off amid all the gunplay. All that remained was the rope that Carson had wrapped around Clay's neck to lead him here. Clay coiled it, fashioned a loop in one end and went to lasso a horse. With his game leg, he wasn't able to hike far.

He set off, determined to warn Suárez that Warnock was hunting for him backed by a gang of cutthroats, intending to rustle the valuable herd. At least that was the reason he admitted to for returning to the Crown K drive.

The telegram Suárez had sent might have arranged for the exact spot the theft was to occur. Telling Barker was a better way to save the expensive breeding cattle. And his warning would keep Sarah out of harm's way. It didn't take much mulling over his real purpose in returning, even if it meant nothing but heartbreak for him.

CHAPTER EIGHTEEN

H IS KNEE FELT better as long as he kept walking.
Whenever Clay stopped to rest, the knee seized
up on him. Now and then he climbed a tree to scout for
the gunmen's horses, but they had lit out and never
slowed. After a half hour of tracking them, he gave up.
The ground turned rocky and then opened out onto
mountain meadows. As serene as those grassy ex-
panses looked, he wanted them to be disturbed by the
two horses.

Lady Luck turned her back on him now. As he hobbled along, he made so much noise, even the rabbits
and smaller varmints ran for cover. Finding the horses
proved even more difficult than seeing a skittish
marmot.

Clay plodded on, heading back in the direction of
the Crown K herd. He expected to see the cattle before
he found the runaway horses, but both equine and bovine eluded him. Close to sundown, he wondered if
Suárez had driven the herd farther north, toward Idaho

Falls, and then west from there. Or worse, he had held up moving the herd until Warnock found them. The telegram sent by the trail boss still worried him. Pacific Star Ranch. Warnock's spread. Why had Suárez been so anxious about not getting a reply—and why had he sent it in the first place if not to double-cross King Barker?

Warnock wasn't likely to have even received it since he was ranging far and wide across Idaho, recruiting his gang. If the rest of his cowboys handled their firearms the way Carson and Phillips had, the Barkers didn't stand a snowball's chance in hell of returning to Hawaii.

The idea of Sarah being laid out in a grave made Clay's jaw clench and his hands tighten into fists. That she'd spend eternity next to her husband gave him no comfort. If he wasn't able to court her, he wanted nothing but happiness for her.

Even as that idea fluttered across his mind, his hand went to the six-shooter in his holster.

"You're not dead, Mrs. Barker, and if I have any say in the matter, you won't be. Not by Warnock's hand."

Talking to himself helped erase the miles he covered. When dusk evaporated and total night fell, he kept walking. The landscape was lit by the brilliant stars pouring their light down without the filter of any clouds. The clear sky also made it cold. Clay wanted to find a place to curl up for the night, but he'd likely freeze to death if he stopped for very long. Making a fire was necessary, but feeding it took a considerable amount of work gathering dead limbs. Without an ax, larger limbs were out of the question.

To occupy himself he swung the lariat around, spinning loops and then recovering the rope into a coil.

He cast the rope at a dark shape, thinking it was a stump. To his surprise, it jerked, got to long, spindly legs, neighed and took off. He had inadvertently tried to rope a colt. Clay changed his direction from due east to a more northerly course to find where the colt had gone. He struggled up a low ridge and looked down into a broad U-shaped valley. He grinned broadly. Lady Luck had finally smiled on him. All he had to do was prove that his vaunted skills were as good as he thought.

"I wanted a horse. Here're a hundred for the taking."

The wild mustangs milled about the way a bedded-down cattle herd did. Standing guard at the edges of the herd were the stallions. Watching the starlit horses for close to an hour identified the leader. Clay checked his rope, then began the slow descent into the valley. By the time he reached the valley floor, the stallion came over, stomping and snorting his defiance. The horse wanted Clay to know who led this herd and what would happen if any mere human disturbed his entourage.

"You're more than I can handle, old man, but I've got to get you out of the way before finding myself a horse I can break. You're just too much for me, big and strong and fast."

He continued talking to the stallion as he advanced. The two faced off, a dozen yards separating them. The stallion issued a challenge, then galloped forward. Clay caught his breath. The horse was about the fastest animal he ever did see. Moving from years of practice, Clay whirled the lariat over his head and cast the loop so it dropped over the horse's head.

The stallion jerked back and tried to dislodge the rope. Clay knew it was impossible to overpower such a magnificent animal and didn't try. He ran toward it, trying to keep as much tension on the rope as he could without getting himself dragged along. As he passed a thick upthrusting needle of rock, he made his move. He circled the spire a couple times, then tied his end to a thick-trunked bush at the base of the rock. Even then he lost his grip on the rope as the stallion jerked and fought.

Clay worried that the bush would be yanked out of the ground, but the double coil around the buried rock robbed the horse of any chance of getting free. Scrambling atop the rock, Clay watched the stallion futilely struggle. Wild-eyed and panicked, the horse reared and bucked and lashed out with powerful front hooves. The rope held. After what seemed an eternity, the stallion wore himself out.

Such a dominant horse held too much in reserve for Clay to think he had any chance of breaking it yet. He hunkered down on the rock. The stallion circled the rock a few times, winding itself inward and reducing the play in the rope. Clay nodded in approval when the horse realized what was happening and reversed course. If it circled enough times, the loops around the rock holding it would disappear. The bush, no matter how deep its roots, wasn't strong enough to withstand a stallion rearing up and yanking hard on it.

When the horse stopped fighting and walked about, as if pacing as he considered the matter, Clay turned cautious. The stallion was both strong and smart. That made for a deadly combination if Clay misjudged a single move.

"There, there," Clay said, balancing on the top of the rock.

The horse glared at him, nostrils flared and eyes squinty with ill-suppressed fury now. He moved around until he reached the far side of the rock, where the tortured bush clung to the ground. The stallion walked around and stood still.

Clay judged the distance and his chances and acted. He vaulted from the rock and landed astride the horse.

He grabbed frantically for the rope around the sinewy neck and wrapped as much of the rope around his right hand as he could before the horse reacted with a mighty heave that almost unseated him.

This wasn't riding a bronco for a prize. He had to stay on the horse's back longer than eight seconds. If he was tossed off, the horse would stomp him into the ground.

"Yeehaw!" The cry escaped Clay's lips before he realized he was egging on the stallion. He grabbed the rope with both hands now, intent on not being thrown.

The ride turned wilder. The stallion put down his head and ran full out away from the rock. The bush's roots were too strained to withstand such an assault. They ripped from the ground. If Clay had wanted to hide his trail, he might have used such a technique of dragging the brush behind to wipe away the tracks. As it was, the bush only bounced around, not slowing the stallion even a little bit. The headlong rush took Clay into the night until his hands ached and his back felt as if it would snap every time the horse bucked, landed and tore out across the valley with seemingly limitless energy—and fury.

Clay fell into an uneasy rhythm with the horse. No matter how it turned and bucked, he clung to its back. The trailing rope tangled between back legs and slowed the breakaway. Not by much, but enough to allow Clay to use what skills he had to wear down the horse a little more. He fought a war of attrition. Whichever of them weakened first lost. In Clay's case, it meant forfeiting his life.

By the time he thought the horse had won, the stallion stopped fighting and stood still, sounding like a locomotive straining to make it up a steep grade. Clay felt it gathering renewed power and determination, but how much more could it summon?

"Settle down, boy. Don't start bucking again."

Clay knew the horse didn't understand him, and if the magnificent beast did, the advice would fall on deaf ears. He used the respite to rewrap the rope around his right hand. He slid his left hand under the rope when the bronco unleashed a new set of jerks, turns and high-flying bucks.

"Gotcha now. You're tiring out. I can tell. I've busted better than you. I have." Clay cried out the words more to keep his own courage up. The horse knew nothing but fight.

And the battle was far from won, even when the wild gyrations died down again. This time the fight drained from the horse sooner than ever before. Its flanks were lathered and its eyes were wide, showing whites all around. Clay wanted that to mean he had broken the horse's spirit and caused just a little fear of losing freedom.

"Go on, trot along. Just enough. No, not that way. This way." Clay's knees dug into the horse's shoulders to change direction.

The stallion broke away from his control again and again, but each time Clay gained a little more dominance. By the time they were both exhausted from the fight that had stretched halfway across the valley, Clay's optimism soared. The horse needed considerable more training but now accepted a rider on his back. For a while.

"This way. Good boy, you're a champion. You're going to be one of the best cutting horses in the West." Clay's words soothed the wildness. A little. But enough.

He leaned about and guided the horse down the valley until they reached a road. Occasionally, the stallion tried to throw Clay, but he was master now.

Eyes blurred with fatigue, Clay knew better than to

rest. If he tethered the stallion and allowed it to regain its strength, the unbroken ways would return. He needed a few more sessions riding the horse; then he would have to break it to a saddle.

Until he had the time, Clay kept the horse heading eastward. Just before dawn, he heard cattle lowing.

"The herd!"

He almost fell from horseback. These had to be the Crown K cattle. The stallion fought him again, but he had learned its ways, how it threw its head high and twisted about, how hard it hit the ground, only to rebound. The horse at the Hoback rodeo had bested him. That defeat now meant nothing. He had shown his real skill by remaining astride this king of the mustangs.

José Vasques called to him before he saw the other cowboy.

"I knew Leo was wrong. You have not left us!" Vasques galloped up, then saw the way the stallion spread its front legs and tried to throw Clay forward. "You have a new horse. A magnificent one, but not broken."

"My gelding was stolen by Warnock and his gang. I need to talk to Mr. Barker. Warnock is waiting to ambush everyone and steal the herd."

"Where is this?"

Clay tossed his head to indicate the road he had just traveled.

"You have returned?" Leo Suárez rode up. "It is about time you showed up. Fred tried to cook and almost poisoned us all. It is hard to believe but your grub is better."

"I never thought I'd hear that," Clay said. Then he rattled off a quick description of how Warnock had waylaid him, omitting the part of how he had killed two of the P Star's henchmen.

"I'll tell King."

The words came from behind. For the first time Clay saw that Sarah had come up and listened to him warning Suárez of the danger they faced.

"All right," he said, avoiding eye contact with her.

His discomfort grew when she walked her horse around to where he had to look at her. If he hadn't been so exhausted—he was an inch away from passing out—he would have turned his new horse's face and ridden away again. The catch in his throat from simply seeing the boss' wife warned him his feelings still ran wild, as wild as the stallion he rode.

He controlled his emotions. Barely.

"Go with her and tell Mr. Barker. We will form the herd and decide what to do." Suárez waved him back toward the camp.

He rode in silence beside Sarah until they reached the spot where they had bivouacked for most of the past week. A single fire remained. Coffee was brewing in a pot hanging from an iron tripod over the flames. The odor made him dizzy.

"Get some coffee," Sarah said. Her tone carried the crack of an order. "You look half past dead. I'll take care of your horse."

"It's still wild. Warnock stole my gelding. I had to catch and break this fine example of horseflesh."

He dared release his hold with his left hand to pat the stallion on the neck. It stirred uneasily but didn't try to buck him off.

"I'll be careful. This isn't my first wild horse."

Sarah dropped to the ground and let her horse's reins trail along the ground. She stepped forward, moving slowly, then grabbed the rope halter and bent her knees slightly. Her entire weight held the horse's head down, letting Clay slip off for the first time in hours.

His legs gave way. He caught himself.

"How's your knee?" She spoke low and soothing, but the words were directed to him, not the horse. She eased and led the horse around. It remained skittish, but she had it under control—or as much as anyone could before it was saddle broken.

"I'm all right."

"You've got a pair of new six-shooters. There must be a story about how that happened."

"Two of Warnock's men weren't using them anymore" was all he said. "What does Mr. Barker want to do about Warnock laying an ambush along the road?"

"I'll stake out your fine new horse and go ask King. He's quite clever when it comes to such things. He dealt with rustlers on the spread and ran them off into the ocean."

Clay considered how she spoke. He guessed that she meant her husband had killed rustlers and thrown their bodies into the sea. Like he had killed Warnock's henchmen and sent their bodies floating down an Idaho river.

He watched her lead the stallion away, forcing himself to admire the horse more than the woman. That was only right and proper. A cup of coffee poured from the pot burned all the way down his gullet, but the strong brew perked him up. His vision cleared, and he felt as if he could contribute to whatever scheme King Barker concocted to fight Warnock.

Returning had been hard, harder than he had expected but not in the way he had anticipated. The horse had presented him a real challenge, but rejoining the Crown K crew felt as if he had come home. He drank down another cup of the bitter coffee and felt better for it. Whipping his weight in wildcats wasn't in the future, not anytime soon, but he had two new six-guns and the determination to see the herd through to the California coast.

CHAPTER NINETEEN

I T'S NOT MUCH of a plan," Clay complained. "It's not
even a plan at all, Mrs. Barker."

"Why do you keep saying that?" Sarah Barker
asked, visibly vexed at him. Her lips thinned and her
eyes flashed fire.

"Because it's true," Clay snapped.

Every minute they drove the herd westward was another minute closer to being ambushed. He had heard
Warnock bragging about taking the herd, he had killed
two of the P Star owner's gunmen and he knew trouble
lay in wait. Only the trap had yet to be sprung. But he
knew it was somewhere ahead, and he worried about
the herd, the cowboys working it, the Barkers and . . .
especially Sarah, he mentally conceded. She refused to
see how her husband was going to be the cause of them
all dying by insisting on pressing on.

"Clay, you—"

He held out his hand, silencing her. Fred came tearing down the road toward them, waving his hat high

above his head and doing everything possible to signal them.

"Stay here. I'll see what's got him so riled up."

Clay urged the stallion forward. The past three days he'd made remarkable progress with the powerful horse. It was far from tamed enough so he could depend on it without thinking. Even more training lay ahead to turn it into a cutting horse. He had picked the best in the mustang herd, and it had been for different reasons. He had intended to keep the stallion away from its herd to make cutting out a mare easier. The leader defended those following it. For all the trouble the stallion presented, the horse was a powerful runner with incredible potential.

There was only one thing he felt a pang of guilt about. Eliminate the leader and leave the rest of the herd vulnerable.

Those words rang in Clay's head as he rode to meet Fred. If he had taken out Warnock, the Crown K herd wouldn't be in constant danger. And if Clay had to bet, Warnock believed the same as he did. Get rid of King Barker and Suárez would turn the herd over to the P Star without further fight. That had to be the reason Suárez had sent the telegram. They were plotting to betray the Crown K owners. Clay wished he had come right out and told King Barker what he had seen. Somehow, every time he started, the accusation died on his lips. The Barkers trusted their trail boss like family.

Like family, Clay mused. Like Henry Oakes and his son, Sully? Only Sully made no effort to hide his debauchery. He was open about his carousing and his father had known it. Suárez hid his treachery so well, Clay doubted the Barkers would ever believe any accusation he made.

"What is it, Fred? You spot an ambush?"

"Nothing like that, Clay. This'll cause us even more trouble. There's been a rockslide that closed off the road. We can travel another ten miles. Then we're stymied. Ain't no way through that avalanche 'less we can figger a way for the herd to grow wings and fly like birds."

"Did Warnock close off the pass to stop us?"

"I didn't see hide nor hair of Warnock. Or anybody else out ridin'. This land's as empty as a banker's soul. The best I can tell, no dynamite was used. The whole danged side of the mountain just up and fell. It happens."

Clay frowned as he turned over everything the scout had reported. One question kept rising to his lips. He finally asked, "Could Warnock have caused the blockage by pushing rocks down from higher up?"

"You thinkin' maybe he intends to rustle the herd on this side of the avalanche?" Fred shook his head as he pondered the matter. "I don't think so. Grass and small bushes are already growin' from under the rocks. That tells me the fall came a week or two back. Besides, it'd be plumb foolish for him to block the road when he'd have to drive the herd along it same as us."

"That's so," Clay allowed. "Do you know any other trail? If Warnock knows about the rocks, he'll wait for us wherever we have to cross this range."

"This is new country for me. I know Montana a danged sight better. I can scout to the south. That's more or less in the direction we'd have to travel, anyway, once we get across Nevada."

"Be careful. Warnock's out there somewhere," Clay said.

"Maybe not." Fred picked at his teeth, then spat. "If he was smart—and the way you talk about him, he is—he'd let us get all the way to California before doin' any rustlin'. Why worry yourself about the trail and all the trouble along the way when somebody else can do that for you?"

"He does know where the Crown K Ranch is and how to get to it," Clay allowed, turning over the idea in his head. "And he is a shrewd character. I'll give him that much. Shrewd and dangerous."

"To the south, then? If you swing that way right now, you won't lose but a day or two."

Clay considered what Fred had suggested. If there wasn't a way through this low range of mountains, they'd have gambled and lost upward of a week since they'd have to retrace their path and go northward searching for a new path.

"There's bound to be a way across. These hills aren't all that high. I wish we had a map of the countryside," Clay said. He came to a quick decision. "Get on out and look around. I'll let Mr. Barker know what we're doing."

"You might tell Leo before that," Fred said. "He *is* the trail boss, not you."

Clay waved Fred back onto the hunt to find a path to the ocean. They had a considerable distance to travel and not a little danger facing them, too. He watched Fred vanish downhill toward a valley that might give them a quick and gentle route westward. A river running along the valley floor meant easier travel and water for the herd. He crossed his fingers for luck, hoping that Fred found the way.

Clay gently tugged on the bridle and reversed direction. The stallion bucked a little, but Clay gentled the powerful horse, then trotted back to the herd. He looked around for Sarah, but she hadn't waited for him as he'd asked. When he neared the front of the herd, Suárez rode up to meet him.

"What is the trouble? What has Fred scouted for us?"

Clay explained the problem with the rockslide and suggested they head south.

"There is no trace of Warnock?" The trail boss sounded as if he was accusing Clay of not finding armed rustlers waiting at every bend.

"Fred had a notion that Warnock and his gang would let us get the herd to California before trying to steal the cattle. They'd be on their own territory, and we'd have done all the work."

"Mr. Barker was right in telling you not to worry so much. That makes sense."

Clay almost asked Suárez outright about the telegram he'd sent back in Idaho Falls. He held back because King Barker rode up. A quick repeat of Fred's scouting set off the Crown K owner.

"We're wasting time. There wasn't any reason to take it slow. Warnock's not got the sand in his gizzard to steal *my* cattle. Now we're delayed even more. Do you trust this Fred?"

Suárez mumbled something that Clay couldn't make out, but he felt the need to stand up for the man.

"He's loyal if that's what you mean. We hired him away from a bad situation. Suárez has told you about what happened. Fred sided with us against his former boss."

Barker's puzzlement told him Suárez hadn't bothered reporting how the herd had been stolen by the rest of the crew hired on back in Wyoming.

"I vouch for him. I trust him with my life," Clay said.

"If we weren't so shorthanded, I'd give him his walking papers," King Barker said, almost spitting out the words.

"I said I stand with him all the way. If he goes, so do I."

"Forsythe, do not say such things," Suárez said in a

low voice. "Mr. Barker is in a bad mood today. His leg, it hurts. When that happens—"

"Don't test me, sir! Leo covered for you when you went on your side trip. No man is indispensable."

"With five, it's something of a miracle," Clay said. "With only three, it's close to impossible in this lifetime." His dander was up now. There wasn't any cause for Barker to take this tone.

"Hawaiians are better cowboys than you find in these parts," Barker said. "And there'd be four of us."

"Sarah?" Clay blurted her name. "You'd have her riding herd?"

"She's a remarkable woman. She grew up on the Crown K working alongside the *paniolo*. She's the equal of any cowboy who ever rode the range. Isn't she, Leo?"

"She rides well," the trail boss said uneasily. "Her sharpshooting skills are second to none. In so many ways, she is remarkable."

"Her marksmanship and cool head saved my life. It'd be a shame if you fired Fred and me since I feel I owe her."

"Please, there is no need to argue. Over what?" Suárez pointed south and said to Barker, "This will be an easier trail. Our scout will find a pass that is lower and speeds our drive. I feel it in my bones, Mr. Barker."

"Time works against us," Barker said. "We must not dally. We mustn't." Without another word, he rode back toward the herd.

"He's right about that," Clay said.

He watched King Barker until he disappeared into a dust cloud. Clay forced himself to look away. He had hoped for another quick look at Sarah Barker. Mooning like a lovesick tenderfoot over a woman he could never have only wrecked his value to the Crown K.

"I work for the ranch," he said more to himself than to Suárez.

The trail boss wasn't paying any attention to him. He rambled on about how to ease the herd down the slope south of the road.

"That way," Clay said. "Get them moving down back there. The slope's gentle enough. If they slide on loose gravel, they won't go far. And we need to move them a few at a time."

The image of cattle tumbling into one another, toppling like dominoes stood on end, made him smile. Then he sobered. They'd surely lose more than one of the valuable animals if that happened.

"Definitely, a few at a time, even if it means we have to ride up and down the slope a dozen times."

"Five or six at a time," Suárez said as if coming to the solution all by himself. "That is the way we must move the herd. Come along, Clay."

They rode back to the herd, where José Vasques joined them. He and Suárez yammered away in their mixture of English, Spanish and Hawaiian while Clay studied the slope. When the pair came to him, he had a route picked out.

"We'll get them downhill in an hour or so," he said. "It'll take a passel of riding, but we can do it before sundown."

Suárez and Vasques took the first half dozen while Clay remained with the bulk of the herd. As he circled the herd, keeping those willing to stray huddled with the rest, Sarah rode over to him. He nodded in her direction, hoping to avoid anything more, but when he tried to put distance between them, she trotted up beside him.

"Mr. Forsythe," she said, "is there any danger from Warnock and his riders?"

"You don't do small talk too well, do you?"

"King thinks you are full of beans," she said. "That there isn't any danger from them."

"He's the boss."

"Clay!"

Her sharp tone caused him to draw rein and look at her. He thought some menace rode down on her. She wanted only his full attention.

"Thank you. I want the truth."

"Whatever the boss says is the truth. I'm not the boss."

"I've seen how you and Leo work together. It's not all that clear who's the trail boss, but you know what I mean."

He wondered if that bothered her. It explained why her husband was as snappish as he was. Leo Suárez was his man and had been for years. A Johnny-come-lately giving orders others obeyed wrecked the order of things. Not for the first time he considered his motives for rejoining the drive. Every time he felt he had his feelings for Sarah under control, though, she said something or gave him a long look that set his heart pounding again.

She was a married woman and that, no matter what he felt for her, put her out of his reach.

"I need to keep close watch on the herd while Leo and José move cattle down the hill a few at a time. They're going to have a devil of a time with some of the bulls."

"I know," Sarah said.

Again she gave him a look, but this wasn't one he could figure out. It made him uneasy. There wasn't any banter in what she said. It came as a resigned, flat statement, but her bright eyes!

"Ma'am."

Clay started to touch his hat brim out of instinct. He really needed to buy a new hat. Somehow taking the guns off Warnock's henchmen posed no dilemma for him, but wearing a dead man's hat would have made it seem that he'd robbed their corpses.

"You look uneasy, Clay. I think I know why. Go help Leo and José. I can tend the herd for a while."

"I can't let you do that. It can be dangerous if one of the bulls takes it into his head to lower his horns and charge. They're not the brightest animals on this earth."

"They're not the only dumb critters," she said almost to herself. Louder, she added, "I'll keep close watch. My horse is trained." She smiled winningly. "And my horse can outrun any bull in this herd."

"Do you know that for a fact?"

"Oh, yes. I've had a few minutes of fun finding out. But you missed those times since you were off . . . scouting. Or something."

Not trusting himself, he said nothing more. He turned the stallion about and sought out Suárez and Vasques. They had returned from taking the first of the herd to the valley floor. From the look of it, the slipping and sliding downhill hadn't posed much of a problem. The half dozen heifers and the bull below scrounged about for decent feed, oblivious to the descent now.

He sighed. He envied cattle sometimes. They had such short memories and forgot any unpleasantness as soon as they found a fresh patch to graze on.

With three of them working in tandem, the move went smoother than it had any right to. Two shooed the small knot of cattle down while the third watched over the growing number in the valley. They switched off so each of them made two trips before resting with the lower herd. Clay was pleased with the way his partially saddle-broken stallion enjoyed the work.

By the time the last of the bulls was escorted down and the herd re-formed, Fred returned. The way was clear along the valley, a river flowed farther down and the drive continued smoother than if they had remained on the higher road.

The rest of the drive went equally as well, but Clay

grew increasingly wary when Suárez announced they had crossed over into California. Not once in the prior two and a half weeks had they spotted Warnock or his men. That had to mean Fred's appraisal of the P Star owner's intentions was right on target.

Clay knew real trouble lay ahead when he learned that to get to King Barker's small dock and embarkation point, they had to take a road passing by Warnock's spread.

CHAPTER TWENTY

"THREE DAYS, THAT is all the time left before we are ready to ship the herd," Leo Suárez gushed. "The past weeks have been hard, but we have arrived."

Clay wasn't as sure. From what they'd told him, Warnock's spread wasn't that far down the road. It would take at least a day, perhaps more, to drive the herd past the sprawling P Star Ranch. The trail after they had skirted the rockslide back in Idaho had been easy. He had to admit he had never been on an easier, quicker drive.

Easy, that was, when it came to tending the cattle. The beeves had fallen into the rhythm of the trail and only a few had strayed. They had been quickly found and driven back, thanks to how well his stallion had learned all the skills that a good cutting horse needed. The mustang was saddle broken now. Clay smiled when he remembered when Sarah had asked to ride the horse. He had been leery since the stallion had never allowed another rider astride his broad back, but he had held the reins. Sarah quickly pulled the reins from him and trotted about, then galloped.

He had appreciated the sight of her long blond hair bannering behind her as she bent low and let the horse show its true speed. It was as if she had been born in the saddle—and the stallion willingly changed owners.

Clay considered giving her the horse when they arrived, but taking any of the other horses used on the drive didn't suit him too much. He missed his gelding and hoped whichever of Warnock's men who had taken the horse was treating it well. But would he want to switch back?

He patted the stallion's powerful neck.

"I'm not giving you up, old fellow."

The horse turned a large brown eye toward him, as if considering whether to buck him off for even considering such a thing or simply to balk like a mule. There were things a cowboy never said to his horse. Hinting that such a faithful trail companion was nothing more than a token to be swapped was one of them.

"Do you want me to scout ahead?" he called to Suárez. "If we're that close to Warnock's ranch, we need to be even more watchful."

"Fred will be back soon. We will stay with the herd. I am familiar with this part of the country," Suárez said. "By the end of the day, we will find good grass and bed the herd for the night."

"On Warnock's property? That's not too neighborly, and I'm sure he'll take it as an outright insult."

"There are patches along the road he does not own. We get along well with many of the other ranchers. We stand together against him trying to buy—or steal— our land."

"All it takes is one of the others to give in," Clay said. "Then it's devil take the hindmost."

"We've been gone a spell," King Barker said. "I can

find out if the Ralstons will let us overnight on their north pasture."

"They are prickly men, Richard and Randall Ralston," Suárez said. He saw Clay's expression and explained. "They are twins and possessive of their ranch."

"I might offer them a heifer or two to soothe their ruffled feathers. The quality of their stock isn't good. The last time we talked, all they did was complain."

Clay saw his final opportunity to tell the Crown K owner about Suárez and the Idaho Falls telegram. No matter how he reacted, the herd was almost to the California spread. Fire him or praise him, it no longer mattered.

They had crossed the West with a herd bound for Hawaii.

"Mr. Barker, why don't we ride ahead? You can talk to the Ralston brothers, and I'll be sure the road's all clear."

"You want to see where we might be ambushed?" Barker laughed harshly. "You've had that bee in your bonnet throughout the drive, Forsythe."

Clay almost snapped back that Warnock was *his* bane as well. As he had done so many times before, he kept his opinion to himself because Sarah rode up and reached over to tug on King's sleeve.

"We need to listen to him," she said. "You know what Warnock said before we joined the drive in Idaho Falls."

"Suárez sent a telegram," he began.

Clay clamped his mouth shut. The words had escaped before he thought. Sarah trusted him. Both of them did, but they had to trust Leo more because of his long history with the ranch—and them.

Both King and Sarah looked at him.

"In Idaho Falls."

His mouth turned dry, but he had to spit out the accusation. It was now or never. Confusion about where his duty lay made it all the worse. Leo had shown himself to be a true friend, even a savior on occasion. But that telegram put them in danger. All of them.

"How'd you know that?" King Barker twisted about in the saddle. The movement obviously pained him. He rubbed his leg and winced.

"I saw the telegram was addressed to the Pacific Star Ranch."

Hearing his name, Suárez came over. He scowled and said, "You spied on me!"

"Explain why you sent Warnock a telegram, then waited for an answer. It never came because Warnock was on the trail and probably never saw it. What'd you have to say to him?"

Clay gripped the reins tightly in his left hand and rested his right on his holster, ready to have it out with the trail boss if it came to that.

"He sent the telegram to us," Sarah said. "Well, to King. He asked for us to ride with the herd. He told us that you'd arrived in Idaho Falls."

"That's right," King Barker said. "We were already on the way. We got the 'gram in Boise. Rather than wait for you to come to us, we went to Idaho Falls."

"I saw Warnock's name on the telegram," Clay said doggedly.

"He never mentioned Warnock. He said he recognized a couple of hands from the Pacific Star. He was warning us, not conniving with Warnock." Sarah fixed Suárez with a hard look. "You never sent a 'gram to Warnock, did you, Leo?"

The man's head rotated from side to side so fast in denial, it would have spun like a top if it'd come loose from his body.

"I would never betray you. I owe you everything. My family is loyal. My grandfather—"

"We believe you, Leo," King said, cutting him off. His face turned red with anger—directed at Clay. "Mr. Forsythe thought the worst of you, though."

"I'm sorry, Leo," Clay said. "You never told us you were asking for them to join us."

"Not everything is shared with hired hands," King Barker said harshly before Suárez answered. "You should take your leave now, Forsythe. Ride on. I'll see you're paid after the cattle are shipped."

"You're firing me?" Clay took a deep breath and held it. He released it slowly. "I deserve it, but let me see the cattle onto your spread. It's the least I can do."

"Oh, do let him finish the drive, King," Sarah said.

She tugged at Barker's sleeve again to get his attention. She pulled him closer and whispered. He tried to pull away, but she persisted and continued filling his ear with whatever arguments she could. King Barker put his heels to his horse and rode off.

Sarah looked grim but said, "You can stay, Mr. Forsythe. It's only a day or two until we reach the ranch. Isn't that so, Leo?"

Suárez glared at Clay, grunted and rode after his boss.

"I apologize," Clay said. "I let my suspicions run wild."

"Leo Suárez would never sell us out to the likes of Warnock. If you— Never mind. There's no reason for you to know his history with the Crown K. Believe me when I say he's the most loyal *paniolo* we could want. To-the-death loyal." She started to say something more, then stopped and fixed an indecipherable gaze on Clay.

It wasn't accusing or deriding him. It was more of disappointment. Sarah Barker lifted her chin into the air and rode away, not even glancing back at him.

Clay sat astride his stallion and wondered if he

ought to quit then and there, no matter that he had
eaten crow by asking to ride the rest of the way to the
ocean. When he had quit before, he had worried Sarah
would be too much of a temptation for him. That was
the furthest thing from his mind now. His mistrust had
poisoned any friendship with Suárez and caused the
Barkers to consider him a liability.

If they hadn't been so close to the end of the drive,
he would have slunk off, tail between his legs. Clay
turned his attention to the herd. Get it onto the ship
heading for Hawaii and his job was done; his humiliation could be left behind.

He walked his horse slowly to the herd, still plodding
along with no sense of urgency. As always happened,
that changed fast. A sudden ripple of fear ran through
the cattle. The leading bull put down his head and
snorted, pawing the ground. Worrying about a snake or
even something larger, like a wolf or cougar, Clay
looked around. His hand flew to his six-gun when he
spotted a rider to the north. He stood in the stirrups
and used his hand to shield his eyes to get a better look.

The rider saw him and galloped away.

The herd was at a standstill. Clay's job was clear.
Keep them moving. He wished he had Leo's slingshot
to pop the lead bull in the rump to goose him along.
Instead, he gave the stallion its head and raced for the
spot where he had seen the rider spying on the Crown
K cattle. That was the way it struck him. Spying.

He found the small rise and studied the ground for
tracks. The soft earth showed the direction taken by
the snoop. Clay looked around again but the rider had
lost himself in a lightly forested area. His six-gun
weighed him down—the gun taken from one of Warnock's hired killers. It would be fitting to turn it against
Warnock and anyone he sent to bedevil King Barker
these last few miles.

Clay turned back to the cattle, knowing how hard it'd be to chase down the watcher. Not knowing how close they were to the P Star Ranch kept him from running down the rider to find out his interest. Falling into an ambush was too easy now since he didn't know the countryside.

"Who'd care if they filled me full of holes?" He spoke with real bitterness.

He had worn out his welcome with the Barkers because of his suspicions about Leo Suárez. From saving him from getting beat up back in Hoback to hundreds of small kindnesses along the trail, Suárez had never shown a traitorous streak. Clay regretted being so mistrustful, but that was his nature.

He shrugged it off. Get the herd to the docks, collect his pay and leave. That was his future.

Fred joined him as they urged along the cattle.

"What've you done to get everyone so mad at you? I asked José about who'd ride night herd, and well, he launched off into a three-language tirade about you. I don't speak Hawaiian and danged little Spanish, but the parts I figgered out weren't too complimentary."

"You might keep your distance," Clay warned. "You don't want to catch my cooties."

"Seeing you and them on the outs ain't right, Clay. All of you have played fair with me. What happened?"

"There's no call for me to pass along everything."

"Even that purty lady's got blood in her eye, and I thought the two of you were gettin' along real fine."

"Sarah?" Clay snorted and shook his head. He had no idea how Fred got such a notion lodged in his head.

"Who else? That heifer over yonder's got her eye on me, but I'm not all that interested. But you and Sarah, now, that looked like a match made in heaven to me. I overheard her sayin'—"

"There!" Clay reached for his six-shooter. "Did you

see them? At least three riders, maybe more off to the side of the road?"

"You've got a sharp eye, Clay. Three cowboys, I saw them. More? Missed them entirely." Fred slid his rifle up and down in its saddle sheath to be certain he could draw it quickly if the need arose. "You reckon those are Warnock's men fixin' to do us harm?"

"I was wrong about Warnock trying to rustle the cattle. You nailed it when you said he'd wait until we got close to his ranch."

"Lettin' us do all the work still makes sense." Fred grinned crookedly. "So you think I was right about Warnock's plans? Ain't usual for folks to believe me to be such a deep thinker."

"Stick with checkers," Clay said. "Chess might be too much for you, but your thinking's looking right on the money." He pointed as six riders crossed the road and galloped away.

"I've seen posses with fewer men," Fred said. "I've been *in* posses with fewer men, but I've never been hunted by posses like that. There's never been no call for the law to come after me with a posse."

"You're in a hole," Clay said. "Stop digging." He smiled ruefully. "I wish I was smart enough to take my own advice with the Barkers."

"With Miss Sarah, you mean."

Before Clay could correct him, Suárez rode up, waving to them. Fred and Clay trotted over to see what he had to say. He pointedly ignored Clay and spoke directly to Fred.

"There is a good pasture two miles down the road. It is owned by friends of Mr. Barker. We will spend the night there, leave early in the morning and get to the Crown K docks by sundown tomorrow."

"Sounds like the end of the trail," Fred said. "A pity since I've enjoyed ridin' herd with you."

Suárez nodded brusquely, glanced at Clay as if starting to include him, then wheeled about and positioned himself at the back of the herd. A few yips and a holler or two, accompanied by a couple pebbles from his slingshot, caused the cattle to low and moan and get moving again at a quicker pace. The lead bull tossed his head and then made his way down the road, strutting his stuff and acting like the king of the world.

Clay kept a few dozen yards to the side, wary of any shift in direction. The bull kept the rest of the herd together but, being a bovine, might have taken it into his head to change directions.

Clay had no call to enforce human will on the herd. It was as if the bull smelled growing green grass and wanted to dine high, wide and handsome.

He shared Fred's sentiment about riding with the Crown K. It had been a decent drive, and he was owed a hundred dollars. He had already paid Fred his due, so it would replenish his poke. He had never been in California before and had no idea what the state offered. He'd find out. If nothing suited him, wintering in the warm climate would give him a chance to consider where to drift come springtime. Texas was always a possibility, and returning to Colorado to see how the Rocking O fared wasn't out of the question.

The way he'd been wrong about so much that mattered, he might have misjudged Sullivan Oakes. He doubted it, but Vic Reedy wasn't likely to be satisfied in Bozeman, even surrounded by family. Cattle and ranching were in his blood as much as they were in Clay's. He and his former trail boss could help out—or maybe buy—the Colorado ranch together. This was as close as he was likely to get to settling down.

Clayton Forsythe, ranch owner. He liked the sound of it.

"There it is," called Fred. "Mighty good-looking

pasture." The cowboy hung back to talk with Suárez to find out if they had to graze the cattle in any particular spot.

The wrangler had barely left his post on the far side of the herd when Clay saw the half dozen men who had been on the road earlier galloping into the pasture. They drew their six-shooters and began firing.

The herd spooked and stampeded. Clay reacted out of instinct. The smart thing was to get out of the way and let the cattle wear themselves out running. They had been on the trail all day and lacked the reserve stamina to go far. But what he saw ahead turned him cold. Both King and Sarah Barker were in the direct line of the stampede.

Clay bent low and whipped the stallion to a flat-out gallop. He came even with the middle of the herd, then outpaced them until he spotted the charging bull. The stallion tried to veer away. The horse showed more sense than he did. He kept the horse angling in front of the stampede as he pulled his rope free from the thong holding it near his knee. Whipping the rope around, he lashed the bull repeatedly. The powerful animal paid no heed.

"Get away. Turn! Go south!" Clay shouted toward the Barkers at the top of his lungs, hoping they heard him over the thundering hooves.

If he convinced the bull to go north, they'd wear themselves out soon and the Barkers would escape. By a hair maybe, but they wouldn't get stomped into the ground.

Clay cried out in despair. King and Sarah weren't budging—and the reason was as deadly as the runaway cattle. Three riders who had to be Warnock's henchmen opened fire on them. Clay saw King Barker snap back in the saddle. He grabbed his shoulder and somehow managed to stay on his horse. A new leaden barrage frightened his horse. Barker galloped south more out of luck than from heeding Clay's warning.

The Barkers' luck evaporated when Sarah's horse reared in fright. As if she moved through molasses, she lifted away from her saddle and took flight. Clay insanely wished for her to grow wings and fly to safety. She continued on an upward arc that held her prisoner. At the top she hung suspended, gravity failing.

Then she plunged to the ground and landed hard. Her horse sped away, leaving her helpless in front of the stampede.

Clay lashed more furiously, but the bull was past noticing or caring.

"Give me every ounce of speed," he shouted in the stallion's pinned-back ear as he bent low.

As if understanding, the horse blasted forward. Although Clay expected some extra speed, the surge took him by surprise. He clung to the pommel as air cut at his face like a dull knife blade. He had ridden past the edge of a tornado with a lesser gale-force wind.

Sarah got to her feet and wobbled, shaken by the fall. Clay steered his mount toward her. He dropped the rope, made sure his footing in the stirrups was secure, then rushed past her. As he did, he bent and grabbed her arms.

Clay felt her shoulders yielding under the strain of yanking her upward. He ignored her cries of pain as he slung her over the saddle in front of him. Then the moans disappeared. The earsplitting roar of the charging cattle drowned out everything, including the pounding of his own horse's hooves against the grassy ground.

Leaning far to the left while holding on to Sarah, he turned his horse and rode at an angle to the stampede.

And then he thought he'd gone deaf. The noise assaulting him simply stopped. He looked behind. The lead bull had taken it into his head to break off the headlong run. It took Clay longer than he'd have liked to slow and finally bring the straining stallion to a halt. He hadn't wanted to throw Sarah to the ground with an abrupt change.

"Are you all right?" He eased her to the ground. She took a step away, dazed. Her bright eyes were cloudy. With hands on either temple, she started to cry.

"My arms. You dang near yanked them out of their sockets."

"Sorry," he said. "I should have let the herd trample you."

Sarah turned in a full circle, looking around as if she had no idea where she was. She faced the herd, now quietly munching grass as if nothing had happened.

"I heard gunfire," she said.

"Those must have been Warnock's men."

"I saw him." She rubbed her head faster, then looked up at Clay. "I saw him!"

"Warnock?"

"His foreman. Roskolnikov. I've never seen a man with a crueler face. When he— King!"

"He was shot," Clay said, remembering the way Barker had almost tumbled from the saddle. "He lit out, going south away from the stampede."

"Clay, please. Roskolnikov went after him. You've got to help him. Please!"

She reached up, wincing as her hands lifted above her shoulders. He had injured her when he whisked her away to safety. But she clutched his left hand and squeezed hard in need.

"I'll see that he's not hurt any more," he promised. She looked so distraught at that instant he would have ridden to the gates of hell for her. "You fetch Leo and the others. But time's a-wasting."

Clay galloped off, wondering if that was exactly what his destination was and if it was worth the risk. But he knew it was. For her.

No matter what she thought of him—for Sarah, it was worth it.

CHAPTER TWENTY-ONE

THE STALLION BEGAN to flag before Clay overtook
Warnock's men. He started to whip the horse back
to a gallop, then relented. The horse had more sense
than he did. If he came across six or eight or more of
Warnock's gunmen, what would he do? There wasn't
any way to tangle with them all at once. And if Sarah
was right and they had taken King Barker prisoner, the
Crown K owner's life hung in the balance if anyone
butted in.

For Clay, his feud with Warnock was personal and
had been ever since the rancher and his men had
beaten him up. Nothing about how Warnock conducted business sat well with Clay, but almost getting
Sarah killed made settling accounts all the more important. That Warnock had kidnapped King Barker
added to the insult.

"He tried to kill Barker," Clay said through gritted
teeth as he rode slower and slower until he finally drew
rein to give his horse a rest.

The stallion had helped turn the stampede and had rescued Sarah and now carried him to a showdown that would mean life or death. He owed it to the horse not to run him into the ground.

And slowing down gave him time to think, to plan, to decide what was the best course of action. This part of northern California was wide-open without much in the way of law. That gave Warnock leave to do as he pleased. From the way Suárez had spoken about the ranchers, only a loose alliance kept Warnock from gobbling up all their land. The tiny patch that was the coastal Crown K spread was not a working ranch. It served as a waypoint between California and Hawaii, with the actual ranching done on the islands, but it was key to getting supplies to and from the ranch.

Clay failed to come up with any plan of attack. Without knowing what he faced, how Warnock held King Barker, anything he did was more of a dangerous guess than a solid plan. He urged his horse forward at a slow walk. His head swiveled from one side to the other. Missing even a single warning now meant his death—his and Barker's.

An elaborate stone arch some distance down a double-rutted road caught his eye. Lettering that had been hammered from wrought iron and fastened to the stone was as much a warning as a declaration of the spread's name. The Pacific Star Ranch. Clay had found the main entrance, but he had no idea what to do now. The road going toward the distant ocean disappeared over a low hill, but Clay knew blindly charging ahead would cost him his life.

He rode under the dark stone arch and shivered in reaction. He had the eerie feeling of being in a grave with the stone arch his tombstone. Clay swallowed hard and forced the premonition away. Warnock intended for everyone coming onto his land to feel that way or he would have put up a more welcoming sign.

Continuing along the road until he encountered Warnock's crew amounted to forcing a showdown he wasn't likely to win. Clay cut off from the road and rode east. If Warnock's men had come onto this property from across country, they would have had to ride from that direction—the direction of the Crown K herd. Ten minutes of slow walking restored his stallion's energy. He picked up the gait and angled around the rise to cross a level patch of ground. He drew rein the minute he caught sight of the P Star's main house in the distance. A hundred yards behind it, a brightly painted red barn stood sentry over a corral crammed full of horses. He rode closer and spotted a bunkhouse. He held his breath as he gave it a once-over. Empty. Not even a hint of movement showed through the windows.

The main house had a deserted look to it also. No smoke curled from the chimney. The utter silence reminded Clay of the grave. Involuntarily he looked back toward the stone arch, but it was hidden by the hill between the house and the main road skirting the ranch's perimeter.

"Horses," he said softly. "There are too many in that corral for there not to be cowboys around somewhere."

Clay edged around the house and studied the barn more closely. Unlike the other structures on the P Star, light oozed between the wallboards and spilled out into the increasingly dark evening. He tipped his head to one side and listened hard. Laughter sounded from inside the barn.

"They're all gathered there." Clay had his suspicions as to why all the hands had crowded into the barn. If King Barker was alive, Warnock was holding him there. It wasn't much of a stretch to imagine Warnock's men laughing and deriding the Crown K owner as he was tortured.

Clay rode as quietly as possible to the corral. The horses stirred uneasily, but somehow recognized the stallion as a leader. Clay's horse kept them from creating a ruckus. He lashed the reins around the top corral rail and inched toward a window at the rear of the barn.

A quick sneak peek dazzled him. A dozen lanterns hung around the middle of the floor blazed like noonday. Clay turned to keep from being seen and pressed his back against the wall. He breathed faster now that he saw what he faced. A dozen cowboys, maybe more, had formed a circle around two men. One giant of a man had stripped to the waist. He stood beside King Barker, who dangled from a rope fastened somewhere in the loft. His arms were pulled straight over his head and his toes dragged along the floor. Clay shut his eyes as meaty thuds sounded. The circle of men cheered and egged on the torturer.

He wished he hadn't envisioned this scene as he rode onto the P Star. Warnock and his men were too predictable, too dangerously predictable in their brutality.

"You give it to him, Ros. You're a whirlwind with those punches. Keep going!"

Clay peeked back, trying to find the man who had called out the orders to the huge Russian foreman. Any of a half dozen were likely candidates. Who spoke didn't matter since they all cried out to see blood spilled.

When the men got tired of that, they made lewd suggestions about what Ros ought to do next.

Clay had wondered if Sarah was right to fear and

loathe Warnock's foreman. Clay decided to never doubt her again. Roskolnikov far surpassed anything Clay had anticipated in outright cruelty. He took in more of the scene, this time looking for ways to rescue Barker. Roskolnikov used the Crown K owner as a punching bag. Short jabs drove into an unprotected midriff. When Ros tired, he switched to uppercuts. Two knocked Barker's head back. Clay heard the crack even over the jeers.

"Hold on, Ros. You knocked him out again." Warnock stepped out from a stall with a bucket of water. He threw it on Barker to bring him around.

Clay thought Warnock's foreman had killed him. A second bucket followed the first and this produced a moan and feeble twitches. Some inner steel kept Barker fighting. He kicked out and caught Ros on the kneecap, knocking the man down. The foreman roared like a wounded animal and stood, ham-hock-sized fists ready to end his attacker's life.

"Wait." Warnock stepped between them. "Ros, back off."

His sharp command cut through the red haze of fury possessing Roskolnikov. The other men hissed and booed. They wanted blood. They wanted Ros to finish the job he had started with his bare knuckles.

Warnock waved them back. The cowboys thought their boss was going to take a turn at their captive.

Instead, Warnock slapped Barker a couple times and said, "You see the predicament you're in. Do what I want. I'll cut you down and you sign over the herd. I've got a bill of sale right here." Warnock pulled a folded paper from the inside pocket of his coat. "Sign and save yourself a powerful lot of pain."

"I'd spit on you if my mouth wasn't like cotton," Barker gasped out.

"Ros, our partner here's being cantankerous. He

won't do business with us." Warnock held his foreman
back before he launched another powerful punch.
"Sign over that fine breeding stock you so willingly
brought to my doorstep. I appreciate all your work, but
you need to learn some manners."

"I'll teach you manners if you cut me down!"

"That's not going to happen, is it? Not with you being so contrary."

Warnock snapped his knuckles and moved a little
closer so he was in range to continue the beating his
foreman had begun. Warnock took his turn hammer-
ing at Barker's breadbasket. After a few blows, he
stepped back, panting.

"I'll add a clause so you can sell me your pitiful
patch of land down by the ocean. It'll make a nice ad-
dition to the P Star acreage. I can use those docks to
start some trade with the islands. Would you like competition? Maybe I can buy a ranch on Hawaii and we
can be neighbors just like here."

"Go to hell." The words came out a hoarse whisper.

Warnock drove his fist into Barker's solar plexus.

Clay reacted before he thought. He had his six-
shooter out of the holster, ready to shoot. The punch
had knocked Barker out.

"Get some more water, Ros. Bring him around. I
don't want him dying until he signs the paper. It's all
got to be legal."

The cowboys grew restive. They wanted blood. As
long as Barker held out, Warnock wasn't going to kill
him, but the instant he signed that bill of sale, he was
a goner. Clay wondered what tall tale Warnock would
conjure up to explain the rancher's death.

He might not even try. They were close to the Pacific Ocean. From what Suárez and Vasques had said,
huge man-eating sharks constantly prowled the shoreline. If Barker was tossed off a cliff into the water, the

perpetually famished sharks would remove all evidence of why King Barker had signed over his herd and his land.

Clay wondered why Warnock was even bothering to get the bill of sale signed. The power structure in northern California must have been shifting, and he wasn't in control the way he had been. A new sheriff? Judges he hadn't paid off? Or had the other ranchers formed a more effective front against him? Whatever had happened, Warnock was walking the straight and narrow, if torture and threats fit that definition.

Clay winced as another bucket of water crashed onto the dangling rancher. King Barker shook himself and moaned. Suspended as he was put terrible strain on his shoulder joints.

"It can be over quick, King. Sign at the bottom." Warnock held up the bill of sale. "It's a good deal. I'm offering you a hundred dollars for the herd, your land . . . and your life. A hundred whole dollars. Sign." He held the page up so Barker could see the contract.

Clay ducked when Ros turned in his direction. From the way the barn's interior was lighted, Ros probably couldn't see anyone looking in, but taking the risk put Clay's life in jeopardy. He thought hard. Barker was holding out, but he had visibly weakened. If he didn't sign the papers, Ros would beat him to death. And even if he did sign, Warnock wasn't inclined to let a rival keep on breathing.

Duckwalking back to the corral, Clay slipped the stallion's reins off the corral railing. The horses in the pen grew restive, giving him an idea. He circled the corral, found the gate and opened it. The gate tried to swing back shut. He wedged it open and jumped into the saddle. His stallion raced off a few yards. This was enough to bring the P Star horses thundering out.

Clay wasted no time racing around the barn. The

sound of the escaping horses brought the cowboys hot-footing it to see their horses vanish into the dark. They yelled and lit out after them. This was all the opening Clay needed—and it was all he'd hoped for. He dropped to the ground again. Barely had he taken a step before his horse reared, swung about and lit out into the darkness. Clay watched the horse vanish, shrugged it off as something beyond his control and pushed open the main door to the barn.

Warnock and his foreman crowded near the rear door, yelling at the men to get their horses back into the corral. Clay walked forward slowly, quietly. He saw a sickle hanging on a nail. He hefted the curved steel implement, judged distance and swung. The sharp blade cut through Barker's ropes with a sibilant hiss. The rancher landed on both feet; then his leg gave way. He fell heavily, the sound alerting Warnock and Roskolnikov. The pair whirled about. The foreman wasn't wearing any iron. Warnock was. He filled his fist with it and fired.

Clay bent, grabbed Barker by the collar and dragged him into a stall. He pulled out his six-gun, not sure what to do. Shooting it out was crazy. He had ducked into a stall and trapped both himself and Barker.

"Get ready to run," he said grimly. "Can you even stand?"

"You'll never get out in one piece. Leave me. Go on, get out of here!"

"Sarah'd skin me alive if I didn't bring you back."

King Barker stared at him. "That's important to you?"

"It ought to be important to you unless you want to die here."

Clay thrust his pistol around the side of the stall and fired. The return hail of lead tore fist-sized holes in the stall above his head.

"You'll run out of ammo before you plug them," King said.

Clay held up a gun belt with a pistol thrust into it. From the length of the belt, it belonged to Warnock's foreman. He had taken it off so he could better torture Barker.

"We've got two guns. How are we going to make them count before the cowboys get back?"

"The shooting will warn them something's wrong. You drove off their horses?"

Clay nodded. He rose enough to press his eye to a hole blasted through the stall. His field of vision was limited, but he saw that Ros had left. He caught glimpses of Warnock moving around.

"We've got to hightail it now. Warnock's all by his lonesome."

Barker grunted. "His foreman's circling to come at us through the main door. You could empty your six-shooter into that one and he'd still come at you. I've never seen a tougher man in all my born days."

Barker slung the foreman's gun belt around his waist. Fastening it in the smallest notch still let it slip down around his hips. Seeing the futility of it ever staying around his middle, Barker swung the gun belt around in his left hand and weighed the gun in his right.

"What are you doing?" Clay demanded.

"Get ready to run like your life depends on it"— Barker laughed without humor—"because it does."

"You're not going out there." Clay grabbed for the rancher, only to be shoved away. Before Clay regained his balance, King Barker stepped out. His left hand held up the gun belt. His right hand clutched the six-shooter.

"You and me, Warnock. We end this right here."

"You're dumber than I thought, Barker. You're no match for me."

Clay pressed against the stall again. Warnock circled out from behind a pile of baled hay. The P Star owner didn't give Barker a fair chance to get ready. He stepped into view the same instant he lifted his six-gun.

Clay let out a loud shout and burst forth, diving to knock Barker down before he caught a bullet. Warnock was fast, really fast. He got off four shots while Clay charged out.

A bullet whizzed past his scalp, cutting off a lock of hair. He crashed into Barker and sent the man reeling to the far side of the barn. They landed in a heap in a different stall.

"You had enough, Barker?" Warnock asked. "My men'll be back any second. You and your lackey will hang side by side. Only this time I'm not inclined to let you swing by your hands. I'm going to put a noose around your scrawny neck."

"You'll never get him to sign the bill of sale that way," Clay shouted.

He heaved Barker to a sitting position. Two of the four bullets had found their target in his belly. One had passed all the way through, but one remained lodged in Barker's gut. The Hawaiian rancher moaned softly, trying not to let Warnock know how badly hurt he was.

"I'll forge your name. Who'll care? I've got a couple dozen men to back me up as witnessing you putting your John Hancock on the bottom line. How many do you have here on the mainland? However many it is, it'll be one less when I get rid of that nuisance with you."

"He's playing for time," Clay said.

He looked toward the main doors. One had swung partly shut. Hand shaking, he aimed where a man pushing the door closed might stand. He fired three times.

A loud howl of pain filled the night. Ros stumbled out, hands pressing into his chest. All three of Clay's bullets had ripped into the giant's body, but none was deadly. If one had been a few inches farther right, Ros would have had his heart punctured with lead. Instead, he lumbered forward, bloody hands reaching for his attacker.

"Keep Warnock occupied," Clay told Barker, not sure how the man would respond. If Ros became furious at his wounds, Barker neared death from his.

Barker flopped onto his belly and braced his stolen six-shooter on the floor. He began firing at Warnock. Clay lifted his gun and emptied it into the attacking foreman. Two more slugs found targets. Ros never slowed.

Clay slammed his gun into his holster, reached behind him and found his whittling knife. It fit his hand perfectly. He dug in his toes and launched himself forward. He crashed into Ros. He might as well have tried to bowl over a brick wall. Strong arms circled him and squeezed down. Clay gasped, then realized the strong steel-band arms around him prevented him from breathing. He kicked futilely. Ros was turning red in the face from exertion. The bullet wounds increasingly robbed him of strength, but his victim would die before him.

Clay twisted about and raked the whittling knife along Roskolnikov's side. This caused enough blood to flow that the foreman's hold slipped. Clay surged and slammed his forehead down into Ros' face, giving himself even more space to move.

The whittling knife slid from one side of the bull-like neck to the other. Clay blinked as blood spurted onto his face. It looked as if Ros grinned from a second mouth. As suddenly as the constriction around Clay's ribs had begun, it ended. The man toppled backward and lay kicking feebly. As Clay watched, the Russian giant died.

Clay dropped to one knee, panting. He had slaughtered plenty of animals in his day, but slitting a man's throat was completely different. He had done it twice now, once with a jagged wolf bone and now with his small knife. With a quick swipe, he wiped blood off the blade and returned it to its sheath on his belt.

"The coward ran" came Barker's feeble words. "He ran from a dying man."

"You're not dying. I won't let you. Sarah wouldn't like it, and Leo told me he hates going to funerals."

Clay got his arm under Barker and heaved him upright. Clay quickly supported all of Barker's weight as the man collapsed, unconscious. Dragging him from the barn, he looked around frantically for a way to escape.

Out by the corral, Warnock shouted for his men. The sound of horses approaching warned that some of the cowboys had successfully retrieved their mounts. Clay started eastward on foot, toward the Crown K herd. Even if he hadn't been weighed down with Barker's shot-up carcass, escape wasn't in the cards. Too much worked against him to make a clean getaway.

That didn't stop him from trying. Better to die than to tell Sarah he had failed to save her husband.

CHAPTER TWENTY-TWO

L EAVE ME. I'M dying. Don't die, too."
    King Barker grated out the orders as Clay car-
ried him along. The rancher tried to pull away but simply regaining consciousness had taken all his strength.
Clay hefted the rancher onto his back, the other man's
arms circling his neck so he could grab his wrists.
Barker weighed him down, but it wasn't deadweight—
not yet, at least. Clay bent forward as if carrying a hay
bale on his back and kept moving.

His knee hurt like he had thrust it into a raging forest fire, and his breath came in ragged gasps. He leaned
forward until he was almost bent double, stumbling
along. The only good thing about trying to escape like
this was Barker's lack of struggling. He lacked energy
even for that.

With his head resting on Clay's shoulder, though,
Barker whispered his repeated demands to be left behind in an ear still ringing from the gunfire.

All that ran through Clay's head was how he wasn't

letting Barker die, not before he got him back to the
herd and Sarah. Then Barker could die in his wife's
arms, but by damn, he wasn't going to die before then.
Clay vowed to keep him alive through force of will.

The noise behind them told of the ranch hands dis-
covering their butchered foreman. Or their boss had
found them and bellowed orders. If they caught up
with their escaped prisoner and his rescuer, even the
stone arch over the main road into the ranch wasn't
going to be a big enough tombstone. They'd begin the
torture all over again until Barker died, then move on
to the man who had caused the ruckus.

This spurred Clay to a quicker step, but his strength
faded faster as a result. When his knee buckled and he
took a tumble, he tried not to fall so that he landed on
top of the Crown K owner. From the way Barker
grunted, he had some life left in him, but his constant
whispers to be left behind faded to the whistlelike
sound of steam escaping from a locomotive piston.
Clay knew the end was near.

He stared up at the night sky and picked out star
patterns as he tried to catch his breath. For a moment
he wondered at the new constellation. Then he realized something was blocking his view of the sky.

With a quick grab, he snared the reins and used
them to pull himself to his feet. The stallion balked at
such misuse but didn't lash out with his front hooves.

"I've never been happier to see a horse in all my
born days," Clay said.

He tugged on the reins and positioned the horse,
then grabbed King Barker under the arms and heaved
him upright. With reserves he never knew he had, Clay
hoisted the rancher belly down across the saddle. It
took him longer to mount than it had for him to get
Barker over the horse's back. His right leg refused to
cooperate. Grabbing the pommel with one hand and

his leg with the other and heaving, he flopped into the saddle.

He settled down, grabbed Barker's suspenders to hold him in place, then realized this wasn't going to work too well. One button popped off Barker's pants and the other wobbled as threads began giving way. Clay's fingers turned sweaty, and he lost his grip on the suspenders.

Behind, he heard Warnock bellowing orders to his men to find the escaped prisoners and kill them both. Clay leaned forward over Barker and gave the stallion its head. The thunderous hoofbeats carried like cannon fire in the still night. There might as well have been a light trained on them because the cowboys homed in immediately on the equine thunder.

"Race, old fellow! Race the wind!"

He used the reins to whip the horse to greater speed. He tried to see where they were running in the dark, but his eyes blurred.

Keeping his burden from sliding off the saddle began taking more effort. After he abandoned his grip on Barker's suspenders, he grabbed a handful of the man's shirt. The cloth tore as they rode, but unlike the buttons on his suspenders, it did not give way entirely.

Clay recognized how the terrain changed from grassy pastureland to rougher dirt.

"The road! We're on the road."

He kept the stallion on the dirt track, galloping full out, until he felt the stalwart animal begin to falter. In spite of the need to put as much distance between him and the P Star hands as possible, he slowed to a walk.

Almost immediately a shot rang out, again causing his ears to ring. Clay hunted for a spot to dismount and make a stand. Keeping Barker with him signed both of their death warrants, but Warnock's gunmen had overtaken them.

A second shot rang out, but from the other side of the road. He straightened. His fatigued brain tried to make sense out of it. How had the killers ridden ahead of him? The road let his horse run faster than the pursuers ever could ride through the lightly forested area.

"Me. It's me, Clay. Got Mr. Barker with me. He . . . he's wounded something terrible."

The truth finally soaked through his fog of pain and exhaustion. He had outridden Warnock's men and reached the Crown K herd. Clay almost bawled when Vasques rode closer, rifle in hand. He had fired the first shot. Fred trotted up on the other side of the road. He slid the rifle back into his saddle sheath.

"Are you hurt?"

José Vasques trotted even closer. He called out in his mix of Hawaiian, Spanish and English. Clay caught the gist of it. Vasques was summoning Suárez.

"He's hurt a lot worse than me," Clay said.

He tried to detail the torture Warnock had meted out but again the words and thoughts mixed in his head and tied his tongue in knots.

"This way. To our camp. Can you follow me?"

Vasques started to resheath his rifle, but Clay stopped him.

"They're on my tail. Can you hold them off? You and Fred? I can find the camp if you point me in the right direction. I . . . I'll get back to help you protect the herd."

"They're gonna outright steal the cattle? That's nothin' more than I predicted." Fred swore and drew his rifle from his saddle sheath. "Keep riding until you see the two trees, then cut off the road and use them as your guideposts. Make believe they're a doorway."

"Two trees?"

Clay worried he would miss such vague landmarks, but dallying much longer meant King Barker's death. He cantered ahead, looking left and right.

He rubbed his eyes when two dark trees rose on the left side of the road as if they had been planted to hold a massive gate. Going between them immediately revealed the Crown K camp. Two small fires burned cheerfully, and the smell of coffee made his nostrils flare and his mouth water. He used the aroma as a guide since his vision turned increasingly blurry.

"Leo. Got the boss here. He's sore wounded. Warnock and his foreman pounded on him something fierce."

Clay grabbed to keep Barker from falling to the ground, but a strong hand circled his wrist and squeezed.

"It's all right. Leo's got him."

Clay recognized Sarah Barker's voice. It came from a thousand miles away.

"I've got you."

Clay toppled from the saddle. Sarah had overestimated her ability to support him. The two of them landed in a heap on the ground. They both tried to move but only became entangled even more. Clay would have enjoyed this more if he hadn't been so embarrassed.

"Your husband . . . ," he said.

"Clay!" Sarah shoved him away. "Why do you keep—?"

"Help! I need your help. Both of you." Leo Suárez barked out his request again, this time in Hawaiian.

Sarah Barker finally disentangled herself and used Clay's stomach as a pivot point as she got to her feet. Clay grunted and doubled over in pain. The world turned red around him, then returned to normal. His hearing cleared and filled with King Barker screaming. This galvanized him to action. He hopped to one foot and made his way to where Barker lay stretched out. Suárez forced a long stick between the man's teeth while Sarah held him down.

The trail boss looked up at Clay and said, "He has a bullet in his belly. It must come out or he will die."

Clay swallowed hard. Barker was likely to die whether or not the bullet was removed.

"Clay, please," Sarah said. Tears welled in her eyes and began spilling over.

He started to tell Suárez to do it, but he remembered what Sarah had said. Suárez and Barker went way back. This might be like operating on a brother. If Barker was destined to die, better to have it at someone else's hand. When Barker opened his eyes and stared at him, Clay almost ran.

Barker moved the stick away from his lips and said in a clear, calm voice, "Do it. I trust you to do what's necessary." When he saw he had convinced his reluctant surgeon, he champed down once more on the stick.

Dropping to his knees beside the rancher, Clay reached for the sheath there and pulled out the whittling knife he had used for so many things. Carving. Killing. The memory of Warnock's foreman dying from a slit throat momentarily blinded him. The knife was deadly. Dangerous.

"Hold him tight," he said, gripping the blade so only an inch of steel protruded past his fingers.

He cut away blood-matted shirt to expose the deceptively small bullet hole. The rim of inflamed flesh made it look like a target. Clay used the thin blade to probe about. The tip nicked the lead hidden inside Barker's gut. The rancher sweat buckets, but he nodded to let Clay know he'd found the leaden culprit. With a sure hand, no matter that he trembled inside, Clay slipped the knife tip under the bullet and lifted in a smooth motion.

The bullet popped out.

Suárez was ready for what had to be done next. He twisted the slug off a rifle cartridge and poured the gunpowder into the bullet hole. Clay winced when Suárez struck a lucifer and ignited the powder. The flare rose two inches and then smoldered, the stench of burned flesh rising.

"Thank you. Thank you both," Barker said in a voice that didn't betray any pain.

Sarah pulled on Clay's arm and moved him away. She looked up into his eyes. He knew that look. He wanted to kiss her but held back. It was wrong.

"You saved him. Thank you."

"Getting him here was something of a chore, but if he makes it through the night, he'll be out of danger. He's got a core of steel. I saw him tortured and—" He bit off the recollection. This wasn't anything she needed to hear.

"Warnock's a monster," she said, her hand hiding her mouth. "I swear I'll—"

"Be careful about that, Sarah," came a mocking voice. "The only time you should swear is when you're signing over the herd to me."

Clay whirled about, his hand going to his pistol. But his leg finally gave out as he spun, and he fell to one knee. As he stared up at Warnock, his pistol pointed straight at the P Star owner, the only thought in Clay's head was how he had failed to reload his six-shooter. He had emptied it back at the barn. Now he was going to die, unable to defend himself.

Or Sarah.

He looked at her and mouthed, *Distract him.*

She frowned, trying to decipher his message.

"Sarah, my dear, here is a bill of sale. Sign it and I'll take my cattle back to the spread."

"I'm not the owner of the Crown K. You know that." She moved to stand between Warnock and Clay, blocking the rancher's view. This was what Clay needed.

He reached behind himself and pushed three bullets out of leather loops on his gun belt. Fumbling for more caused him to realize these were the only cartridges he had. Three. Palming them he lifted his six-gun from his holster and laid it on the ground. As he did so, he thumbed open the gate.

"But, Sarah, you're the sole owner now that King is dead."

"Don't tell him," Clay whispered, but he still spoke too loudly.

"Tell me what?" Warnock stepped out of the shadows. He motioned for Suárez to move closer to Sarah and Clay to make it easier to cover all of them. "King can't be alive, not after everything that I did to him."

"No," Suárez said.

He stepped in one direction while Sarah moved in the other, forcing Warnock to divide his attention.

If Clay had told them where to stand, their positions couldn't have been better. He ejected all the brass from the six-gun's cylinder. He leaned forward, hoping he hid what he was doing from Warnock.

He didn't. A bullet tore into his leg. He flopped flat on the ground, writhing about as the pain knifed into his thigh. Clay looked up and thought he was hallucinating. King Barker stood behind Warnock, six-gun steady in his hand.

"I took this from your foreman. I want to return it," Barker said as he fired.

The air filled with gun smoke as everyone traded fire. When Clay got a look again, King Barker once more lay on the ground, staring into the night sky. Only now a new element had been painted into the picture. Sarah gripped the pistol that had once been Roskolnikov's. She fired twice before the hammer fell on an empty chamber.

"Get down!" Clay screamed as he dove forward.

His shoulders hit the woman behind the knees, snapping her backward. Warnock's slugs missed her as she fell.

Wrenching around violently, Clay got out of the tangle of Sarah's legs and his arms. His six-shooter was already in his hand. Matching Warnock's lightning draw wasn't necessary. All he had to do was not miss.

He fired all three rounds as fast as he could pull the trigger. The ringing in his ears died. A deathly silence descended like a funeral shroud. Doing the best he could, he helped Sarah sit up.

"Did Warnock hit you?"

She pushed him away and crawled to King Barker's side.

"You foolish, foolish man," she said, sobbing. She laid her head on his chest, then sat up abruptly. "You're alive!"

"Course I am," King Barker rasped out. "What's another slug going to do to me?" Barker moved his hand to show a new bullet wound in his side.

Clay crawled over to join them. He lifted more bloody cloth away. "The bullet went clean through. Stop the bleeding and you'll be as good as—" He started to say *as good as new* but that was a lie. He finished lamely, "As good as before."

Even that was far from the truth. As bruised and battered and shot up as King Barker was, recovery would stretch months into his future.

"Put pressure on the wound," Sarah said, more to herself than either of the men.

Clay hopped up and looked around for Warnock.

"Where'd he go? I thought I hit him. He ought to be dead."

"He limped away," Suárez said. "We must go now."

Rifle fire in the distance warned that the fight wasn't over.

"José and Fred are defending the herd," Clay said.

Dizziness made him stagger. The hole in his thigh didn't require any more aid than Barker's new wound. Warnock's round had passed clean through muscle without hitting a vital artery.

"The P Star riders must be trying to steal the cattle. Steal them. Help José and Fred. Help."

Clay smiled when Sarah touched his cheek. She spoke rapidly, but he didn't understand a word of what she said. He reached out for her, held her, felt her hair brush his cheek, and then he slipped away into darkness without pain—without pain or Sarah.

CHAPTER TWENTY-THREE

THE WORLD BOBBED like a cork on a floating fishing lure. Clay shook his head to get the cobwebs out, but all he accomplished was rattling gravel around inside his skull. He opened his eyes. Darkness. He closed them, took a deep breath and smiled. Fragrance. And warm arms circling him.

Clay snapped fully awake when he realized those were Sarah's arms, and she rode behind him on his stallion.

"What's going on?"

"Stop fighting me. I'm not strong enough to hold you in the saddle. I might succeed in doing that if you took three or four more rounds and banged up your other knee. Since you haven't tallied as many injuries as King, you have to keep your wits about you and not thrash around."

"Where are we going? My horse? He's still not completely saddle broke. What happened with Warnock?"

"So many questions. If I were cruel, I'd make you figure them all out for yourself. But I'm a nice person."

Clay wasn't going to argue, but this was improper, unless—

"King? He's dead?" His heart hammered until it threatened to explode.

"He's riding with Leo. He took another bullet after you blacked out, but he'll live. He's too weak to walk. There's hardly any problem riding, though. He's on my horse, which is why we're riding double."

"He's not dead?"

"Don't sound so glum. You saved his life." Sarah lowered her voice. "I don't know how to thank you for that." Her hot breath gusted across the back of his neck and sent new tremors throughout his body, different ones from the pain in his leg or the way his head throbbed.

"I didn't kill Warnock, did I?"

"You saved King, and you risked your life to save me. Don't think you have to do everything." She chuckled. "What you did was more than any two other men could have done. There's no call for you to monopolize being so heroic."

Clay cleared his throat and wondered what to say, what to do.

"I have to earn my trail money someway." He looked around. To their left marched the Crown K herd, making its way slowly in the darkness. "Why are we moving the cattle in the dark when dawn's only a few hours off?"

From the depth of the shadows, day might break sooner than that. He wasn't going to crane around to get a better look at the eastern horizon. To do so would have put him almost face-to-face with the woman. He grew more and more uneasy at riding like this with her.

He had saved her husband and his reward was to suffer having her so close and not be able even to kiss her.

"If the amount of blood spilled counts, you've more than earned your keep," she said. "I had to cut through your trousers to patch up the leg wound. You're going to hobble about for a spell until the bullet hole and your injured knee heal some more."

"Did Warnock fetch his men? Is that why we're on the trail so early?"

"He owns this part of California. The nearest law is twenty miles off, but he has enough men working the Pacific Star to hold off a cavalry company. Carrying a bullet or two of yours in him is not going to improve his disposition."

"My killing his foreman won't make him any more hospitable, either."

Clay shifted around to get the whittling knife moved so it didn't press into the middle of his back. That knife had seen uses its maker had never intended. He closed his eyes and remembered the hot gush of blood over his face and hand as he cut Roskolnikov's throat. It had been either Clay or Warnock's foreman.

That simple statement brought Sarah Barker even closer behind him as they rode. She outright hugged him now. King must have told her what Roskolnikov had done to him and this was Sarah's way of thanking her husband's savior.

It bothered Clay more and more, but telling her to keep her distance wasn't in the cards. He wanted to enjoy the feel of her hands on his belly, the pressure of her arms circling his body, the heat of her breath on his neck for as long as possible. This ride would have to provide him enough of a memory to last a lifetime.

"He'll be a trapped rat," Clay said. "A wounded, trapped rat and all the more dangerous for it."

"I agree. There's no reason he won't swoop down on us and steal the herd."

Sarah's grim tone turned away whatever good feeling he had about being so close to her.

"Are there any other cowboys Suárez can get to come help us fight him off? The Ralstons apparently have no liking for him. And Leo said the others in the area all fought Warnock over trying to steal their land."

"The other ranches are spread out. The best way to keep the herd from being rustled is to get the cattle aboard the ship as fast as we can. Once it's set sail, the ship's beyond Warnock's reach."

"Is it in port?" Clay asked.

"I hope so. It's supposed to be." She hugged him a little tighter, then stood in the stirrups and leaned forward. "There's the road to the Crown K. We'll have the cattle aboard within a couple hours."

"A couple hours," Clay said with a mixture of regret and doubt.

Once the ship sailed, he'd never see Sarah again, but that was for the best. He had saved her husband a couple times and still found himself with the guilty thought of wondering what might have happened between Sarah and himself if King Barker had died. He might not sleep easier at night knowing she was once more in Hawaii riding the Crown K spread, but removing the source of such depraved thoughts was best for both of them. Sarah obviously loved her husband. Wanting King to die so he could make a play for her was wrong.

"You sound strange, Clay. But you've been strange the entire trip. Why have you avoided me at every turn? You're the most contrary man I've ever come across. You have feelings for me. I can tell. Everyone can. It's about all José talks about. Leo's too much a stick in the mud to ever gossip around the campfire, but Fred sees it, too. But you deny it. I—"

"Listen," he said urgently. "What's that?" Clay had the sinking feeling that he knew. Gunshots. Lots of them.

"The ship! We've got to ride straight to the dock, Clay. Hang on."

She sat back and pulled the reins around Clay's body as she kicked hard with her heels. The stallion grew wings and flew, hooves hardly touching the ground as it raced past a small ranch house and down a broad road toward the ocean. The surf pounded and salt spray made Clay squint.

They rounded a bend in the road. It took him a few seconds to make out the dark silhouettes. Then flames leaped high into the air.

"They're burning the dock! The ship! The ship's on fire!"

Sarah's arms clamped down hard around Clay, making it hard for him to breathe.

Clay saw the upper sails billowing in the breeze. "The ship's moving away from the dock. See?"

"But there are fires on deck. Several of them."

The stallion slowed and came to a halt at the base of the dock. Sarah leaped off and drew the six-gun she wore in the holster strapped on the gun belt around her trim waist. It took two full turns around her to keep it from falling down.

"The gun belt," Clay called. "Give me your gun belt."

"They're burning the dock. We have to use it to load the cattle onto the ship," she cried. Sarah unbuckled the belt and cast it aside.

Clay almost fell to the ground, his leg refusing to support him, forcing him to hop along. He scooped up the discarded gun belt and slipped six rounds from the loops. He repeatedly shouted at Sarah to wait for him, but she ran pell-mell along the dock, pistol waving about in front of her. Clay loaded his six-shooter and trailed her, ignoring the pain as he rushed along, dragging his leg behind.

"Warnock!" she shouted, and fired.

Clay saw a figure outlined by the dancing fire at the very end of the dock. Something explosive erupted and blew away ten feet of the dock. Heavy tar scent wiped away the brisk salt odor of the ocean.

Clay stumbled along faster when he heard the hammer of Sarah's six-gun click down on an empty chamber. Over the roaring fire came taunting laughter. In his rush, Clay stumbled and fell to his knees. He fought to get to his feet and stop Warnock, but Sarah had moved to stand between him and the rancher.

"You'll never load the cattle," Warnock exclaimed. "Not now. Sign them over to me, and I'll let you and your worthless brother live."

Sarah continued to pull the trigger. One dull click after another mocked her. She reared back and threw the six-shooter at the rancher.

Warnock dodged it easily. He lifted his own pistol and sighted in on her.

"You were stubborn, Sarah, but I hadn't thought you were stupid. Goodbye."

Two shots rang out. Rolling to the side, Clay got a clear look around Sarah. He cocked his six-shooter again to take his second shot. He glanced at Sarah. She stood unmoving. But Warnock pulled back his gun and stared at it. He had fired and missed.

Clay's round had hit the P Star owner square in the chest. Warnock took a step back and then collapsed. Even if Clay had wanted to rush to the man's aid, there wasn't a chance now. Another ten feet of dock collapsed from the raging fire. Warnock lay on the section that fell into the water.

"Sarah, get back. The whole dock's collapsing. Sarah!"

He tried going to her but hopping on one leg hindered him too much. She stared into the fire. From this angle it looked as if her blond hair was on fire. Sarah took a step back, then spun around and ran into Clay's arms, sobbing. She almost bowled him over. They were in danger of being set ablaze as the dock vanished one section after another.

"Let's get back," Clay said, "to where it's safe."

He leaned heavily on her, then stopped. He stared down a rifle barrel. One of Warnock's men would again determine whether they lived or died.

"Don't you go raisin' that smoke wagon," the rifleman said in a shaky voice. "Mr. Warnock, he tole me to stand here and not let anybody 'cept him go back to dry land."

"You can't shoot us down in cold blood. Your boss is dead."

Clay got his dander up. He hurt, his leg refused to support him and Warnock had threatened Sarah along with burning down the dock. He'd had all he could stomach.

"Dead?"

"I drilled him through his rotten heart." Clay spat out the words. "He tried to kill me enough times between Bozeman and here."

"No, that's not true. Is it? That you, Clay? Clayton Forsythe?" The cowboy stepped closer. The towering flames devouring the dock illuminated his face.

"Lanky Lou," Clay said.

"You know him?" Sarah had recovered from her shock.

Clay hissed for her to be quiet. "Lou and I rode with the Rocking O. He hired on with Warnock when our drive was over. I didn't."

"You kilt him, Clay? Why'd you go and do a thing like that?" Lanky Lou Larson raised his rifle and took aim again. "I worked for him."

"Doing what, Lou? Killing people? Rustling cattle? That's what he wanted. Did he order you to steal the Crown K herd?"

"I've been tendin' the horses, not cows. I prefer handlin' the remuda and only jist arrived in these parts. What's goin' on?"

"Either lower the rifle or kill us, Lou. You were a decent man when we rode together."

"You really kilt him?"

"And Ros. I slit the foreman's throat with the knife I use for whittling." Better to tell Lou himself than have him find out later and think Clay wasn't being truthful.

Clay fought a little with Sarah but pushed her behind him for the sake of her safety. He haltingly advanced. When he was sure Lou saw him clearly, he slipped his gun back into the holster.

"I've got no quarrel with you. You weren't the one who shot my boss or did this to me." He thrust out his leg with the bloodied cloth to show where he had been injured. "Warnock did this to me. What he and his foreman did to King Barker was even worse."

"You sayin' he gunned down Mr. Barker? I heard of the bad blood between them."

"Warnock and Ros tortured him and shot him. They shot me and they tried to kill Sarah here."

"It's all true," she said. "Every word Clay is saying is the Gospel truth."

"You wouldn't hurt a fly, Clay, and you say you kilt 'em both?"

"They tried to hurt Sarah. They shot up King Barker, trying to steal the Crown K cattle. Warnock wanted me dead, too."

Sarah started to add something. Clay gripped her arm tight enough to quiet her. Lanky Lou had to come to his own conclusion.

"I never knowed any of this was happenin'. Honest, Clay." Lou moved the sights off them, then lowered the rifle. "I had no idea he was settin' fire to this here wharf. I jist showed up with the horses at the ranch house and he tole me to come right on out here and stand guard." Lou looked around. "This ain't the P Star, is it?"

"It's the Crown K wharf. Or was. And that was Crown K range you rode across to get here," Clay said. "You've been duped, Lou."

"Dock," Sarah corrected. "It's not a wharf unless—"

Clay silenced her again. Too much information only confused Lanky Lou. He was a steady worker, not a quick thinker.

"I reckon this means I'm not gettin' paid by the P Star, don't it?" Lou laughed ruefully. "That's always the way it is with me."

"If you're looking for a job, the Crown K needs some temporary help," Clay said. "I'd be willing to hire you on."

"Clay!" Sarah moved around and started to argue.

He ignored her. Avoiding another shoot-out was more important than her hurt feelings at getting in the last word.

"I'm not the foreman, but I'll put in a good word for you. I know you're a hard worker, and you say you prefer horses to cattle?"

"Those are my druthers. I hadn't figgered that out ridin' with the Rocking O, but I came across a big herd of ole mustangs on the way from Idaho and—"

"And you broke a few. My stallion was their leader."

"You always could break the worst bronco," Lou admitted. "I wondered why I didn't have to work all that much when I cut out three mares from that herd. They musta been lookin' for the stallion you caught and weren't up to fightin' me. Maybe I'm not as good as I thought, eh?"

"I'll wager you're plenty good, Lou. You willing to hire on? For a week or two?"

"If you'll have me. I always looked up to you, Clay. Never saw a better bronco buster. And nobody ever had a bad word to say about you, except for—"

"We can hash that out later," Clay said.

He felt darkness closing in all around him. He had pushed himself as hard and as far as any human could.

Clay motioned. Lanky Lou ambled over. They shook hands on the deal.

Lou looked past Clay and said, "I s'ppose part of the work'll be rebuildin' that dock. I'm good enough with hammer and nails if somebody hands me sawed planks."

Clay shielded his eyes as the last gouts of flame ate away at the dock. Rebuilding would take a considerable amount of work. Looking out into the small harbor, he saw tiny fires on the cargo ship's deck being put out one by one.

"The ship's still seaworthy from the looks of it," he said. "We can get to building a new dock and set sail by the end of the month. Maybe sooner if you're as good a carpenter as you claim, Lou."

He needed to lean on Sarah but that wasn't right, not with King Barker somewhere back in the direction of the ranch house.

"That's not good enough," she said. "The ship has to sail within the week. We don't have time to rebuild the dock."

"So what're we going to do, Mrs. Barker?" Clay asked.

"We'll show you how we do it in Hawaii. And stop calling me *missus*. You seem to think King is my husband."

"He's not?" The loud roaring in Clay's ears almost drowned out her reply.

"He's my brother."

CHAPTER TWENTY-FOUR

"Can't the ship sail to another dock?" Clay asked. He kept switching his attention between the ship bobbing on gentle waves in the harbor and Sarah Barker beside him. He found it hard to meet her gaze, yet he wanted to do nothing but stare at her.

"We'd have to drive the herd another hundred miles, and there's nothing to say we'd be allowed to use the dock. That's why we built this one." Sarah shifted her eyes to the end of the burned dock. "The one that is now nothing but burned timbers, what remains of it at all."

Clay refrained from saying it made an appropriate grave for Warnock. They'd never found his body, but he knew none of the Crown K workers had spent much time in that pursuit. The harbor water stirred constantly with the fins of great white sharks. If what Suárez and Vasques said of those creatures' hunger was halfway true, Warnock's body would never be found.

"Why does the ship have to sail so soon?"

Clay didn't understand such things, but if he'd been the ship's captain and Warnock had tried to set fire to the vessel, he wouldn't anchor a half mile off. He'd drop the sails and be headed for some other port and some other cargo.

"Storms brew down in the South Pacific and sweep north this time of year. The captain thinks he has a month before the seas get too heavy to make a safe trip. It's different with cattle aboard from having bales of durable goods. Cattle panic in heavy seas. We lost one ship when a steer kicked its way through the hull."

"A week to load, then two or three weeks to reach Hawaii," Clay mused. "I've never seen it done, but if you get barges, we might be able to move the stock to the ship."

He wondered if such barges even existed. Certainly they were absent near what had been the Crown K dock.

"How do you paddle a loaded barge? You can't pole it out. The harbor is too deep. Or do you put sails on it and expect the wind to cooperate?" Sarah laughed as she wet her finger and held it up to show the breeze had died. "This isn't as big a problem as it seems, Clay. We're used to such transfers. Hardly anywhere in Hawaii has a dock worth mentioning for loading cattle to ship between the islands."

He looked over his shoulder as Fred sauntered up. The cowboy scratched himself, waited for Clay to motion him closer and then stopped at the base of the burned-out dock before speaking.

"I've been on a couple drives where we had to float wagons 'cross rivers all swole up from spring runoff. One time we did it during a real frog strangler of a storm. We put floats on the sides and let the horses pull us across."

"The horses did it all by their lonesome?" Clay was skeptical.

"Well, now, we did have ropes fastened to trees along the shore. We did some pullin' but the horses did all the real work. The ropes mostly kept the wagons from gettin' swept downstream."

"We float the cattle out the same way, only there's no way to use guide ropes," Sarah said. "Oh, don't look so skeptical, Clay. We have a hundred head. If the weather doesn't get too stormy, we can move them all in a day."

"Might be worth the money to hire on more help," Fred said. "Lou tells me some of the P Star boys might be interested, the ones that didn't hightail it when they heard their boss was dead."

"Well, yes, they might," Sarah said uneasily. She stood on tiptoe and whispered in Clay's ear, "We don't have the money. We don't have *any* money. We have to get the breeding stock back home if the Crown K is going to keep operating."

Clay had guessed that something like this was the reason so few trail hands had moved the herd from outside Hoback. The Barkers were teetering on the brink of bankruptcy and had bet everything on the new cattle.

"I don't trust them too much," Clay said hastily to keep Sarah from concocting a lie. "We can handle a hundred head if we take a few at a time. Right, Miss Barker?"

"Right, Mr. Forsythe."

She brushed against him and moved, just a little like a cat stropping up against him. He tingled all over at the touch. Then his good feelings evaporated. Too soon the herd would be aboard the ship and Sarah, her brother, Suárez and Vasques would sail back to Hawaii.

"Will your brother oversee the loading?"

"I . . . I don't think he's up for it," she said. "You know how to do this, don't you, Fred? You said you'd worked on a wagon train or drive where you had to float wagons across a river."

"That's a long way," Clay said, judging the distance to the ship. "Is there any way the captain can move closer to shore?"

"He's set his anchor and is afraid of coming closer because of the debris from the dock," she said. "That's nonsense. He's being contrary, but we have to work with him."

"There's something else," Clay said uneasily. He pointed to a gray fin speeding through the water. "How do we keep the sharks from dining on prime beef?"

"That's not as much a problem as you might think. Chum," she said.

Clay tried to figure out what she meant.

"Oh, you landlubber. Chum. Bait. We go beyond the harbor mouth and throw bushels of bloody fish into the ocean. The sharks go for the smell of blood."

"We keep feeding them out there while we float the cattle from land to the ship?"

"Don't sound so skeptical. We know how to do it," she said.

He hoped her confidence wasn't bravado.

"Let's get to it soon," Clay said, eliciting a quick nod of approval from her. That restored a bit of his mood, but not much since whenever he spoke with her was closer to being the last time. He turned to Fred. "Get some flotation together. Ask Suárez and Vasques to help. And tell them about the chum."

"You ramrodding this, Clay?" Fred grinned ear to ear.

"Reckon so," he answered.

He heard no complaint from Sarah, so he assumed

the responsibility. Clay began pulling pieces of timber from the harbor and piling them to make rafts. The Crown K had a single boat. Unless he wanted to force his stallion into swimming out and back while pushing the cattle along, he needed something to ride on.

The rest of the day passed quickly. Clay built a crude raft while the others fashioned floats for the cattle. By early afternoon Vasques brought five cows down to the waterfront. It took longer to strap on the floats than he'd expected. The cattle turned cantankerous at the unexpected gear slung around their bellies.

"Board the boat," he called to Suárez and Vasques. "Fred and me'll paddle the raft on the other side."

"I've got a few clumps of grass to dangle in front of them to keep them swimming," Fred said.

Clay saw Suárez and Vasques exchange amused looks and knew this wasn't going to amount to a hill of beans. A carrot or sugar for a horse might spur the animal on, but not a cow. They were too set in their bovine ways. Grazing mattered; following a handful of grass was something to ignore.

"Let's get 'em into the water," he called.

Clay waited to see if Suárez objected to him taking over the movement. Suárez hopped to the boat, one of the cowboys and not the trail boss now.

"Lou, get the boat out beyond the mouth of the harbor," Clay called. "Leo's told you what you have to do."

"Dead fish," Lanky Lou said with some distaste. "Bloody, smelly fish. But he tole me. And I have to keep my hands out of the water or I'll lose 'em." He set out in the boat to where the ocean met the harbor.

Clay took the time to be sure the cattle were securely strapped to their floats. After he was satisfied and Lou was out of sight, Clay gave the go-ahead.

Clay and Fred pushed their raft into the water with a loud splash. They lifted their paddles and started work. The raft hadn't been designed for easy passage through the water, and it dipped low in the stern. Then it righted itself and their paddling sent the raft toward the cattle. Clay looked over his shoulder as he stroked in unison with Fred.

"It looked as if you need me for ballast," Sarah said, settling down at the back of the raft. "It's a nice day for a cruise, isn't it?"

Clay had to laugh. For her as a passenger it was. He and Fred paddled until their shoulders ached and the muscles in their arms threatened to explode from exertion.

They banged up against the nearest cow swimming frantically. On the other side Suárez poked and prodded with his oar to keep the cows moving in as straight a course for the ship as possible.

"Let me help," Sarah said. "I've done this since I was a little girl."

She knelt at the edge of the raft, leaned out and grasped a slick horn. Twisting hard, she turned the cow's head in the direction of the ship.

After an eternity for Clay, they neared the ship. Sarah got to her feet. Her sea legs proved steadier than his.

She waved and called, "Captain Garmond! Get the sling ready."

"Miss Barker."

The captain stood at the rear of the ship. After acknowledging her, he barked commands to the deck crew. They moved a hoist with a double-strap sling over the side, then cranked it down to water level.

"Who gets to fasten the sling?" Fred sounded uneasy about the chore. "I can't swim. Well, I paddle around but divin' and holdin' my breath? Not something I'm much up for doin'."

Clay heaved a sigh. "It's up to me, then."

"We can do it together. Two divers make it easier. I've done this before, Clay." Sarah shucked off her outer garments.

Clay stared, wondering how far she would strip, embarrassed that the thought had even crossed his mind. She was in full view of the ship's crew as well as the cowboys. She stood with her clothing piled in the middle of the raft.

"Well. Go on. You'll drown if you dive with your boots and coat and vest and all the rest."

Clay's embarrassment grew as he stripped off as much as he could while retaining his modesty in front of her. Sarah took far too much glee in his discomfort.

When he was down to his union suit, he said, "Let's get those beeves onto the ship."

"Last one in's a rotten apple!"

Sarah dived and cut cleanly into the water. She continued her dive and disappeared under the nearest cow.

Clay's dive was less graceful. He sent a big splash up, positioned himself and kicked hard to go underwater. The salt water stung his eyes. The other thing different from paddling around in a lake was how buoyant he felt. He worked harder to dive and get under the cow.

Sarah already had one end of a strap ready. She passed it beneath the cow. He grabbed it, surfaced and fastened it to the hoist. By the time he dived back, she was ready with the second. Again the work went smoothly. When he surfaced, she came up for air.

"I was beginning to think you could stay underwater forever without taking another breath," he said.

"When you live on an island with nothing but ocean stretching to the horizon, you learn to swim like a fish."

"A mighty attractive one at that," Clay said.

Sarah laughed. She mouthed something. He read her lips and blushed at such a suggestion.

"Free the floats," he called to her. The cow was soon held only by the hoist. When the deck crew began turning the capstan to raise the cow, the animal began kicking and complaining.

"Time's a-wasting," Sarah said, moving to the next cow.

The two of them saw to the loading in what Clay thought was record time. When the fifth cow was lifted to the deck, Clay clung to the side of Suárez's raft. The trail boss shook his head, turned and held out his hand. Vasques silently passed over a greenback.

"What's that about?" Clay asked.

"I bet him you would take more than five minutes a cow. Back on the island, the crew can lift a cow in under a minute."

"That's because they've all got fish blood in their veins," Sarah called from the raft. "And they've done this all their lives."

"I'll get better," Clay promised.

"Good. I do not want to be here until next spring," Suárez said, but his broad grin told Clay he was only joshing.

With a loud splash, Clay returned to the raft and sat beside Sarah, his feet dangling in the water. The salt caused the bullet wound in his leg to burn like fire, but he ignored it. She pressed close to him, their damp bodies moving as the raft bobbed on the waves.

"Get to paddling, you two," she said. "Leo's right about how long this is taking. And, Clay, get your feet out of the water. Movement can attract the sharks."

"Aye, aye, Captain," Clay said.

She smiled and said, "Don't you forget it, either."

They completed the transfer of the cattle from their

pen behind the Crown K ranch house to the ship before it got too dark. The last transfer had to be made using a torch to light the way, but Clay was practiced enough with the cattle and hoist straps by then that he finished the transfer in almost pitch-blackness.

Back onshore, he shook off the water and carefully dressed.

"The ship sails with the morning tide," Sarah said. She twisted her long blond hair to wring out the last droplets of water.

He started to ask if she was sailing with the ship, then stopped. He knew she was. The Crown K in Hawaii was her home. Of course she was leaving.

"Miss Barker, all your gear is loaded," Suárez said to her.

He shifted from one foot to the other, more nervous than Clay had ever seen the trail boss. Sarah said nothing, waiting for Suárez to say his piece.

He finally blurted out, "Mr. Barker isn't up to making the trip back. He has lost too much blood."

"He's on the mend, though?" Clay cut in.

"He is weak, but it will take many weeks to fully recover."

"I'll talk to him," Sarah said. She started but Suárez had a little more to say.

"He wants you to run the Crown K." Suárez fumbled out a sheet of paper and handed it to her. "This deeds his half to you."

"Oh, really. King knows better than to do this." She took the paper and held it up, trying to read in the dark.

"He will sail in the spring after he has recuperated." Again Suárez stopped her. "I would stay here to look after him."

"José is staying, too?" she asked.

"He misses his family. He will sail with you back to Hawaii." Suárez smiled just a little. "He would miss those cows as much and wants to keep them safe aboard a ship filled with hungry sailors."

Sarah nodded. She turned to Clay and said, "I'll be back as soon as I thrash this out with my brother. He can be so pigheaded at times."

Clay watched her disappear in the dark. Suárez hesitated, as if he wanted to say something more, then followed her. Alone, smelling the scent of the burned dock mingling with those of the salt and fish and feeling the cool wind from the sea, Clay watched the ship rolling gently on the waves. The loaded cattle caused the ship to ride lower in the water. Movement now was more ponderous. He wondered what it felt like to be on board once the ship sailed beyond sight of land. Never in his life had he been anywhere that the prairie or the mountains weren't visible.

This was the first time he'd been to California. With the P Star in turmoil over the loss of the owner and foreman—or at least the ranch would be when everyone learned about Warnock's death—this wasn't the place to linger. No matter that he might help King Barker and Suárez, there wasn't a job for him here. No cattle, a few horses. Drifting south would give him time to decide what to do. If he rode far enough, he'd be in Mexico. There were ranchos there needing bronco busters like him.

Maybe he and Lanky Lou could partner up and find some trouble to get into as long as it had nothing to do with feeding ravenous sharks.

A sloshing sound marked the beaching of a boat. Two sailors climbed out. He waved to them, but they ignored him.

José Vasques came down the path from the ranch house, lugging two large cases. He loaded those into the boat, then joined Clay.

"Miss Barker must weigh down her trunks with gold

bricks." He laughed and said, "At least I did not have to load Mr. Barker's. His weigh twice what hers do."

Vasques moved to look past him. Clay saw Sarah hurrying down with two gunnysacks tossed over her shoulder.

"Did you square things with your brother?" The words caught in Clay's throat. *Your brother.* Not her husband.

"King is too weak to make the trip, if we run into any foul weather. He likes the idea of wintering over here and seeing snow. Leo will look after him until he's back on his feet." She swung the gunnysacks off her shoulder and handed them to Clay. "Here. Load them into the boat." She preceded him, lithely stepping in and finding a spot at the prow to sit.

Clay thought she matched the figurehead on the cargo ship, only she was aboard a small boat and living, breathing and far lovelier than the painted wood sculpture.

Vasques hopped in and sat amidships. Clay found himself unable to help push the boat into the water. He refused to do anything that sped Sarah on her way.

She twisted around and pointed at him. In an almost schoolmarmish way, she said sternly, "Clay, get in. Now. Climb aboard."

He understood. The boat belonged to the Crown K and had to be returned. Vasques and the sailors—and Sarah—wouldn't be returning to solid land anytime soon. Awkwardly stepping in, he almost fell into the water when the boat slid away faster than he'd expected. The sailors snickered, then settled down on the oars and began rowing strongly.

"We could have used them getting the cattle out to the ship," he said to Vasques.

But Vasques paid him no attention. He waved to two shadowy figures on the shore.

Suárez and, from the way he stood, King Barker.
Clay started to wave, too, and then stopped. He'd be
back with them in a few minutes. Fred and Lanky Lou
were tending the cattle on the ship. If Clay worked at
it, he could get them to row back and save him the effort. He crouched in the boat, gripping the hardwood
bench seat. By the time they reached the ship, he had
gotten used to the rocking motion and even liked it.
Riding a bronco was far more unsettling.

Vasques helped Sarah up a rope ladder, then scrambled after her. Clay admired the *paniolo*'s agility. He
picked up the gunnysacks and started to hand them up,
but Vasques reached the railing, rolled over the edge
and disappeared. The sailors worked fore and aft to
attach rope to the boat, making him wonder what they
intended.

"Come on, Clay. Bring up the bags if you can climb
the ladder." Sarah was leaning over, watching him.

"What're the sailors doing?"

Clay got no answer from Sarah, and the two salts
grumbled. They obviously considered him lower than
the bilge.

"Do you need help?" Sarah taunted him now.

He slung the gunnysacks over his shoulder, then
tested the ladder. He was almost tossed into the harbor
after he climbed two rungs; then he matched the roll of
the ship with the swaying ladder. While not as agile as
Vasques, he reached the railing without incident.

"Good," she said. "Look. They're unfurling the
sails. The tide is favorable."

"I'd better . . ." His words trailed off.

The sailors had hoisted the boat so it hung from da-
vits. They secured it and then dashed to a mast and
clambered up to the crossbeams to help lower massive
sails. When the wind caught the unfurled sails, the
ship lurched.

"Am I supposed to swim ashore?" he asked.

"Only if you don't want to come to Hawaii." Sarah lowered her voice and said in a husky tone, "With me."

Clay was speechless for a moment. "I didn't think—"

"That's your problem, Clay. You don't think. And you don't act on your feelings. I want to be with you and have since seeing you in Idaho. Don't you want to be with me?"

"Yes, of course, from the instant I saw you. But I thought you and King—"

"That's not all you've been wrong about," she said. "What would you like to do once we reach Hawaii?"

Clay saw the small figures on the shore moving back to the ranch house. Leo Suárez let King Barker lean heavily on him.

"You need a foreman on the Crown K. I can do that job and make you proud."

"We've got some nasty broncos, too. Are you willing to challenge them?"

"I need a new mount," he said. "I've left behind a gelding and a stallion."

"That's not a problem. And your stallion's below-decks. He had no trouble swimming out to the ship, though the crew had a few problems lifting him from the water. He is quite high-spirited." She snuggled close to him and whispered, "Like you."

"All my gear is back there onshore."

Sarah pointed to the gunnysacks on the deck at their feet.

"Your six-shooter, your clothing, everything from your saddlebags."

"There's more there than my tack," he said. All his gear would fit in only one sack and there were two.

"Do you want a real Hawaiian hat?"

He blinked and nodded, not sure what to say.

She untied the string around the second bag and

pulled out a Stetson. She held it out to him and said, "A genuine Hawaiian cowboy hat."

He took it, ran his fingers around the brim, then settled the hat on his head. It fit perfectly and would have gone unnoticed in any Western bar or rodeo or trail drive. Some things in Hawaii were exactly the same, it seemed.

"I like a woman who plans ahead." Before she said a word, he pulled her into the circle of his arms and kissed her.

She pushed away. "Not in front of the sailors. They'll get jealous."

"Let them. I've got a six-gun and a hat now. I can take 'em all on." He kissed her long enough for her to gasp when they broke apart.

"We can discuss your position later. In my cabin." She brushed her fingers across his cheek, then went to speak with the captain on the quarterdeck.

He watched her take every step on the ladder up, then touched his vest pocket and ran his finger around the wolf-bone ring he was carving. This was a token of how she had saved his life from the wolf pack. It would be fitting if he fancied it up and gave it back to her. He had detail work to do on it, but the finished ring would be well received later, after things settled on Hawaii, on the Crown K Ranch. It was the kind of wedding ring that'd appeal to a spirited woman like Sarah Barker.

Clayton Forsythe rested his elbows on the railing, watching the sunrise over the land and the ocean waves grow all around the ship. Only when José Vasques called him to help tend the cattle in the hold with Lou and Fred did he leave his post. He went below to do as good a job as possible to win his place on the Crown K Ranch and in Sarah's heart.

Ready to find
your next great read?

Let us help.

Visit prh.com/nextread

Penguin
Random
House